THE RED ROOM

by Françoise Mallet-Joris

THE RED ROOM
THE ILLUSIONIST *(under the name Françoise Mallet)*

THE RED ROOM

Françoise Mallet-Joris

translated from the French

by Herma Briffault

Farrar, Straus & Cudahy   *New York*

© 1956 by Françoise Mallet-Joris
Library of Congress catalog card number 56–6154
Manufactured in the United States of America
by H. Wolff, New York
First printing, 1956

Translator's Foreword

One enters the world of Françoise Mallet-Joris with mingled dread and delight, for this young writer holds a magnifying glass up to nature and ruthlessly says, "This is the way I see it, these are the details of life as I see them, these are the endless perspectives opened up by every act we commit." It is the same magnifying glass that the Flemish painters of the Renaissance held up to nature. Here, in this graphic writing, are the familiar people and scenes depicted by Bruegel and Bosch, the revelries and carnivals, the haywagons loaded with drunkards, the ship of fools, the well-fed burghers disporting themselves among monsters and beggars, the lascivious sinners undergoing weird metamorphoses—and here, too, is the same acceptance of life for the exciting thing that it is. In this writing, as in Bosch's surrealist painting, the eroticism is alternately tender and violent. The vision we are given of life is apocalyptic;

v

Inferno is never far away from the Garden of Earthly Delights through which the meditative Hélène wanders, and we with her.

In this dynamic, dense, teeming world, everything is alive, from the gargoyle knocker on the bedroom of Hélène's dead mother to the gilded caryatids supporting the bed in the Red Room. And the Red Room, where Jean and Hélène love and hate, lives with a life of its own, "like a venomous flower."

But for all the flamboyant imagination, this is disciplined writing. In descriptive and narrative passages alike, there is a complete absence of the cliché, that easy-to-lean-on crutch; instead, there is always the unexpected adjective, the challenging thought, the surprising verb. The writer uses the French language, but she molds it to suit her purpose, and to expound her point of view, which is Flemish.

As with the Flemish painters, no inch of canvas is left empty: even the seemingly empty portions throb with life. When the author describes a sky which the crying seagulls render "as palpable as torn cloth" one is reminded of the expanse of sky in Bruegel's *The Fall of Icarus*. And nothing is left to chance: each item in the crowded canvas has its significance. It is not merely by accident that the motif of the caryatid appears in the Red Room; that motif, which is associated with the temples of Diana, the maiden goddess who was never conquered by love, also appeared on the sculptured façade of the house where Hélène first knew Tamara.

Few characters in modern fiction are as convincingly alive and real as Hélène is. But, as Jean remarks, she is "a female Dorian Gray" upon whom, as yet, the violences to which she has been submitted have left no visible trace. Her life is a search for new and strange sensations, but, being Flemish and female, she is no æsthete; instead, she finds "beauty, cruelty, voluptuousness and suffering, all equally delicious." To her, the one odious thing is humility, and she prays to the God of the Old Testament for punishment, not pardon. She fears old age, not out of vanity but out of an unwillingness to lose the precious gifts of the senses.

And yet Hélène is terrified at the feeling that her heart is gradually being encased in a hardening shell and longs for someone to break through that unnatural carapace, so that she may go on living, even if it means only to suffer. In sum—and this is an important point—Hélène deeply senses a great truth which Pascal has stated: that the worst part of damnation is not the fire, but the gradual hardening of the human soul. It is this nascent moral perception on Hélène's part that gives *The Red Room* its true stature, and lifts it above the realm of mere astonishment, into the realm of art.

HERMA BRIFFAULT

I •

Under their globes of glass, the stuffed birds were prettily sleeping. The presence of winter—vulgar winter, befurred and jangling her crystal adornments—was scarcely felt in the small white and gold drawingroom. A lighted lamp not far from Tamara bathed her rapt face in its soft glow. I was observing her.

More precisely, I was watching her. Was my charming stepmother about to betray herself? Would it happen that day? Her puffy ogress face, that new matronly face of hers, was more hideous than I had ever seen it, just now, when Jean began to sing. There was no longer a doubt: the idea of deceiving my father had entered her mind and she was considering it. But with what dissimulation, what caution, what discretion! Her lowered eyelids, her artful smiles that were barely too amiable and so need not be hidden from anyone, could mean only one thing. But it was not passion, and it was barely desire. It was a kind of voracity. How much more contemptible than all other sins, that stealthy lust which is nothing but the shadow and mockery of true, impetuous, desperate desire!

I watched and waited. A time would surely come when something would give way in this respectable edifice with which she was trying to surround and defend herself. We would wait, and, while waiting, would study that ruined face we once loved. Angles, minerals, ridges, all had vanished from a landscape that was strangely lit; now, in the broad light of day, one saw only complacent prairies. However, a vestige of charm remained, Tamara was still beautiful. Beautiful to Jean, whose eyes lingered on her gentle curves; beautiful in the Venetian mirror that hung between the white curtains and an ornate piece of furniture; and beautiful to that fifty-year-old man who, through loving her without knowing what she was, had made her become what he loved; to that peaceable man standing behind her and leaning against her, and whose weight she perhaps loved, Tamara was still beautiful. But how irritated she was, though, in the midst of all this comfort, to realize that I did not find her so, I, to whom she scarcely ever spoke, I, whose very existence she often seemed to ignore. Just the same, something remained to me of the Tamara I had known: her compelling eyes.

We were sitting there in the winter twilight, in the silence that follows the midday meal, as though posing for a family portrait. Tamara was half reclining on the white sofa, one foot tucked under her, gracefully pensive and very conscious of how charming she looked in a costly negligée of leaf-brown satin. Father, standing behind her, was endowed with all the indispensable attributes of an industrialist in repose—beaming smile, coffee cup, fat cigar—and so perfectly symbolized beatitude as depicted in the movies that he seemed unreal. Seated at the piano, Jean Delfau was strumming with his right hand, and his sharp face had become softened by a hint of revery. He was waiting for my father's departure, and for mine, too. Would that day be crucial? Anyway, sure of himself and more than sure of her, he was in no hurry. And there I was, too, in a big armchair, a little apart from the others, ill-dressed as a nice young girl should be, with charcoal smudged fingers and modest mien which wonderfully concealed my disdainful awareness.

"Well, now," sighed Father, pulling himself out of his comfortable rumination, "I must go down to my study. And I may look in at the warehouse presently, so don't expect me back home before seven. Goodbye, my dearest."

With a graceful movement, calculated to attract Jean, perhaps, she raised herself up towards Father, who gave her a long kiss, a stupidly long kiss, and yet, in a way, pathetic. His constant and obvious desire for her was both touching and embarrassing.

Before going off, he shook hands with Jean.

"Try to cheer up my wife," he said cordially. "She's apparently in very low spirits today."

"Oh no, just a bit chilly,' she protested, clasping her arms and shivering most becomingly. And he indulgently smiled.

This banal exchange of words would have been comic to me had I not heard it so often. In the old days, I had laughed when he talked about how sweet, how loving Tamara was. But sweet she had become, sickeningly sweet. And she now put on quite a good show of being devoted to him. Men who have that much conviction, I reflected, are the ones that get what they want out of life; I was close to envying him.

He left the room. And I, silent and stupid, very much in the way, remained in my tapestried chair, staring at the Venetian glass chandelier, the exaggeratedly heavy draperies, all that white and gold urbanity with which Tamara had managed to surround herself, and I looked at Jean, who had once more begun softly to sing, accompanying himself with one hand. It was now an Elizabethan air, both lively and sad:

> *Now our partings must be done,*
> *Joy once fled does not return . . .*

I reflected that he must be thirty-five or so; a fine network of wrinkles covered his face, like sparse foliage through which peered a fox's sharp nose. His hair, thick and dark, brought out the pallor of his fine features, which bore countless signs of mistrust, irony, and perhaps also a little weariness. But his affected drawl, his studied gestures, even his unconcerned way of flirting with Tamara, betrayed a rather disagreeable amount of self-sufficiency.

I doubted that he was in love with my seductive stepmother. But you could see by the way he acted, for he made no least effort to hide it, that he felt sure of her. And how could she be expected, after two years of a boring marriage, to hold out very long against this still youngish man, with his established reputation as a stage designer, his near-celebrity, his wealth—for he was assuredly well-to-do—who had come from Paris at my father's request, arriving in Gers covered with glory and scandal?

Just think! In three months, Father might be the mayor of Gers—a rank he had coveted for a very long time. What an ambition! To gather votes, he had launched what he called "a prestige campaign" and one of his ideas was the reorganization of a theatrical company in Gers. The Grand Theatre of Gers had been, for almost thirty years, nothing but a popular playhouse where laborers and fishermen went, on Saturdays and Sundays, to applaud old actors in Germanic-dialect farces. And even that public had gradually dwindled. By posing as a Patron of the Arts, Father had discovered a way of winning votes, since voters will do almost anything for a little entertainment. Some new recruits had been cleverly chosen and added to the group of old actors. The new play which this renovated theatrical company was to put on was already in rehearsal. A fever of excitement reigned in Gers, where the backers of the Mayor, old Maalens, who intended to run for reelection, were conniving to find an overwhelming retort.

The play chosen, *La Reine Berthe*, happened to be the work of a certain Van Beck, undoubtedly an estimable man of letters, but more particularly esteemed as President of the Municipal Council. Lievens, the juvenile lead, also happened to be the son of a municipal councillor; and if the other members of the honorable electoral body had had children and if they had showed the least inclination for the stage, a place would in all probability have been found for them in the heterogeneous Grand Theatre Company. The part played by Jean Delfau in this brilliant commercial venture was, first of all, to prove that Father was no penny-pincher. Max Villar had been the one to get in touch with him, Max, the celebrated painter of Gers, formerly Tamara's intimate friend, promoted, since her marriage, to family friend. Max asked Jean to design the sets and also to take charge of staging the play. The second proposal was Max's idea, for he knew that the opportunity of trying out his talents would tempt Jean more than the financial inducement, since he liked to pose as a rich dilettante and had no least need of money.

A young and rather well-known actress, Sandra Marelli, had also come down from Paris to star in the show for about a dozen performances. Everyone said she was Jean Delfau's mistress—but then, what didn't they say on his score!

"All this gossip is incomprehensible to me," Father had said, with his usual naïveté. "After all, the poor boy is almost a cripple."

That was quite a serious word to apply to the partial paralysis which immobilized Jean's left arm, and that infirmity did not seem to bother him much. With almost provocative ease, he sketched, he strummed the piano, using only his right hand, and that hand was so rapid and skilled in all the motions of everyday life that he almost seemed to hold his left arm against his chest negligently, in a gesture that was a part of his nonchalant attitude.

From the way Tamara was looking at him, it was obvious, to me at any rate, that my father's pity was badly misplaced. Jean was still singing, in a pleasantly melancholy and rather muffled voice, observing Tamara without seeming to, and Tamara was enjoying the game like a young girl. Not daring to use her charms openly, in front of me, she flushed resentfully and remained mute. In the old days she would simply have said, "Aren't you going to your class, Hélène?" Despite myself, I still expected just that. Instead, she said nothing, merely sighed, playing the part of the irreproachable wife who does not want to give the least cause for suspicion. Did she perhaps think I was fooled? I imagined there was a glimmer of irony in Jean's shrewd glance.

Another sigh. Languidly she put some stray locks in place, smoothed her severely drawn-back hair, patted her heavy black chignon. No, she'd never bring herself to do it. And I would go away, disappointed once more. She would not admit her duplicity in front of me, not yet, not just then.

"I must get to work," I said. "So, I leave you to yourselves."

For a second Jean's gaze rested upon me, sharp, scrutinizing, then returned to Tamara.

"Very well, darling," she replied, without even seeming glad to get rid of me.

I shut the door softly. As I climbed the stairs, the sound of Jean's voice grew fainter, and the last notes died away just as I reached my room:

Joy once fled does not return . . .

Sitting on the stairs leading up to the second floor, I was on the lookout, at my post of observation. From there, I had a view of a rather dark little landing, connecting with my stairway, and which led from one room to another. It was the scene of quite a few amorous intrigues which I had watched with amusement. Since my father's remarriage, his circle of acquaintances had widened and grown younger. Instead of businessmen fond of beer and interested only in money, he now saw a collection of forty-year-old couples who deluded themselves into thinking they were still young and often met to drink, dance, and reassort themselves into new couples, more or less openly,

6

more or less durably. There is something infernal in this de-
bauchery of small towns where, for lack of other relations, all
the couples know each other just a little too well.

These were the couples I saw crossing the dark landing, less
ardent as the weeks passed, breaking off, then renewing their
intrigues or half-heartedly beginning others. The couples might
be new but the individuals were always the same, and I saw
their familiar faces pass and repass before me as if on a stage,
in different plays. Some of the women's faces showed a sensuous
desire that alcohol touched with poetry, others smirked coquet-
tishly, coldly calculating their fall from grace. There were men's
faces, heavy with lust, slack-lipped, fat-chinned, to which alcohol also provided an excellent alibi. There were hard, precise
faces, like Madame Freud's, as she stood arranging her hair in
front of the small looking glass, wondering which man she
would next favor with her stale baby-tricks, and practising expressions, as if assuming a mask—lips sensual, eyes clouded with
desire, and all the rest of the respectable prostitute's repertoire.
Joris, the sculptor, whispered to his agate-eyed "disciple" as he
pressed his shoulder, "Confess, you liked her? Admit it, you
did like her?" And the disciple laughed like a tickled girl.

Even vice became small, sank from its sombre grandeur into
repulsive depravity. My father at least brought a kind of whole-
someness to these laborious orgies. Tamara saw to it that he did
not go too far, but that evening I saw him, among others, corner
that blonde widow with the milk-white shoulders, and disregard-
ing her coy simperings, kiss her avidly, with such naive and
evident relish that it was almost pathetic. For I had learned how
rare is even such desire without grandeur; I had seen those couples who go off in corners to confess their flirtations to each
other simply to bring about a show of jealousy and thus restore
a semblance of vitality to their decomposing sex-life.

That evening I waited longer than usual. I waited patiently,
stubbornly, for a couple who had not yet passed before my eyes:
Jean and Tamara. It was already late and I had not seen them,

but I still waited; if need be, I would wait until the very end of the evening, until the last guests should have taken a far too noisy leave, banging the heavy street door behind them. I wanted her to come there, I wanted to see her in his arms, giving the lie to everything she pretended to be or tried to make me believe. I needed to despise her still more.

But a heavy step shook the stairs. Max Villar, our great national painter, rigged out to look very Bohemian and untidy, as was his custom on special occasions, came to sit down heavily beside me. I knew only too well why he was there: Tamara was snubbing him, all her attentions being for Jean Delfau, whom she was showing off like a new dress. And Max, still devoured with his old love of her kept following her around, receiving with a hang-dog look one rebuff after another, continuing to hope against all logic, that she would some day yield to his desires again.

While waiting, he put an arm around my shoulders and spoke with forced gaiety.

"Well, Lovely Lena, everything okay? What are you plotting, perched up here on the stairs? Why aren't you spinning round and round like the others?"

"I wasn't invited," I said without bitterness.

"I'm beginning to think I wasn't invited either," he groaned. "Do you know how many times she's danced with him? Four times straight!"

He did not need to tell me whom he was talking about. I understood at once. His face was becoming terribly worn. I could read on it the ravages of the two years spent, since Tamara's marriage, in waiting for the least look from her, they were engraved in deep lines. He had been handsome, with the face of a laughing faun, but his tangle of curls now hung down sadly, a symbol of his profound defeat, and new lines appeared each day on that face that had once been jovial. They were wrinkles of sadness and discouragement, even of resignation, not the wrinkles made by anger, and that was what I could not forgive.

Tamara went by on the landing, dancing with Jean. Then they again disappeared into the drawingroom. Max sighed. He would not even reproach her, and it was only with a lamentable remnant of pride that he said, "I'll tell her tomorrow what I think of her, I'll speak out my mind!"

We both knew quite well that he would do nothing of the sort. That he now went back to Paris only rarely, that he had stopped painting canvasses that scarcely sold and had descended to painting family portraits was explainable: he wanted to put down his roots more solidly in Gers, so he could be near Tamara, follow in her wake, breathe the air she breathed and perhaps, one day, when she would be very tired, he could hope to hold her once more in his arms. And so he went on living nearby. He had given up his career, and he would do even more: he would see her only in public, would be content with a smile, a glance. And were she to have lovers, he would protect her from gossip, would receive her letters for her, would uphold her lies. And were my father to drive her out, he would take her back, and with what joy!

Again, Tamara and Jean passed by on the landing. With his valid right arm, Jean held her expertly by the waist, and she gazed up at him with simulated diffidence. He tried to kiss her, she resisted briefly, being very careful not to leave his arms. How well she pretended modesty, how well she imitated the hesitations of a wife who has not yet been unfaithful! At last she gave in. It was a long kiss, so different from those, imperious, swift, and desperate kisses I had known. Her body yielded under that kiss, I could see it, sheathed in a red gown, slowly and pliantly yield. That kiss lasted for an infinity of time, docile and as if mindless, and when the sound of footsteps came to interrupt it, I saw Tamara's face, her half closed eyes, still completely absorbed in that unfinished kiss. I looked at Jean. His expression

9

was calm, a little sad, but as another couple passed, I saw the flicker of a hard, triumphant smile on his face.

I felt Max wince beside me. That was what kept me from laughing. Oh, if only she had known I was there! After going to such trouble to play, before me, me the one who knew her, that rôle of affectionate wife, devoted if not passionate, whose social life was nothing but a sacrifice willingly made to her husband's ambitions! And was she just playing a rôle? Was she still capable of amusing herself? Or was she managing, by an admirable *tour de force*, to reconcile Jean's kiss and their future illicit union with her new and respectable middleclass character?

"Oh, the rotters!" said Max under his breath.

"If you were the man, you'd think it delightful."

"Oh, sure! But I made love to her *before*. It's not the same thing, now."

"You belong to the past, he belongs to the future," I said lightly.

"What do you mean, he belongs to the future? Did she take you into her confidence? Did you find out something? Is she his mistress? Is she in love with him?"

There was not the least anger in his voice: nothing but panic and grief and that eternal resignation that I loathed. For my part, had I ever been resigned? Had I ever weakened for a moment in those two years? Had I for one sole moment stopped despising her? And yet there was great temptation, on some miserable evenings when I felt hemmed in by solitude, imprisoned and alone there in my room at the top of the house, isolated from sounds and warmth and the sense of well-being that Tamara spread around her, and without anything but the view from my window over the roofs of the town sloping down to the harbor, and alone there in my room at the top of the house, isolated from

Sometimes I was close to tears and forgetfulness and dissolving pardon. But I had always held out. Never had I gone downstairs to the floor below, where Tamara and Father were laughing together. Never had I responded to her advances, laughed at her jokes, taken part in her pleasures. And when I saw Max's state of prostration, the debasement which marked his whole being, I forgot the coldness of solitude, the anguish of unshed tears. I was only proud to be there, still unbroken, confronting him.

I wanted to seize him by the arm, shake him, tell him loudly that his love was base, degrading, rotten, and that my hatred was tonic and fresh. That he was lost, caught in a bog, and that a little anger would be enough to pull him out of it. But had I not myself, two years before, known the pleasures of subjection in the arms of Tamara? No one could have pulled me out of that lethargy, and no one could pull Max out. I could do nothing for him. Disdain cannot be communicated: it is not a soft substance like their love, quickly spread, quickly shared, and which, when you merely approach it, soils you. Contempt is shining and compact and round like a medal; it has its own delights, and it cannot be shared.

That is why I said to him, "No, she's not his mistress. No, she did not take me into her confidence. Don't worry. She'll come back to you some day . . ."

"You have it in for her, eh?" he said with melancholy.

"Oh no!" I said sincerely. "I don't have anything against her. Not now."

And it was true. I had nothing against her, now that she justified my contempt.

I I •

Before going to the Beaux-Arts Academy, where I was following a course in drawing, I was in the habit of taking an early morning walk in the steep and almost deserted little streets of Gers. That morning, at the beginning of winter, it was still dark, with the soft and gentle darkness of the dawn, behind which you feel the coming of light. People who were strangers to me passed in groups, very quickly, without talking, a little numbed with the cold, perhaps, on their way to offices or factories, towards light and warmth and noise. For the moment, under the winking street-lamps, they were nothing but shadows, and they passed near me, also nothing but a shadow. I felt completely alone, and therefore happy. I crossed the silent park. On the edge of the pond, some dimly seen animals—stray dogs and cats, enormous rats—were fighting over some whitish bones. Sometimes, at the end of a street, I glimpsed the garbage truck, a sombre mass lit dimly by a lantern, and its soft sucking sound echoed in the sonorous streets, like the moan of a huge wounded monster. I then went down to the harbor, passing by the post office on the little square.

The fishermen had already gone off towards the invisible horizon where the lake merged with the distant wide river and the uprooted reeds with the floating seaweed in a great backwash, green and icy. There were only a few people mending nets—some women and an old man. Here and there, through a window of a cottage, one could see a solemn looking housewife preparing breakfast in a room of unplastered brick lit by a single light bulb hanging at the end of a wire. Almost no sound was to be heard. That hour was for me alone, I could secretly enjoy its quiet sadness. Without fear of anyone, I could relax for a moment. The town was no longer made up of hundreds of mocking or leering faces, spying glances, scandalmongering mouths, human beings ready to speak to you, cling to you, contaminate you.

I was at peace during that hour, and it ended upon a moment of glory. With the first glimmer of dawn, the new buildings standing here and there on the hillside grew bigger before my eyes, like fantastic and still indistinct white cliffs, and the lake, slowly touched by the light, unrolled like a big yellow snake. Then I slowly returned towards the upper town, crossing without seeing it the Rempart des Beguines, while the bakers passed, blowing into their little brass trumpets to summon the servant maids who came running out for the hot bread wrapped in a big white paper, and I traversed that odor of love, musing that it was towards love that I would like to return from my nocturnal town.

A man came towards me, passed by. I felt him staring at me and I hurried my steps. No one must penetrate this hour of peace, or it would be spoiled . . . But the man must have turned in his tracks, for I soon heard him walking behind me, and a hand fell heavily upon my shoulder.

"So, one must go out at this hour of day in order to meet you, young lady?"

I at once recognized the pleasantly muffled voice of Jean Delfau. How I hated him for catching me like that, off my guard! I was filled with a childish fury at the intrusion, the indignation of an actor who, during his monologue at the beginning of the play, sees a character of the third act come on stage. To my mind, Jean Delfau was, above everything, the future lover of Tamara. His rôle was all ready for him, well defined, and there he was, appearing suddenly in the darkness, standing in front of me, looking at me in that ironical way of his, as if he guessed something of my confusion.

"I imagine you didn't come out just to meet me?" I said rather curtly.

He began to laugh, not at all hurt by my coldness.

"If I had known I would run into you, I most certainly would have come out, of course! But since I did not know . . . And anyway, to tell the truth, and at the risk of shocking you, I did not come out—I was just coming in. But don't let me keep you. No doubt you have a rendezvous?"

His rather mocking, yet not unkind words, infuriated me. He

sounded so exactly as if he were speaking to a little girl who was something of a ninny and utterly unimportant! He would not have spoken differently if Tamara had been there.

"No. I was not going to any rendezvous. I wanted to be alone, that's all."

"Heavens! And I have disturbed your solitude! It's unforgivable! But are you aware that you're quite pretty when you think you're alone?"

I blushed in spite of myself, less at the banal compliment than at the fact that I was not entirely indifferent to it. Even a slightly naive young girl could attract a blasé Don Juan, and this encounter was, in the long run, rather romantic. What would Tamara say to it, Tamara, so sure of her conquest and so proud of exhibiting her triumph before the eyes of the ladies of Gers, who were all competing for the attentions of Jean Delfau? I liked to think about how annoyed she would be.

"I was going to the Academy," I said in a sweeter tone, starting off again.

He followed me, his tall, bony silhouette floating in a raincoat that was slightly too big, a newspaper slipped beneath his left arm, which was bent as though naturally.

"And what do you do in that pompously named place, may I ask?"

"Taking a course in drawing."

"Well, well! In other words, you and I are fellow workers! You must show me some of your efforts. What sort of things do you draw at that Academy? Poppies in a vase? Antique plasters?"

His bantering tone nettled me. Obviously he expected my work to be the usual silly stuff done by young girls. I resolved to show him my drawings, for I knew some of them would, at least momentarily, capture his interest. And though I wanted very much to see Tamara sink to the point of accepting Jean Delfau's advances, it might also constitute a pleasant revenge to deprive her of the possibility. Why not? I was not overestimating myself in supposing that he could be momentarily attracted to an eighteen-year-old girl, if only out of curiosity. He was certainly flirting with Tamara for no other reason.

"I would be very glad if you would have a look at my drawings," I said modestly, blushing again, and voluntarily this time. "I only hope Tamara won't object."

His brief smile just escaped being smug.

"I don't believe our meeting . . . on an artistic plane could offend your stepmother."

He was making fun of me, almost openly. But his hard eyes flashed with curiosity. We were still walking in the narrow streets and he did not seem to think of leaving me.

The town was waking up, more and more people were in the streets, and within an hour the first boats with orange colored sails would return to the port. Behind the bluish glass of the bakeries could be seen those wierdly shaped hot rolls, golden brown, which our bakers make and which look like glistening shells or sponges. Jean stopped to survey them. As for me, my mind was on something else. I was mulling over this new idea of mine: I might capture Jean Delfau's attentions. There would be a double advantage in it: to fool Tamara, who would endure all the inconveniences of adultery without its benefits—the whole town was already predicting that she was going to succumb to the stage designer's charms, if she had not already done so—and I would run no risk of falling in love with him.

For I wanted no more tenderness in my life, no more vulnerable emotions, no more degrading submissiveness. Henceforth I would tolerate nothing but desire, which I believed to be the only sincere emotion—I was still too young to guess that desire, too, is sometimes shammed.

We kept on walking. The street-lights went out. Jean Delfau took me by the arm, and I allowed it.

Had I not long ago decided to take a lover? But up to then I had not been able to visualize anyone in the rôle. The choice, in Gers, was very limited. There was Max, who would have obligingly made love to me, with one eye on Tamara. There was Stani, in my class at the Academy, who felt that only a rich marriage could pull him and his family out of their dump in the Rue d'Ecosse. There was a crowd of young men without money or looks who were always loud in their praise of my father's abilities and my stepmother's charms, my artistic talents . . . What wouldn't they have praised in order to become the son-in-law of the important Monsieur Noris, future mayor of Gers? And there were some married men who, in the evenings when they had had a few too many drinks, could be made to forget their usual caution and the fact that I was not yet of age. Nothing very tempting! Well, what about Jean Delfau?

Meanwhile, Gers was gradually emerging from a bluish mist and a pale winter sun had risen behind the wet roofs.

"I'll say goodbye here," he said, as we arrived on the Post Office square. "So if by chance you were *not* going to the Academy, you won't have to take the trouble of making a detour."

His conspiratorial air exasperated me.

"You're referring to my 'rendezvous', I suppose!" I exclaimed. Then, seizing the opportunity he had given me: "I despise love!" I said fiercely.

"No doubt you've had a sad disappointment?" he queried with gentle irony.

"Quite right," I said, smilingly.

"And of course, you swore to renounce such deceptive pleasures forever?"

"Not at all. I simply do not want to be deceived again."

"And have you found a sure-fire recipe for that?"

"Sure-fire, possibly not. I haven't tried yet. But I would try not to have any illusions and would try to prevent the man I picked from having any."

"The man you picked! What a little Amazon you are! And have you already picked that fortunate man?"

"No."

Our glances met like two supple and resisting blades. Again there was that satisfied smile on his face.

"How interesting," he said. "Well, young lady, keep on look-ing. You will certainly find him."

And upon these ambiguous words, he left me, going off with hurried steps.

He must be wondering about my confusion and congratulat-ing himself on having made such an impression upon me. How easy it was. How easy everything was when you did not care. By the time I reached the Academy, I was gayly humming a tune.

It was cold in the Academy courtyard. Under the big tree which made the shadows even denser, Stani was stamping his feet, waiting for the doors to open.

"Things all right with you this morning?" I asked.

"No . . ."

"Depressed? Your affair with Colette isn't progressing? Co-lette's in a bad humor?"

His handsome tanned face clouded.

"Colette? She's chucked me out. She's a stinker. Girls are all alike. They kiss you, they pet, and it's Darling this and Darling that, but when it comes to talking about getting married—zero. They're as slippery as eels."

I was amused at the look on his disgusted face. He did noth-ing but chase heiresses, and didn't seem to realize there were no simple-minded ones left.

"And marrying for money is your only hope?"

He gave me a bewildered look. His eyes were the most beauti-ful imaginable, big, golden, slightly slanted, with heavy eyelids, like a Turk's. I had not escaped being more than a little stirred by those good looks, and it was this very feeling that separated me from Stani. I had too keen a recollection of having suffered for a face I loved; I didn't want to begin another affair like that with Tamara, and so I was quite satisfied just to exercise my power over Stani.

"You'll not easily find the girl you're looking for," I said. "The suspicious girls aren't the only trouble. There are the papas who threaten to cut them off. If you don't look out, you'll have some dreadful creature on your hands and not a penny in your pocket."

"Oh, I know, Lena. But what else can I do? You should see the hole we live in! I'm not just thinking of myself, I'm thinking of mamma! She lived on a great estate in Poland, and now she has to live like I don't know what and can't even buy a new dress when she wants one. Oh, she doesn't complain, she's very brave, but . . ."

I resolutely stopped him short in his tirade of filial love.

"You oughtn't to talk so much about your mother," I said kindly. "It's not your style. Now, don't worry. Three days from now I'm going to introduce you to Madame Périer."

"That old woman?"

"She's not so old . . . I'm sure you'll like her a lot. And then, think what it would mean to your mother . . ."

"Madame Périer already has some one," he timidly objected.

"You mean Fontanas? You're much better looking than he is!"

"Honestly?" he asked, with such a stupid smile that I felt like kissing him. "Well," he added with a sigh, "when are you going to introduce me?"

And this was easy, too! The vanity of some people, the cupidity of others. If I had known this in the past, I might even have been able to manoeuvre Tamara. With Stani and his good looks; Jean and his talent, his fame; and Tamara steeped in hypocrisy; I felt confident of making them do as I liked. It was such fun to think of holding the strings to these dissimilar puppets that I forgot the solitude which was waiting for me at home and the morning hour when, for a brief instant, I had been touched by the recollection of love.

I returned to the sweet disdain which for two years had soothed me with the same words: "You alone hard, you alone new and intact, you alone strong and invulnerable."

Under the spell of those words I forgot the rancors of the

past. Let Tamara be unfaithful to my father, let Stani prostitute himself to the overripe Odette Périer, let Jean conceitedly believe that Hélène was in love with him, this was necessary to my peace. No one now could wound me.

Jean came to call and, with his ironical and condescending smile, asked Tamara's permission to go up to my room with me and look over my drawings. I was careful to show him first of all the stupidest ones—antique heads and bowls of fruit drawn at the Academy. He was more interested in some rapid sketches I had made of fishermen, shopkeepers, people in cafés. Then he picked up a pile of my latest drawings and looked at them for a long time. In those sketches, day after day, I had recorded, as in a diary, the ravages made by her new life on Tamara's face. From the day of her marriage, when she was radiant with joy, still beautiful, still with a tinge of cruelty on her arrogant lips, until these last months, I had wanted to show, in gradual touches, the empty sweetness, the weakening, the progressive sagging of those features that had once been so proud, and fix them, as if forever. And through those portraits, I could live again the days when I had particularly detested Tamara. There was the day when she had asked Father, with kittenish persuasiveness, for her first expensive fur coat . . .

"But are you being very reasonable?" Father had asked, a little scared at the idea. And she had said, with a girlish pout, "Of course, it's not reasonable, but I do so want it!" I had caught that little pout and had exaggerated it almost into a grimace.

And the day when the drawingroom had been newly decorated and she had asked Father to carry her over the threshold in his arms. He had lifted her from the ground. "You've become very heavy!" he had said, and she had laughed a full, self-satisfied laugh. It was the laughter of a spoiled wife who likes herself, feels comfortable in her flesh, enjoys it. I had caught the laughter in my sketch, grotesquely distorting the triangular face. And the last of my drawings showed the new amorous face of Tamara, succumbing to Jean's embrace, swollen with sensuality, dishevelled, undone, in a sensual yielding that lacked real warmth, being more like a drunkard's heavy drowsiness.

Jean surveyed this drawing for quite a few seconds. Did he recognize it?

"You're not very fond of her, are you?" he said at last.

"No," I replied, "I'm not very fond of her."

"Why not?"

He had resumed his ironical tone. He looked disproportionately tall in my low-ceilinged room.

"What, in particular, do you have against her? The life she led in the past? That she seems to enjoy my company? You are certainly conventional!"

I fairly jumped with anger at the insult. He had wounded me in my most sensitive point.

"Why no, that's not it. I have nothing against her for the life she leads, what I object to are the pompous names she gives that life, making it a travesty of excuses, instead of plunging into it recklessly. Her hypocrisy, her half-heartedness—that's what I reproach her. And . . ."

But I did not go on. The secret of Tamara's undoing belonged only to me.

"How you do flare up!" said he, smiling. "What vehemence! Why, you're a terrible little fanatic, Hélène! Who would have guessed it from your calm, pretty face? So, if you'd been in Tamara's place you'd have acted differently? With more enthusiasm and less caution?"

"Yes," I said, without reflecting, "yes, of course."

"Just how?"

He seemed amused at my embarrassment. What could I do? After all, it would be easy for him to defy me. I remained silent, feeling rather silly before the challenge.

"You see? You don't know a thing about it. There you stand, without moving, exactly like Tamara. I really don't see what you have to criticize in her."

His mocking tone utterly exasperated me.

"You know very well," I said angrily, "that you behave differently with Tamara, and so, consequently . . ."

"Is that a reproach?" he demanded quickly.

I did not reply. Fortunately, I blushed. He drew near. I was standing with my back to the window, near the bed. With unexpected gentleness he put his arm around me, holding me close for a long time before kissing me.

I took no pleasure at all in that kiss. I thought, "He would kiss any woman who said those words and blushed and fluttered her eyelashes and showed she was ready to give herself." What easy preys to women all Don Juans were! But the easy prey was becoming a little too eager, I was losing just a little of my self-possession. Out of breath, we drew apart. The windowsill outside had a white fur edging of snow, and the stripped branches of the big linden tree set dark bars against the bright blue sky. I was struck by that banal pattern: it was an omen, I would have to be careful . . . not careful as Tamara was, but in a quite opposite way.

"You know," he said in his muffled voice, which had a gentle sound, "once more you're behaving like Tamara?"

"Yes," I said, trying out the provocative tone. "I know. But there must be some way of not being like her, from a certain moment on."

I was thinking of her pretended resistance. He stepped towards me, then stopped, as if struck by a thought.

"There's one sure way," he said, with his indefinable smile, half ironic, half bored. "And that's for us to stop right here, definitely."

He strode towards the door, then turned back.

"Your drawings are very good," he said, "really very good. But you must learn to check your imagination . . ."

And he went downstairs, where Tamara was waiting. Decidedly I had been wrong to pity him. He was not the easy prey I had thought.

In Madame Périer's little drawingroom, half-Moroccan, half-Turkish, there was a considerable crowd. Draped in a kind of leaf-brown sari, and wearing silver earrings, Madame Périer was trying so hard to look languorous that her thick black eyebrows were frowning with the effort.

"She's not too bad," said Stani.

Odette Périer received her guests half reclining, in a pose that evoked the harems of Delacroix more than the image of Madame Récamier. Her abundant flesh, which burst all bonds, was voluminously displayed on a divan upholstered in Persian silk. The lovely white bosom revealed by her low cut gown would have been seductive, one had to admit, had she not surfeited the eyes of the local gentry with it for some twenty years.

"She doesn't look her age," Stani went on earnestly, trying like a not very talented schoolboy to whet his appetite.

"Well, shall I introduce you?"

"Oh, not yet!" he said, recoiling from the heavy bovine gaze that had settled upon him.

Everyone was crowding around Madame Périer, men were bringing her drinks and ices as if they were gifts specially chosen, rather than the refreshments she herself was providing. And she accepted them like that, with the majestic nonchalance which enabled her to act like a guest at her own receptions, the most favored and fascinating guest, around whom the other guests thronged.

Odette had not always been so calmly regal. There had been a time when her rival, Madame Vallée, reigned supreme in Gers, flaunting her extravagant bonnets and a very dirty little monkey an inspired relative had brought back from Brazil. But

"Come along, now," I said gaily, "let me introduce you to Madame Périer."

Seeing through Jean's behavior the other day had restored all my good humor. Stani hesitated.

"I'm not sure that I . . ."

"For heaven's sake, you were the one that asked to be brought here, weren't you?"

"Yes, but . . ."

Again he had that honest look that was so unbecoming.

"You're going to talk about your mother. I feel it. Did you mention Madame Périer to her and tell her how useful she can be to you?"

"Yes."

"Well?"

"She told me to come here with you and she said you were very nice to have fixed it up for me. But I'm not sure she understood."

"She'll understand even less when she hears that you wouldn't even let me introduce you. What are you afraid of? That she's going to rape you right here in her drawingroom? After all, who knows, she may not even like you!"

"Oh, yes she will," said Stani naively. His handsome tanned face, his almond eyes, were magnificent. It was a face not made for noble sentiments; he should have nothing to do with such things. We advanced towards Odette.

"Stanislas Mierowicz, one of my friends at the Academy," I said.

"A young artist, how delightful!" she said in her pensive voice. "Are you exhibiting in October?"

Her tone was almost absent-minded, but her eyes flashed and she surveyed Stani with the slightly annoyed admiration of an amateur discovering a favorite artist's painting never seen before.

"I hope so, Madame," replied Stani with admirable detachment.

26

the providential death of a great aunt, who concealed her enormous fortune just where it was least expected, in a neat little house in Amsterdam, had placed Odette at the head of an important cocoa firm, with several ships and immense plantations—poetic images which were expressed in an annual income astounding to the people of Gers. "Who would have thought it?" my father had naively commented. "A woman so lacking in practical sense . . ." As if the languid Odette had any part in the distant decease of the great aunt! And in the wink of an eye Madame Vallée had been eclipsed by the sumptuous receptions, the exquisite dinners, the impromptu country excursions offered by Odette, her imperturbable rival. Disheartened, Madame Vallée had left town and gone to Barfleur, not far away, to vegetate among her souvenirs in the society of her venomous husband and her stinking monkey that no longer had her prestige as an excuse.

Tonight, the society of Gers was by way of making amends to Madame Périer for having misjudged her ever since Jean's arrival two weeks before. A scandal had threatened which would have deprived the beautiful Odalisque of her throne: everyone had thought she aspired to annex Jean.

Odette Périer shared with her late rival, Madame Vallée, a pronounced taste for artists, whom she was always careful to pick young. For more than fifteen years, her admirers had all been painters. The fact could be easily explained: the Academy of Beaux-Arts had the honor of being the finest and most celebrated ornament of Gers. Besides, ambitious young men of the business world had other things to do than spend time saying sweet nothings to a mature lady who loudly proclaimed her intentions of remaining a widow. Well, when Jean Delfau arrived, that lady's first care had been to send her car and chauffeur to meet him at the station, with an invitation to accept her hospitality. Innocently, or perhaps out of curiosity, Delfau had at first accepted. The generous thought of the Odalisque, for whom the very words "stage designer" or "theatrical director" called up

23

the image of a starveling, had been to save him from the hotels of ill repute in the harbor and from the outrageous prices of the only first-class hotel, the Carlton. She had invited Jean in all honesty, for Fontanas reigned over her charitable heart. But the people of Gers were malevolent, gossipy, quick to imagine and prompt to blame, so that by the evening of Jean's first day at Madame Périer's, despite all her past kindnesses, floods of champagne, avalanches of sandwiches, numberless loans, and the adulteries facilitated and even consummated beneath her roof, Odette was in danger of losing her throne. Everything was topsy-turvy. Some rather familiar joking went on about Art and Madame Périer. The bets that had been laid in November on the possible "winners" of her heart and on what painters would show their work at the exhibition she patronized dropped to zero. And this, with the exhibition only one month away. Some young men who had little standing with the Academy and who put all their hopes of future glory in Odette, seeing their career ruined, used pretty inflammatory terms in accusing the good lady of betraying Art. Had she publicly burnt a canvas of Leonardo, the emotion and indignation of certain people would not have been more intense. Some people took a moderate stand, arguing that Jean Delfau was above all else a stage designer and that a stage designer was the next thing to being a painter. But the intransigents replied that a designer, who was also a theatrical director, was not an exponent of Pure Art, and no matter what, this Outsider was not going to exhibit his work in the October Academy exhibition and that Madame Périer, by depriving the entire town of winning its bets, gravely sinned against her social duties. Was she going to lose, just for a passing whim, the consideration and esteem and indulgence of her fellow citizens?

A week passed. Jean Delfau, no doubt weary of the languorous attentions of Madame Périer and unimpressed by the prices of the Carlton, had transferred his belongings to that hotel. It was also observed that Fontanas had recently acquired a new car

and that Jean was assiduously frequenting the Noris home. It was understood that he was paying court to Tamara, an unconventional woman, to whom public opinion was not well disposed anyway, and that Madame Périer, if not always faithful to artists, was at least faithful to Art. Then the storm died down.

The extraordinary crowd at this evening reception proved that Gers regretted its error in having momentarily misjudged such a respectable lady. Surrounded by young men who were authentic artists and citizens of Gers, Odette was happy. The refreshments were plentiful and of excellent quality. From time to time could be heard the clatter of a Moroccan weapon falling from its place on the wall, or the soft deflating plop of an upholstered ottoman collapsing beneath a too voluminous guest.

"Delfau seems to be very chummy with your stepmother," said Stani.

"You think so?"

"Can't you see? I'd say the event is about to take place."

"You think he's in love with her?" I asked with something of a shudder.

"No," said Stani, speaking as an expert. "But he's got to have some woman or other."

"He has the Marelli girl."

"The Marelli girl runs off to Paris every other day. He's got to have a woman here to protect him from the husband-chasers."

I had a lightning flash of understanding.

"So he's being tormented by a lot of husband-chasers?"

"For goodness sake! A thirty-year-old bachelor, rich as Croesus, who is probably bored—what a godsend! Why, the mammas can think of nothing else! Where are your eyes?"

Perhaps that explained his sudden recoil, his hardened expression, his words, "The best thing would be to stop right here." If he was on his guard against me, the game would not be as easy as I had thought. Stani must be right. He was not noted for his intelligence, but he had a sharper intuition than I when it came to questions of money.

"You must come and show me your paintings one of these days," the Odalisque languorously murmured. A circle of people already had surrounded them, spying upon them, gauging the brooding look in Odette's eyes, the impassivity of Stani's face.

"What day?" asked Stani, with ever increasing calm.

"Why, let me see . . . What about Thursday?" said she, half surprised, half flattered by this sign of eagerness. Silently Stani kissed her hand, with a very convincing look of admiration, before stepping aside. I wondered if I had not misjudged him.

"Was I all right?" he asked, entrenched behind the buffet.

"Splendid! How did you manage it?"

"I thought of mamma . . ." he said fondly. And as I burst out laughing in spite of myself, he walked away, with an offended air.

I V •

The cloakroom was a small space contrived on the mezzanine floor. The ceiling was uncommonly low. A big mirror covered one of the walls, the other walls were bristling with hooks and hatracks. There were two small windows, overlooking a misty garden.

"An Alice in Wonderland room," said Jean, surveying it with some astonishment. Of course he had been in it before; but one passed quickly through this little cloakroom when someone was waiting outside, and when voices resounded on the floor above. Today, no one was waiting for Jean. Tamara was at the hairdresser's, Father was in his room, and I had drawn Jean into the little nook to have a talk with him. No one was waiting for him, nothing hurried us, and the door shut behind us made everything seem out of proportion in this closed space. I would never have believed that this almost nonexistent little room, which seemed as tame and inoffensive as a bathroom or a kitchen —indeed, the kitchen seemed to me to harbor more mysteries than this innocent cloakroom—that this little enclosed space could suddenly become a trap which altered all dimensions and likewise all plans. For a moment, I was frightened at so unexpected an atmosphere and was afraid of Jean's eyes, which had taken on a gentler look as I led him in there by the hand. The misty garden, seen from the low windows, seemed inordinately big, like a hostile land whose evil spell we would have to thwart. The frozen shrubbery, the rosebushes without flowers, still, inoffensive skeletons, the gravel paths which seemed to go off into nothingness (the fog swallowed up the white railings), everything had lost its friendliness. In order to recall the words I had memorized and sworn to say to him, I had to struggle against the sudden fraternal feeling of castaways. However, I managed to pull myself together and to speak without trembling.

"I had resolved, when I next saw you, to call your attention to something."

"Well, what is it?"

"I'm not one of these young girls out for a husband," I said, struggling against embarrassment. "I absolutely have no . . . no such ideas. I wouldn't like you to misunderstand."

"And why am I being honored with this information?"

"Don't you think it might simplify our relations?"

His keen eyes sparkled with malice.

"Do you, by any chance, imagine I'm afraid of you?"

And as I remained silent, not knowing what to reply, he drew me towards him with his one valid arm, in a slightly awkward gesture which strangely moved me. He did not kiss me, but merely held me close, with something of tenderness.

"Supposing we leave this place, child? If your father or Tamara caught us here, we'd look rather silly, don't you think?"

The sudden intimacy of his tone, the proprietary way in which he took me by the shoulders, dissipated any stray impulse of tenderness in me. I followed him, apparently docile. A warm wave of satisfaction swept over me at the idea that of all the women he had ever kissed, I was perhaps the one that had followed him with the least pleasure.

We were soon walking outside, climbing the steep little streets, pacing the big boulevard lined with naked trees. I imagined he was tactfully leading me to his hotel.

"Gers is an extraordinary little town," he said.

He had cleverly slipped my arm beneath his paralysed arm, and was talking to me in his drawling society voice. He seemed very relaxed, and I tried to be equally so.

"Really extraordinary. This being a theatrical director—a job I considered quite simple and for that reason accepted it, just to try it out, for as you may know I have had little experience in it up to now—well, it turns out to be the most difficult thing I ever attempted in my entire modest career. Not only are the actors here completely ruined by all those years of playing nothing but farces, but they have a frightful accent and they cost me quite a lot of energy. In addition, they're always cooking up something, contriving dark plots. Just imagine! A certain Mademoiselle Futa, daughter of I forget what influential man, has asked to replace Marelli! Marelli, the only one who may prevent this play from being a flop! As for the juvenile lead they've given me, I suppose, again, it was for a political reason that your father was forced to choose him. I must suppose that, otherwise your father's not to be forgiven. How do you feel about all this, young lady?"

"Oh, as far as I am concerned, the activities of Gers leave me cold. But I know it's always like this. Two years ago, when they tried to organize I forget what biennial celebration which was supposed to bring together all the painters of the country, well, there were so many plots, bribes, disputes, reasons why such and such a painter had to be invited, that the whole thing became too complicated and so remote from art that finally the biennial was held at Barfleur!"

He laughed in a free and easy way and went on talking. I only half listened, more interested in watching his face, which was cleared of all boredom and irony, showing only contentment and the flushed excitement of a little boy explaining the mechanics of a new plaything, because he was telling me about his life in Paris, about the actresses whose costumes he had designed, about his house, his car, in an effort, perhaps, to dazzle me. That a man seemingly so discriminating and talented should give such importance to the material advantages of his life surprised and amused me. I was glad not to discover anything superior in him. Unable to think up responses to his chatter, I tried the silent admiration tactic, and he seemed to fall for it. No doubt he thought I was in love with him and the act of giving myself to him would preserve this flattering illusion. I would not deprive him of it. I had my proud and solitary satisfaction, why not let him have his? That way, to the end, we would remain all the more apart.

The boulevard was deserted. The trees thrashed in the wind, their branches making a dry chopping sound of broken firewood. The trolley cars passed, momentarily dazzling us with their lights which were already turned on. In the distance, at the end of the avenue, the old-fashioned little railway station thrust up its pretentious cupola of many-colored mosaics.

"Even so, this stay in Gers is very restful to me, despite the ill will of my strange company of actors. It's astonishing how little there is to do in a small town like this. Rather charming. One's whole life moves to a different rhythm, slowed down . . ."

"Don't you enjoy your life in Paris?" I asked, without thinking.

"Oh yes, of course!" he replied very quickly, almost curtly. "As I've just explained! Do I look like a man who has a hard life?"

"Why . . . no . . ." I said stupidly, taken aback by his unexplainable aggressiveness.

"I practice an art I adore, I have a delightful house in Paris, a charming woman's companionship, I have a . . . a complete financial independence. One could not hope for more, could one?"

"Certainly not," I said earnestly.

But why had he asked the question so angrily? His arm pressed mine till it hurt, and his face had lost its self-satisfied expression which had so amused me. I was seized with a vague uneasiness.

We had arrived in front of the station, dimly lit behind its many glass panes. A few melancholy porters in blue smocks were idly sitting on their handcarts, in the waiting room. We crossed the wide stretch of black and white tiles which lay beneath our feet like a checkerboard. The minute hand of the enormous round clock moved forward with a clicking sound. At the top of some stone steps was the station platform, and from it came smoke and confused noises, the tooting of a whistle. We exchanged glances. I had almost forgotten that this man I was with was the same man who had been in the cloakroom, the man who had looked at my drawings, in short, the man I intended should become my lover. Why were we taking this walk, why were we exchanging these useless words? Out of a certain delicacy, no doubt habitual to him, he was trying to spare my girlish modesty by accustoming me gradually to him. I must show him that such precautions were utterly needless.

"We've gone past your hotel," I said. "Aren't you staying at the Carlton?"

"Yes, my hotel's the Carlton, all right," he said in a tone I could not fathom. "But what would we be doing at the Carlton?"

"Making love, for heaven's sake," I said with some irritation, finding this professedly blasé seducer terribly slow.

31

He burst out in a gay laugh.

"Making love! My poor dear Hélène, how rashly you are making the plunge! And how cold the water is! Frankly, do you have the least desire to go into a hideous luxury hotel and give yourself to a man you scarcely know? Believe me, I can speak from experience, that's an adventure that wouldn't satisfy you at all . . . or me, either."

A reply was ready on my lips, but I held it back. I wanted to say, "Do you imagine I'm trying to satisfy myself?" But no, I must absolutely not let him see through me.

"Well, then?" I said simply, my lips trembling a little.

"Then, wait. Wait until I tell you to come with me, Hélène. Or rather, no, for I'll not say anything. Wait until the moment comes, all by itself, when you feel or I feel that this thing should happen between us. And then, the moment will be pleasant to us both. I know this hurts you, for you are proud and you want to choose the time and place. You haven't yet learned that we can't force such things, that desire is as imperious as happiness— perhaps more so. No matter what, one must wait for it, nothing is to be gained by hurrying it up."

His kindness tinged with mockery wounded me to the quick. He was treating me like a greedy child, like a more daring Tamara, and on top of it, like an ignoramus who did not know how to be attractive to him. I felt incapable of reply, I could not find the word to wound him in my turn by making it clear to him that I expected no other pleasure than the pleasure of release. But if I wounded him, that would be to lose him definitely, and then what? Stani? Max? The young fellows with ambitions who might think I was in love with them and talk about marriage? The married men who would complicate my life with their sentimentality or contaminate me with their lust?

I made no reply to Jean.

"Why are you trembling, Hélène?" he asked. "How wrong of you to be sad! Isn't it enough to know that what you want I want? And that I was touched by your suggestion, as much as I could have been had we gone through with it?"

His voice was again tender, as it had been in the little cloakroom. But what did his tenderness matter to me? I disengaged myself from his light embrace.

"So, you don't want to?" he said in a tone I hoped was indifferent. And he laughed again.

"How you detest me this minute, Hélène! And all this because I'm not doing with you what any other man would have done—much to your regret later on."

He was now putting on his man-of-the-world act, no doubt flattered at my offer, sufficiently flattered to count it of little importance to possess this little minx. The people passing through the station were staring at us. Despite myself, my eyes were brimming with tears; they must think we were saying goodbyes.

"Isn't Tamara leaving soon for Italy? Haven't we still three months before the opening of *La Reine Berthe*, that admirable tragedy? Why don't we just explore this strange little town together? Come, come, Hélène, don't pout, and let's get out of this station where we've been making a display of ourselves for twenty minutes, now."

Outside, the little square was already in darkness. Beyond it, an ornate gilded door glimmered.

"What is that strange edifice?" he asked. "Be kind, reveal to me the mysteries of Gers. That should be exciting."

"It is the entrance to the Zoological Gardens," I said curtly. "There's absolutely nothing exciting about it. Father must have talked to you about it more than once."

"Oh yes, now I remember, he made his famous speech about it: 'Citizens, our town could be another Berne, another Antwerp! Alas, it is only Gers, with its abandoned Zoo . . .'"

His imitation of my father haranguing the populace was rather good, but made me barely smile. I was exasperated at his easy indifference, I felt like running away after my inglorious defeat. But to run away would be to confess, so I stayed on, trying to imitate his perfectly off-hand manner. After all, wasn't I really just a little relieved that the date of accounting had been postponed? Not too bored, I followed him down the deserted paths of the Zoo. Night was falling. The gravel path encircled vast grey structures, massive and vaulted, like Assyrian palaces or like gigantic whales washed up there, high and dry. From the rotunda of cages, where only crows fluttered and hopped, a slight odor of wild beast came with each puff of wind. The well-kept lawns, sole beauty of this deserted garden, were empty. No one was near the little kiosk, where good children used to sit stiffly erect under their starched bonnets to listen to the military band. The benches were empty, and under the rains of so many autumns the toy-like bandstand had lost all the gilding from its slender balustrades. I was walking in these pathways as I would have walked alone, with a curious melancholy pleasure. The gravel crunched under my feet, a bird cheeped, I forgot whose was the arm slipped under mine. Some ducks and swans were swimming on a green pool, and, standing on a little artificial crag and watching us go by was a big pink flamingo, melancholy vestige of the vanished splendors of the garden.

"Don't you think we're better off here than in a hotel bedroom?" asked the voice of that unknown man at my side.

"Yes," I said sincerely, "much better off."

A hush fell upon us and everything in those winding paths, as the darkness deepened. To the right, the station rose above the garden, and from it came the hooting of whistles, confused sounds which grazed without breaking the calm of this basin. On the other side of the wall was a narrow street, full of lights, brothels, dens of vice, and the station, a badly lit cavern, with its minuscule travellers dragging their valises, its little trains spitting out foul blackish fumes. But of all this agitation nothing came to us but a distant and confused hum, almost pulsating, and the evening air remained sad and pure, as if before a rain. A divinity must be watching over the garden, a little rustic god, not very impressive, who preserved the peace of the groves and shadows. Jean was no more than a man looming up out of the night, the black trees, the sleeping water, a man I was going to kiss for the first time.

It was a real, a first kiss between us. He felt it, and almost at once, regaining consciousness, I felt all the dupery in it. That kiss, more than my words even, must fill him with confidence. But after all, what did it matter to me? Did he not himself, that minute, believe he was fooling me in the same way?

At the end of the garden, which we had reached, there rose an artificial terraced mound, to the side of which clung a great rectangular building, faded, windowless. It was the Aquarium, which the schoolchildren still visited sometimes, but which now contained nothing aside from a few varieties of tropical fish and two giant turtles, except some trout, judiciously distributed in the various glassed-in compartments. The entrance, surrounded by artificial putty-colored rocks, gaped like a mouth of Hell. We went in. From behind their walls of glass, in the greenish twilight, enormous trout swam majestically round and round in the glaucous water. One long catfish, astray amongst these common species, seemed to have conceived a profound bitterness, and rolled ferocious eyes behind its moustaches. In the rotunda which was cluttered with rattan chairs, two idle soldiers were contemplating the giant turtles, manoeuvring among the rockwork. We sat down in a corner. Jean's hand was holding mine, which, for a second, I thought of withdrawing. There was something ridiculously romantic about sitting there in the deserted Aquarium, hand in hand. But he drew me to him.

"Come, come, Hélène, relax," he murmured. "Why spoil this peaceful hour?"

And I relaxed, and I explained nothing. Since he wanted it, since he demanded it, today again, after two years, I would know that peace which comes from oblivion, the voluntary renouncement of all thought. I abdicated nothing of myself, since it was with a clear head that I decided to give him that hour, that evening. I was not fooling myself, I was not pretending to love him. But from the fish turning slowly in the green water, from those paths that had opened up only for us, from the nearby darkness which was gathering around this refuge, I would take the bitter sweetness, the pleasure of sadness, since I knew their worthlessness. I lay my head on Jean's shoulder, and his arm encircled me.

"There, that's the way I like you," he said softly. "You are not trying to be hard, you are not making complications, you are not being sentimental, but you are sweet, infinitely sweet."

My body yielded, passive beneath his kiss and his caress. However, something inside me, tenacious as a little flame, murmured: "Yes, the sweetest, for an hour . . ."

The soldiers on leave, dragging themselves away from the contemplation of the turtles, had discreetly withdrawn. We were alone in this weird under-water domain. The turtles were swimming with a soft gurgling sound. The air was suffocating, with a curious perfume of plant-life which came from the shrubbery surrounding the rotunda. We did not speak. All at once a little door opened behind one of the bushes and a care-taker appeared, pipe in mouth, as decrepit looking as his establishment. Was it because of his association with the fish? Whatever the cause, there was something about him that made you think of a sea-going captain, retired, however, and taking it easy. But his beard and the way he sucked at his pipe were indisputably maritime.

"Hullo!" he shouted in a sonorous voice, which echoed the length of the Aquarium. "Bless my soul, a couple of love-birds! I was going to close down for the night when I saw those young fellows leave, but I'll give you twenty minutes more!"

Jean started to decline the offer of the gallant seacaptain, but the old man, in a voice made to command, shouted him down.

"No, my dears, don't move! You're very comfortable here, and you paid the entrance fee. I'll not let it be said you were thrown out before time. For once there are customers in my shanty! And a young couple in love, at that! No, no, don't move!"

And he went back into what I could not keep from thinking of as his cabin. I realized that Jean was a little chilled by the amiable old sea-dog's gushing words.

"Don't worry," I reassured him, "I'm quite aware you're not in love."

He laughed so gaily that his face underwent a transformation: he did not look a day older than twenty, and apparently he had a lighter heart than ever before in his life.

"Hélène, you're delightful. I like you very much. I believe we're going to understand each other quite well. As for being in love . . ." As he spoke, his fine wrinkles of irony and sadness had reappeared. "It's been a long time since I was in love."

"So you've been in love?"

"Been in love! You forget I'm an old man, dear child! But it was so long ago, so very long ago . . . In fact, I must have been only nine years old when it happened to me for the last time."

"Nine years old! And you were in love with a little girl?"

"No, not with a little girl, but with my German nurse. I should tell you that, like you, I lost my mother when I was quite young."

"And you've not been in love since then?"

"Since then, I've learned to be on my guard," he replied, almost seriously.

"That governess' name," he went on, "was Lydia, and she had beautiful dark blue eyes, curiously shadowed. I adored her, perhaps because already, even then, I was rather separated from others of my own age. It all happened in a little provincial town. That Lydia, who must have had other things to worry about than my adoration, had no meanness in her but was rather cold and indifferent. One day, though, she seemed quite changed, began to pay attention to every least thing I said, to help me with my studies. And, despite my father's veto, she took me to the cinema to see a detective film, and after that she bought me an enormous pineapple cake which she allowed me to devour. I enjoyed all that bliss unquestioningly. Why should I have asked any questions? After all, I was only nine years old. Well, when I was in bed, still sticky with pineapple, she came to kiss me. I very much liked to be kissed by the ladies when I was small. I still remember vividly how she kissed me in the neck, the smell of her powder, and the exact taste of that pineapple cake. I also remember her voice, which was rather low and very tender, as she whispered to me that I must be very nice and tell my papa how much I loved her, how much she loved me, how much . . . Well, in other words, she wanted a raise in her salary! Next day I had a bad indigestion, and was sickened forever at the thought of pineapples and my governess. I think it's from that time on that I've always been a little afraid whenever I'm offered too many good things. I'm always afraid of the request for a raise that will follow . . ."

"For instance," I said maliciously, "when young girls let you think that you're not unattractive. . ."

"Yes," he said, smiling. "I'm always a little afraid that such advances are addressed to the stores of Delfau, Gunther and Company, rather than to my modest self."

"Well, be reassured," I said, "Gunther and Company inspire me with no kind of interest. I am only interested in Jean Delfau."

When we came out of the Zoological Gardens, night had at last fallen. We did not return by way of the boulevards, but instead followed the narrow street which, to the left of the station, brought us straight home. Around us, the green and red signs of small cafés scintillated. "Café du Grand Polisson," "Le Symphony's," "Chez Guillaume," "Chez Anna," "Bar Allegresse"—it was to these bars and night clubs that the notables of the town came for their diversions. On the second floor of each café were furnished rooms. Sitting at the windows of those rooms, as if on display, were some imposing creatures, devoid of beauty but very decked out, waiting for customers. Farther up the street were respectable looking houses, without signs, where frightened married women could have assignation with their lovers. But in these dingy bars which filled the street as far as the harbor, the transient visitor in Gers, or timid men, or men in a hurry, were sure to find a welcome. The probable price of the establishment could be judged by the amount of elegance in the *accoudoirs*, the window balustrades against which the women behind the windows leaned. Some of them were padded with chintz, cheap and gay: such a house would be open to all comers. Other windows—you might say, other show-cases—had their rails upholstered in leather or brown velvet studded with gilt nail-heads, or small pads covered with fake Chinese or Persian stuffs. We caught a glimpse of a pretty and well-dressed Negress, showing off well against an *accoudoir* of orange colored chintz.

"Decidedly," said Jean, "I find this town attractive."

The more sumptuous cafés had English names, and their window draperies of red velvet, their fringed window balustrades, gave them a weird aspect of boxes in a theatre, so that one was astonished to see a dull-eyed woman in a kimono suddenly appear. Jean seemed to take a great interest in these window displays.

"Don't worry," I told him, "they are there every day, from 4 or 5 o'clock on. You'll see them again."

"Do they open their windows in the Spring?" he asked. "That must be charming. I'm very fond of prostitutes; you know their price right away. Unfortunately, they are a little too sentimental, the movies have contaminated them. But a few remain incorruptible."

I could not think up a comment, and he may have thought I was offended, for his right arm encircled my shoulders affectionately.

We were now standing in front of my home, its high grey façade loomed above us.

"I'm going to Paris for a fortnight," he said rapidly. "I'll come back a little before Christmas. Will you be here? Will I see you again?"

"I can't imagine how you could avoid seeing me," I said, with some bitterness. "I never budge from here, as you well know. And you will see Tamara again . . ."

I had hoped to secure from him, before his departure, a promise to drop Tamara. It would have amused me to observe her surprise and disappointment at not receiving any news from him. Jean certainly owed that much to the infatuated young girl I had pretended to be. But he only laughed.

"To end up with," he said, "things will be just the same, won't they?"

His light and mocking tone was close to wounding me.

V ·

"*Isn't* there any mail today?" Tamara asked, as she came into the diningroom.

"Nothing," said my father, who was opening some big envelopes and surveying some textile samples.

"Are you expecting something special?" I asked her.

She raised her eyes to me with surprise, flushed, and then pretended to be absorbed in buttering a piece of toast.

A week had passed since Jean's departure, and I had soon

noticed Tamara's impatience for the arrival of the mail, her
haste to be first to reach the diningroom, her disappointment
at the reply which was always the same: there was no mail for
her. Did she regret having posed as virtuous too long, did she
regret her assumed indecision which had worn out the seducer
whom she had decided to let gradually conquer her?

"You have nothing to say, Tam? Are you blue?"

"Blue, me? Why should I be blue?"

Her tone was too aggressive, and her laugh was forced. I went
on talking, as if oblivious.

"Life is duller without the rehearsals."

"Yes, I've noticed that, too," said Father innocently. "Well,
I hope Delfau will come back for Christmas. After all, he must
not let his Paris affairs take precedence over the *Reine Berthe*
rehearsals."

"Are you sure he'll be here for Christmas? Hasn't he written
to you, Tamara?"

My direct question forced her to raise her eyes.

"What?" she asked in a low voice.

Father thought she had not heard.

"Hélène is asking you, my dearest, if you have not had some
news from our friend Delfau."

"If I had had, I would have told you," she said, with irritation.

"You could have forgotten to."

"Oh, Tamara would not have forgotten," I said softly.

Her face, that minute, was shattered with emotions: dissimulation, wrath, and a resentment too spiteful to be called suffering.

"By that what do you mean to say? What are you insinuat-
ing?"

Her cold, cutting voice made Father look at her in stupefaction.

"Oh I say, Tam, what's wrong with you? Hélène said nothing to hurt, it seems to me. Hélène, what's up?"

For a moment we all three sat there transfixed. I looked her in the face, I feasted my eyes on her indignity. From now on she could never even play the hypocrite with me. Unmasked, she had lost all her venom.

"I believe . . ." she began.

"You must have misunderstood my words, Tam," I interrupted. "I'm sorry if I hurt you."

She made a quick recovery.

"Why, not at all," she said, with affected dignity. "I'm the one who . . ."

"Come now, my dears," said Father, who seemed to be in a jovial mood, "you're both bored, that's all. Boredom upsets your nerves. You'll have plenty of amusement, when our friend Delfau returns and the rehearsals begin again."

V I ·

In the little garden leading up to the church, the stiff, frozen grass stood up like long white needles. Beneath the dim light of some high placed lanterns, a crowd of people thronged.

"It's hellishly cold here," Max whispered. "Why in the world did Tamara want me to attend!"

I wanted to say, "You had no idea of refusing, had you?" But I stifled the malicious thought. What did it matter? In imagination I could still see Jean's arrival at the little station, the previous night. Tamara had gone to meet him and I had gone with her, following like a chaperon, a little grumpy, but amused all the same, rather admiring the skill with which Jean managed the difficult situation.

Tamara had talked a lot about the receptions that had been organized, and about this Mass at the church of Sainte-Marie-des-Pleurs which she thought might interest Jean, because of its originality, about the little party that was to follow—all the notables of Gers had accepted the invitations—and as she talked, she played the part of a society woman, the wife of a man destined—just imagine!—to become mayor of Gers! And in the midst of that stupid chatter I had felt a kind of understanding spring up between Jean and me.

That day, Max had given me an enthusiastic report. According to him, Tamara had said she was completely disgusted with Jean, and she had also said that she owed too much to my father to "deceive him like that." I had every reason to believe that this was not a dodge, for a joke I had indulged in before dinner, on the subject of Jean Delfau's charm, had been greeted with glacial silence. The whole affair had been settled once and for all, I thought. Tamara, more attached than ever to Father, would be able to convince herself in a week that she was the one who, out of pure virtue, had broken off with Jean. She now affected a serene behavior, overdoing it a little, the way a woman would act who had pulled herself together at the very edge of the abyss. Renouncing Jean had provided her with the makings of a new comedy, and she now sometimes looked at him with a mixture of coldness and virtuous pity that was enough to make you die laughing. Max took this behavior at face value and stood ready to play the part of semi-Platonical comforter.

The choir could be reached only by way of a long stone corridor, and the rough-hewn walls, the faint lighting, the rather funereal look of a catacomb had its effect on the crowd, which was as dense that Christmas eve as in other churches, only quieter and more meditative. It was Tamara's idea, she had had it the previous year, of attending midnight mass in this fine old baroque church of Sainte-Marie-des-Pleurs, situated a little outside town, rather than at the church of Saint Joseph, which was frequented by the best society, was well heated and situated in the very centre of Gers, but which was, after all, nothing but a horrible red brick building. By attending the midnight mass here on the previous year and by boasting about what an original idea it was, Tamara had set a fashion, as could be seen by the great number of other luxurious cars that arrived when we did in front of the sombre edifice.

We joined the flood of people slowly advancing in orderly fashion and in a silence broken only by a few faint cries of children, arriving at length beneath the baroque vaulting, then passing between the columns of black and white marble and through doors framed in imitation skulls of polished marble. The place reserved for us was in the front of the church, at the foot of the raised platform on which the Mass was to be said, that imposing platform draped in old velvets which suddenly became reduced in size when you raised your eyes towards the walls that were tortuously carved with draperies of stone and where, apparently ready to fall and crush you, gigantic black and white marble saints stood out, transfixed in flight. Some rows of prayer-stools had been arranged this year for the patronesses of the quarter and for the more numerous well-to-do families that were expected. And it was on straw-bottomed chairs that the inhabitants of the quarter sat—fishermen, stevedores, shopkeepers—peacefully leafing through their prayer books which, for the most part, were opened only once or twice a year. The children had to be settled down, women moved about, now scolding a tired little boy, now blowing the nose of an infant who was already coughing in the icy air.

In front of me, Jean and Tamara exchanged cool comments of an esthetic kind. My father gravely consulted his missal. Max, relegated to my side, was open-mouthed in astonishment.

"It's absolutely sinister, isn't it?" he whispered. "And we're dying of the cold, to boot. Well, it's supposed to be picturesque . . . Where are the whores?"

"Down there at the far end," I whispered, a little embarrassed

at his flow of words. It was well to the back of the church, indeed, that dark mass of physically and mentally prostrated
women, from whom people drew apart, more out of offended
modesty than disgust. There they were, the prostitutes of the
harbor and the prostitutes of the station. They had come, out
of respect for an old custom, to take their part in the celebration, play their rôle, and proclaim by their presence the existence, in everyone there, of an undying hope. That night, not
one of them would sin, not one of them would put on powder
and rouge; and those dozens of naked faces which seemed a
little startled and ashamed at showing themselves so denuded,
those shawls and those dark clothes which were worn only once
a year, that mourning of a day which is really the mourning of
the soul, would always keep the midnight mass at Sainte-Marie-
des-Pleurs from being just like any other mass on Christmas eve.

Those women standing in the farthest corner of the church,
I told myself, were barely tolerated there, while Tamara was
displaying herself on a velvet prie-Dieu, dignified and re-
spected, her mind exclusively preoccupied with the little supper
that was to follow the mass. And Madame Périer was there, with
Fontanas. And the somnolent municipal councillors were also
present, except for the Protestants who were somnolently attending their own chapel services elsewhere. And Max, who
had come out of simple curiosity, was pretending to mumble
something. Jean was the only one who showed a certain embarrassment, which I could easily understand. What were we
doing there at that ceremony? In other times, when I was just
a child, I had had a kind of vague piety, to which my taste
for religious pomp contributed something. I had enjoyed those
processions in which I walked with Julia behind me, her hands
on my shoulders, and I had even liked the poignant banality of
organ music. All that was far in the past, and this pacific God
who tolerated and even welcomed Tamara in His church—yet
wasn't her lukewarm faith the worst sin?—the God of that
woman, the God of that town was not my God. If I had had

45

one, he would have been more like the Jehovah of the Old Testament, the pitiless and jealous god whose nostrils flared at the odor of burnt sacrifices. My God would not be capable of pardon.

The crowd had become more silent, and up there, in a wooden gallery, the orchestra, composed chiefly of brass, had settled itself out of sight. And suddenly, making everyone there gasp and scattering my thoughts, there resounded the first blare of the trumpets, filling the whole vault with a long cry of triumph, a fulguration of sounds so complete that the congregation gave a long sigh of emotion, almost of fear, when it was over. Despite myself, I was borne up by that wave of delusive sound, which offered soaring wings to everyone. Tamara had stopped whispering to Father and was sitting with her face lifted, as if she were being flooded by a slow tide of ecstasy which gradually erased all care. How I hated those brass instruments for giving me the same pleasure!

"All this is an imposture," I told myself, as the Mass began. Imposture, those brass trumpets full of promise, all those responses being given in clear voices, and all those demands for pardon! Pretexts for weakness, pretexts for lack of zeal, that's what those words were, under their fake aspect of joy and sweetness. If I had made a prayer, it would not have been like any of those prayers being said that night. "O God," I would have said to that God who would have been mine, "O God, do not pardon me anything. Do not ever let me be like all these people. I would rather sink to the depths of wickedness than to be like them. Do not fogive me my trespasses, for I will force myself not to forgive anyone. Leave me whole and strong as I am, and, if I happen to weaken and fall short of what I want to obtain from myself, then punish me as much as it is in Your power, for I shall refuse Your indulgence forever."

And the responses continued to rise, and the Elevation tinkled at last, as frail a sound in that immense nave as the tinkling of a bell on the collar of an animal lost in a deep forest, and heads bowed, like a field of grain suddenly bent down by a passing wind. And I said again to myself: "Do not let me bend my head, O God, ever."

Then I perceived that it was the first time I had prayed for perhaps ten years, since my first childish stammerings. And I became silent. The Mass ended. The brass trumpets blared forth again for a moment while the clergymen in the wooden stalls stood up, with exasperating slowness, for the crowd was already restless, eager to be gone. The orchestra tackled the last hymn of joy, and in an immense hum of impatience and excitement, the crowd began to flow towards the door, but not peaceably as it had entered; instead, jostling and shouting, holding babies up in the air, yelling out Christian names, losing hats that were trampled underfoot, and all those faces were stripped of their gravity as if unmasked, flushed with animation at the thought of the imminent festivities, of the warm house where a decorated tree and a smoking hot supper were waiting. The people crowded to one side a little to let the prostitutes pass, but the haste was too great, the throng closed in again at once, separating them, and gradually the black shawled heads were mingled and lost among the many brightly hatted heads. With all his big frame my father was shielding Tamara from the crowd and, while responding to her prattle, was protecting her with his arms as though she were a child. He almost carried her towards the car. Max, in a hurry to escape this atmosphere which he found disagreeable, had already reached the exit. Jean held me discreetly by the hand. We had not yet had occasion to talk alone together since his return.

"You see, I came back for Christmas," he said, as we tried in vain to make our way through the crowd. "Will you let me see you one of these days?"

"Whenever you like," I said.

"Shall we say tomorrow? I'll meet you at 3 o'clock in front of the Zoo, does that suit you? And don't worry, we shan't go again into the Aquarium."

"Very well," I said soberly. I was glad to see everything getting settled so easily. This was the final test, the one that would leave me entirely liberated. I did not fear it, but I counted on that small amount of bloodshed to deliver me from a last doubt of myself: I did not want to owe anything to ignorance.

Outside, in the car, Father, Max, and Tamara were already waiting for us.

"Come, come, hurry up! Our guests will be there before we are!"

Leaving behind us the almost empty sombre church, where already the tapers were being extinguished, and laughing gaily, we embarked for the Christmas celebrations.

V I I ·

The room was red, violently red. The walls were covered with faded red silk, the bed, supported by gilded caryatids, had a canopy of crimson velvet; the counterpane was dark red with large tassels. The armchair might be called cherry red, except for its filth and threadbare state which gave it the look of a weird animal suffering from a skin disease. But you could boldly affirm that the window draperies had ruby tones, and that they had that surprising odor of plush, faded flowers and dust, which reigns in call-houses and also in the drawingrooms of aged spinsters. A curtain of crocheted lace veiled the window, and when Jean turned on the light, it flared out of two wall brackets of bronze, set on either side of the door, filling the room with shadows and blood-red glimmerings.

"This is the room," said Clara Vaes, not without pride. "It's

the nicest room, Monsieur. You'll not find another like it anywhere in Gers. At the Decker's you'd have nothing to approach
it! That's why I only give it to important folks, judges, civil
servants, doctors—oh yes, they come here, I don't have fishermen and sailors coming here. And it's because you're from Pairs
that I'm giving you my red room. Afterwards, you'll not go and
complain about not having found every comfort here!"

She had pronounced these words emphatically, pulling herself
up to her full stature—which was very short—and Jean had not
been able to keep back a smile. That little barrel of a woman,
adorned with dangling earrings, laces, bowknots, her cheap jew-
ellery jangling as she gesticulated and trotted about, now trying
to put on a haughty look, was indeed laughable. But I did not
feel like laughing. A moment later, we would be alone together
in that room with its immodest and gilded caryatids, the log
fire laid in the fireplace. I had wanted this, and yet I could have
wished to keep Madame Vaes there, and would have done so
had it been in my power. I thought about the innumerable
young girls for whom this moment had been or would be the
most marvellous and thrilling moment of existence. I thought of
the white flowers, the veils, the blushes and tears with which
marriage is surrounded. I thought of the women hiding themselves in this very house with their lovers, I thought of Tamara's
laughter when Father easily lifted her in his arms and carried
her towards their bedroom. I thought of the fear of girls when
they leave their parents and run far away towards this feared,
this waited-for moment. I thought of Max's despair, and of my
own excitement in the old days when I went towards the Rempart des Béguines. I thought of all the literature of the world,
crystallized around this quite simple act, and I was afraid.

"All you have to do is set a match to the fire," Madame Vaes
was saying meanwhile, seemingly unable to tear herself away.
"And if you need anything, there's the bell. The bathroom's to
the right. Naturally we serve drinks in the rooms, perhaps you
want some champagne?"

"No, really, I don't believe so," said Jean, smiling. "Not unless you feel like a drink, Hélène?"

No, I did not want Madame Vaes' champagne, but I did have a cowardly desire to befuddle my mind, it was mounting in me, and only the fear of being seen through by Jean kept me from satisfying it.

"As you like," said the stout creature, trotting towards the door. "Here, we don't force drinks on people. It's not the same thing here as it is at the Decker's; I can pass up such little benefits!"

She went out, in a great jangling of her fake jewelry.

Jean folded his raincoat expertly, cast a look over the room, the armchair, the far too big bed, as embarrassing as a nasty and tenacious thought. For his part, he seemed to be calm and perfectly self-possessed: he was used to casual experiences of this kind. At Jean's age—and just how old was he, exactly, I wondered, resolving to ask him later on—at Jean's age, a man must already have seen quite a few rooms such as this. Jean must be able to leaf through his memories like a catalogue: the blue room with Alice, the room at the Carlton with Sandra Marelli, the room in Paris where there had been a succession of faces. There had very nearly been a room with Tamara—but what did it matter, since there was the room with Hélène? He had given up Tamara easily; would he renounce me like that, if another woman came along? Without a doubt. This hour, for him, was only one such hour among many, neither more nor less exciting. I was for him only a face, a name. Later on he would say, "Oh yes, Gers, that's where I had an affair with a rather nice little redhead called Hélène." And perhaps those words would arouse the imagination of a man I would never know or the jealousy of a woman whose name I would never know and for whom I would always be just a girl who had had an affair with Jean, a young girl in Gers . . .

"An amazing setting, this!" said Jean pleasantly. "What,

Hélène? You haven't lit that fire yet? I've almost never seen a girl as lazy as you are!"

Yes, it was true, he had seen all kinds of girls, I reflected. Even my anxiety was nothing new to him. His mocking voice had tried to sound reassuring. He must have a special voice for these occasions. I suddenly loathed the idea of his being tactful with me, and I tried to adopt his gay tone.

"You want a lot! We've only been alone for two minutes, and already you want to put me to work!"

"And what about the woman's sphere, what are you going to do about that? Come, I can certainly see you're incapable of lighting a fire. I'm going to have to teach you that, as well."

The "as well" made me blush, and I bustled about to show him that in the matter of lighting fires, at least, he had nothing to teach me.

"First of all, sprinkle the logs with kerosene," he said, picking up a bottle that stood to one side of the fireplace and handing it to me. "This will make it catch quicker."

"You're the one that doesn't know anything about it! A log fire isn't lit with kerosene! What a crude method!"

Reassuringly, the fire caught and crackled, began to roar, filling that alarming room with comforting shadows. We were sitting on the floor in front of the fireplace, and from time to time a spark flew out, forcing us to move back suddenly.

"I'll eat humble pie," said Jean. "You do know how to light a fire. In fact, you are almost perfect . . ."

His arm was around me, he drew me to him. "The psychological moment," he must be thinking. My apprehensions should have been soothed by the fire, the pleasant semi-darkness, his tender voice. But the trite proficiency of it was wounding. I would have preferred a most total lack of feeling. His gentle voice made itself again heard.

"For heaven's sake, Hélène, you mustn't be afraid," he said. "I'm not so terrible . . ."

51

"I'm not afraid," I said, through clenched teeth.

"Then why are you so tense and rigid, as though you expected me to behave like a brute with you? We're comfortable here, the afternoon is ahead of us, the situation is romantic, there's nothing to be frightened about."

It seemed to me he had put a little irony into these remarks and my uneasiness was transformed into anger.

"I'm not romantic," I said in an exaggeratedly hard voice. "You don't need to be tactful with me like this, you don't have to lead me gently towards that bed as though I were a sentimental young girl needing to be got round by fine words."

"That's true, I'd forgotten that you're a strong-minded woman, Hélène," he said in his drawling voice. "But surely you must be aware that strong-minded women have their moments of sentimentality, too. Come now, be just a little loving. You can fight with me later on."

"If I were loving, as you say, do you think I would have come here with you?" I said, letting myself go. "If I were loving or romantic or sentimental, I would never have agreed to give myself to you like this in the first room we came to, at the first sign you gave me, without knowing whether you will want anything more than this with me, without knowing if you are still in love with Tamara or with Mademoiselle Marelli or the maid or no matter who. But I'm not sentimental or romantic or loving, and so it's all the same to me."

"What passion! What fire!" he said, purposefully exaggerating the drawling mockery of his voice. "There are unexpected sides to you that are quite attractive, my dear Hélène. All right, since it's agreed that you will coldly surrender yourself to the most sinful of orgies, perhaps you recall why we are here?"

"I certainly do," I said, with a little less assurance. "You're the one, it seems to me, that doesn't remember."

He looked smilingly at me for a moment, but his eyes were hard.

"Very well, then, undress," he said casually.

I tore off my clothes in a rage, and his eyes upon me were like a dash of cold water. The fire roared in the chimney, attuned to my wrath, from time to time crackling with sparks wrathfully. It was hot now in the room and it was not from cold that I was trembling. It was not from fear, either, as I stood waiting near the bed, repressing even the gesture that would have hidden my breasts. I was trembling with anger.

I watched Jean as he loosened and took off his tie, carefully folded his jacket, smoothed out his shirt. He drew near, but did not touch me.

"Get into bed," he said in a flat voice.

Then we were lying down together, stretched out on the bed like stone statues on a tomb, in the silence of the red room.

His hand lightly touched my shoulder. I flinched.

"You're frightened," he said with a kind of triumph.

"No, I'm not frightened. It's just because I'm not frightened that I'm here," I said fiercely.

I did not want to pretend any longer, I wanted him to know that I did not love him, I wanted him to dispense with all superfluous delicacy, as I was doing. But I had not expected his eyes to reveal a hurt. Had I carelessly touched a sensitive point? I was about to forget my anger, but then he flung himself upon me and there was nothing more between us except a struggle, in which I tried to have the initiative of defeat. Several times we rested, panting, trembling, without tenderness, and already showing vicious tooth marks. These respites were only for our tired bodies, and Jean's frowning brows proved to me that sensual plesure did not disarm him. At last I greeted the pain and held back a cry that would have been a cry of triumph as well as a cry of suffering. Then, as Jean broke away from me, I at last allowed myself to shut my eyes.

I may not have experienced the same pleasures that I had formerly known with Tamara, but at least I had the good fatigue which follows the act of love, a fatigue bordering on intoxication and forcing one momentarily to disarm. Yes, I could shut my eyes; was not Jean himself resting? But again we were separated in this quiescence, and neither of us made the least gesture of affection.

"You don't feel too badly?" he asked politely, after a few minutes.

"Not at all."

"I'm glad to see you take it so calmly. Most young girls make a big thing over this."

"Not me," I said. I had tried to find a stinging retort, but could think of nothing better than that "not me" which was rather inadequate.

"Really?" he said, with unexpected sweetness. "But it's a little sad, isn't it?"

And suddenly we were again in each other's arms, this time without struggle or resistance, but with a kind of mild, mocking tenderness that left me defenceless.

"Really?" asked Jean, with quick, gentle kisses. "You don't attach any importance to it? You will never be in love with me?"

There was no trace of meanness or anger on his smiling face. He seemed suddenly relaxed, rejuvenated, and the gentle look in his eyes revealed their almost infantile blue. I did not reply to his questions—my final prudence. But I kissed him with more pleasure and I discovered, still without boldness, a body that was also new. The assuagement that had come to me from this act at long last consummated was great, and I felt I was paying little for it with a few minutes' truce. The dark room, the fire, everything predisposed me.

"So we're no longer mad at each other, Hélène?" Jean said, with a touch of malice.

"No," I said cautiously, "not for the moment . . ."

His laughter rang out like a child's.

"You're very far-sighted," he said. "But why should we quarrel? We have agreed that we will not fall in love with each other, that we will make no demands upon each other—which adds up to a dead calm. It's a little dull, but very restful." He reflected for a moment before continuing more seriously.

"Fundamentally, you are perhaps the most disinterested creature I have ever known. You don't demand a thing, do you?"

"No. I don't demand anything of you. But neither did Tamara demand anything of you."

"Tamara demanded more than you'd think. First of all, to let her believe in her rôle. What she wanted wasn't an adventure; she was tired of the rôle she was playing, wanted to change to another, escape from boredom, play the heroine. And I let her. Why not? After all, I'm a man of the theatre."

"But why let her do what she liked?" I asked. I did not want him to think I held a grudge, as he might have thought were I to avoid talking on the subject. "Why, if you didn't desire her?"

"I enjoy seeing people put on an act," he said, smiling. "It amuses me more than to hasten by a day or a week the moment when a woman like Tamara will belong to me. No," he added, as he saw me give an involuntary start, "don't think I'm still expecting anything of Tamara, Hélène. And don't think, either, that I've been amusing myself like that at your expense. When a Tamara plays the part of the respectable woman, overdoes it, thinks she's pulling the wool over my eyes, or when a young middle-class girl who's dying to go on the stage pretends to be crazy about me and sends me flowers every day, or when an actress imagines that she'll manage to extort a fur coat from me and some recommendations on top of everything, I prefer just to note all the trouble they go to in order to 'arrive' than to take advantage of it. That's not being very mean."

"No," I said, but without much conviction.

A shadow of suspicion clouded his face. I had soon become acquainted with that expression, and it disturbed me. I remembered his enthusiastic eulogy of the prostitutes in the station district, the story of his governess, and once more I felt an obscure force suddenly reviving in him, ready to wound, ready to strike out blindly, like an animal brought to bay. Why did he hide, behind his trivial manner, his irony and cynicism, this strange fear of being duped? Why was there suddenly that shade of cruelty on his face? Without saying a word, I listened as he went on.

"If all they were after was my money, it would be quite simple, and I even rather like women who are frankly whores. But what they want is a part in a play or to be introduced to celebrities, or they count on my slight fame to make them the rage! But the worst kind are the women that demand sentiments and fidelity of me . . . That, well, that's the limit . . ."

"Aren't you faithful?"

"Not at all. From taste and by principle."

"Why by principle?"

"Well . . . to begin with, because faithful men aren't loved. You have to be just a little on the minds of the people who love you. And then, it cuts short all illusions. I let no woman imagine that I consider her unique. If she imagined that, she would become unbearable and possessive. On the other hand, I quite well tolerate a woman's being unfaithful to me. Will you be faithful, Hélène?"

"To whom?" I asked innocently, without imagining that this painful and stormy embrace could create between Jean and me any sort of tie that would suppose a possible infidelity.

"To whom! Why, to me, Hélène! After all, I'm your lover!"

An almost childish indignation could be read on his face, where cynicism and childishness succeeded each other constantly, but I had no idea of laughing at it, being completely lost in amazement at the idea that Jean, the possible lover of Tamara, had suddenly metamorphosed into the lover of Hélène. Since I had admitted that the former relationship could have had importance, I must logically accord a similar importance to the latter relationship.

This reflection plunged me deep in thought. So there existed between Jean and me, on acount of that brief, painful embrace, a new bond: how enduring, I still could not say. I surveyed this man at my side, to whom I was still so unused. Yes, they were his fine, sharp features, dangerously ironical, his thin lips, his grey-blue eyes that could be charged with so much sweetness— and yet, something in him seemed changed. Perhaps it was simply that I was looking at him more attentively.

Whatever he was, I had to admit it, Jean was my lover. I wondered how long it would last. I could probably not expect much constancy in a man who would leave for Paris three months later. But at least, these three months would be con- secrated to me—or would this be, for him, merely a parenthesis until Sandra Marelli's return?

"How long are you going to be my lover?" I asked.

"What do you mean by that?"

"Well, that I'd see this . . . this affair in a different light, depending upon whether we were to be together for three days, three weeks, or three months."

"Roughly, I'd say about three weeks," he replied with such seriousness that I believed him, feeling just a little disap- pointed, until he burst into a laugh.

"Little idiot! You don't even know what you want, whether three days or three months, as you say. How could you know today, my poor dear? You should give up cynicism, it doesn't suit you. And you're eighteen years old! Three days or three months!"

He was still laughing, and so irrepressibly that I was not of- fended.

"I thought you didn't like people to be sentimental?"

He made a face, as if confronted with an insoluble prob- lem, then his eyes cleared.

"I don't like false sentimentality," he said, "I even have a horror of it. But all the same it's possible to have a feeling of understanding, isn't it?"

"Yes," I said hesitatingly, "yes."

I realized I was on new and slippery ground where I ran a great risk of losing my equilibrium. Without having encoun-

57

tered any other pleasure than the very relative one of a reckless pursuit of pain, aching and sore as I was, I had nevertheless found a new appeasement which the love of Tamara had never brought me, and which had caught me quite unawares. I had feared a too keen pleasure and had come armed with ingratitude before the pleasures Jean would reveal to me; but I was not prepared to undergo what followed, this warm comradeship of bodies that have wrestled, this almost stifling intimacy of this room, the sweeter and more familiar words, the arm slipped beneath my shoulders, the cigarette smoked in silence, and especially, on the face that I tried to think of as the face of an adversary, a peace that I truly had to respect. Desperately I tried to think of some words that would break the silence, words that would resurrect our rivalry, restore anger, that domain in which I moved with ease. But I could think of nothing, and I lay close to Jean, a little envying his tranquility, refusing to share it, but casting covetous looks at it, breathing it in, as if it were an appetizing odor.

The fire was dying down in a long sigh of contentment, sunlight penetrated the narrow window, and in a nearby courtyard the dreadfully shrill, off-key, gay little voices of children were singing a melancholy roundelay. The caryatids watched over us, grotesque and a little frightening. Stretched out beside me, that unknown man took my hand in his.

"Now, now, Hélène, none of this mournful yearning! Do you have some regrets?"

"I don't regret anything at all. I'm waiting . . ."

"Waiting for what?" he asked, astonished. And then, almost tenderly, "You mustn't expect too much from me, dear . . ."

Could I explain to him that it was not from him that I was expecting anything? That I wasn't worried on his account, but on mine? The test had begun. I was going to have to struggle harder than I had thought to come out of it victorious, indifferent. I was thinking about that as he jumped out of bed and quickly dressed. I stared unseeingly at him, but he must have thought he was under observation for he suddenly said, "You see how clever I am? But I can do better than that. Just look."

He came over to me, buttoning his shirt and, seizing his tie, he knotted it with one hand, like a conjuror performing a trick.

"What do you say to that? Don't you think I might get a job in a circus?"

I had forgotten his disabled arm, while we were in bed together. Was I to think that he had used the same dexterity to prevent its coming into contact with me as he had used in knotting his tie and in getting into his tweed jacket? I felt sick at the thought. A while ago, when I had pretended not to be afraid of him, had he believed I was making an allusion? I wanted to ask him, there were many other questions I wanted to ask. But he was looking impatiently at his watch.

"Hurry up, child. I'll be late for rehearsal. And God knows they're already none too easy to get along with, those old hams. After all, we have more than three months ahead of us for palaver."

That was so. We had three months. Quickly, I got out of bed.

V I I I ·

With its rose-bushes, its hedgerows, its dark and glistening clumps of rhododendrons, the garden had changed but little since my childhood. To the left stood what remained of a kennel, where Father had used to keep two setters chained. The paths crossed each other at right angles and two stone statues were becoming, each year, more covered with moss and weeds; gradually the fierce lions, to whose manes some hardy perennials clung, had been given a civilized look by those strange wigs and now evoked peaceful poodles, dyed green to suit some fashion or other. I realized, as I entered the garden, that I had not walked there for some time.

I wanted to find again a calm and a serenity which would erase the troubled moment. Not that anything had completely upset me, but those motions which Jean and I had gone through, and which imitated the gestures of love, had stirred in me a residue of feelings and sentiments which I had thought dormant or even consumed. I went down the neat paths towards the clipped hedges to find again Indifference, that little companion of mine which had held me by the hand during all these long months. I walked beneath the hard, shining leaves of the rhododendrons, in that grotto formed by their protective branches, to seek a naive and childish cynicism. But even the acquaintance with this geometrical garden, even the view offered by my high window overlooking dozens of gardens like it, all geometrical, all bordered with box hedges, all holding in their centre a statue covered with green growths, differing only in the subject—although the panorama included more than one Diana, more than one Pomona raising towards the sky an intact basket of fruit, saved by miracle from the encroaching plant-life, and more than one lusty Gardener—all toppling down the hill towards the inviting lake, with what dignity their degree of incline allowed, even that spectacle did not restore me to the detachment of the last few months. The world had suddenly recovered its colors, and not only its colors, but its teeming aliveness, its density. Like grass inhabited by millions of insects, everything was vibrant, everything around me was moving and even the trees, even the animal life of the world, even the suddenly heavier air, all infringed upon my solitude. I felt more surprise than displeasure at this, I felt at home in a path I had already trod, but which held out hopes of being more peaceful. I entered it without great resistance; perhaps I was weary of the deserted spaces I had inhabited and which hatred no longer peopled. I was sure that what was coming to life and stirring within me was not love. But what was it?

I walked in the garden of my childhood, touched the bark of the oak tree, caressed the heart-shaped leaf of the catalpa, penetrated the grotto of the rhododendrons, again full of mystery. I saw, touched, smelt the decaying leaves, the black branches of the lilacs without flowers. These things again imprisoned me, the wind excited me, and every time a sound reached me from the house, far off down there—the ringing of a bell, the banging of a door—every time a figure passed behind the tall windows or appeared upon the white flight of steps, I felt a sudden and poignant shock, recalling me to existence. And the hedges alligned in vain their absurd exactitude.

The morning had left me in a reflective mood, a little uneasy, and at lunch time, as I entered the drawingroom without having paid any attention to the subdued murmur of voices, I had barely glimpsed Jean, who was sitting close to Tamara and talking peacefully with her, when I became disturbed beyond measure, flushed, and stammered as I held out my hand to him and, as I turned aside to hide my embarrassment, I upset a glass of port wine. I picked up the glass, proposed cleaning up the stain which was spreading on the carpet, blushing all the while. I felt Tamara's eyes upon me, following all my movements, at first with surprise, then with suspicion, and my disturbance became still greater when I heard Jean addressing me in a mocking voice.

"Well, there's a sample for you of the awkwardness of the awkward age!" he drawled. "Is it my fascinating presence that agitates you to this degree, Hélène?"

Tamara gave a contemptuous little laugh. Perhaps she thought I was secretly infatuated with Jean, but surely she did not suspect him of paying me the least attention.

"Well, what do you expect," she said, in a most motherly and most exasperating way. "She's only eighteen . . ." I sponged the carpet without a word and she went on chatting with Jean, as if I did not exist. Had he been there a long time? Unjustly, I felt slighted at having been left uninformed of his presence.

"As it happens, we were talking about you, Hélène," said Tamara suddenly, turning towards me.

I started. "About me?"

"Why yes, you. Monsieur Delfau is very interested in your drawings, and I told him I had felt for a long time that you had talent. Even when you used to come to see me when I lived on the Rempart des Béguines—do you remember?—you were already drawing some rather nice things."

I blushed again. Decidedly, this was my day for blushing. And beneath the eyes of Jean, who seemed to be very intrigued, I completely lost countenance.

Fortunately, Father appeared at this critical moment, as usual bringing with him a whirlwind of excitement and concerns.

"Well, well, Delfau!" he cried, sitting down beside Jean. "How are the rehearsals getting along?"

"You must have judged for yourself, Noris. They told me you dropped in yesterday afternoon?"

"Yes. Unluckily you hadn't yet arrived, but I had a chance to have a look at the sets and costumes."

"Do you like them?"

"They're absolutely wonderful! Wonderful . . ." said Father in a slightly embarrassed way. "While I think of it, I would like to . . . oh, not criticize, but make a remark, a small observation. You know I'm a Philistine, an absolute Philistine in such matters, but well, here you are. The sets, the costumes—which are as I say very very well done—seem to me a little . . . how shall I say?"

"A little . . . ?" asked Jean, apparently enjoying Father's embarrassment.

"A little mingy, there, I've said it. You'll excuse me, for it's not at all a criticism of the designs made to the designer, you understand, it's merely a suggestion I'm making to you as a friend."

"Mingy!" said Jean, slightly irritated and trying to hide his irritation under a double amount of politeness. "Why, my dear Noris, it seems to me I was even a little too free with the expense accounts you opened for me. I don't see how . . ."

"You don't get the point," said Father, who was becoming more and more involved in his explanations. "What I meant to say was . . . See here, I'm launching a campaign of prestige, you understand, and the elections are not far off. Old Maalens went to fantastic lengths, spent a fortune at Christmas, and I've got to eclipse him in a month and a half. To do that, I counted on the Grand Theatre and on you, my dear Delfau. Don't you think it might be possible—without in the least prejudicing your esthetic conception, remember, the people here are not very subtle—don't you think you might add something to show I'm not close-fisted? To point up what I mean: the other day there was a question of that scene of the beggars, one of the most successful, I believe, in the play, well, just imagine, someone dared to insinuate that I had specially chosen a play with a beggar-scene in it to reduce the costs of the costumes? Naturally, the person who said that was a supporter of Maalens, the old fox, but all the same . . ."

"Well, after all, see here," said Jean, divided between anger and amusement, "you can't expect me to dress your beggars like lords, can you? That would evidently give a richer look to the thing, but would risk introducing a preposterous note that Monsieur Van Beck might not like to have in his play."

"It's not just the beggars," said Father, who was red as a beet in his effort to convince. "It's the other costumes! They are extraordinarily elegant—yes, yes, I assure you—but you might add some frippery to them, some tinsel, how can I explain, some ornament . . ."

"A little gold, for instance?" Jean suggested with a smile.

"That's it, gold, lots of gold! That's what I was trying to say!" Father's outburst was immediate and cordial. "And the same thing in the sets. Let's not pinch pennies, for heaven's sake! No penny-pinching! And what difference does it make to you? A little gold can't do any harm."

"Quite right," said Jean, disarmed by so much simplicity. "A little gold never did any harm."

"Delfau, you're the man I was looking for! You get the idea at once, you're a real man of talent, you . . . Yes. Gold. That's what will please the people here!"

His face was crimson with enthusiasm, he slapped Jean repeatedly in the back, and Jean smiled vaguely, making no objection.

"And now that's settled, suppose we have some lunch?"

Tamara, looking a little tight-lipped, it seemed to me, preceded them into the diningroom. Father and Jean followed, still talking animatedly, and I trailed at the rear, waiting for a sign of recognition which did not come.

Jean's indifference astonished me a little. No doubt, it was necessary not to make a display of our understanding, all the more so since my show of embarrassment might have put Tamara on the track. But after all, he was carrying his dissimulation too far: throughout the meal he did not even once look at me. From time to time he addressed a compliment or smile to Tamara, whose attitude towards him was cold. The rest of the time he listened to Father, who continued to talk excitedly. The two men seemed to get along wonderfully well, despite their difference in looks and personality: my father, big, red-faced, neatly combed hair, pearl grey cravate, stickpin, waistcoat, watch chain, discoursing in his emphatic, electoral way, punctuating his words by striking the table with the flat of his hand; Jean, sitting opposite him, seeming more unconcerned than ever, listening with an absent smile on his lips, now and then running his well manicured hand through his longish hair, throwing out a pleasantry, and smiling, while his eyes were gazing elsewhere, across the wide bay, beyond the garden. I cast him an occasional glance, still surprised to see him once more reinstated in his mocking, weary, indifferent attitude, remembering as I did the passionate combat of the previous day, remembering that enemy body close to mine, and the sudden fraternity, born of the stillness of the room, the crackling wood fire, a voice outside, singing, as if coming from another world.

The meal ended, with Jean and Father still talking.

Tamara remained silent, as I did, tapping the table with her fingers. A vague uneasiness hovered in the air of the dark diningroom, and the gilt parakeets of the Cordovan leather on the walls had a rather baleful look.

"I must absolutely have this diningroom redecorated," said Tamara, as she always did upon leaving the table.

But Jean, following her, did not reply, as he usually did, that the diningroom was all right as it was. Even Father seemed aware of the embarrassment that reigned for he observed, almost suspiciously, that no one seemed to be in good form that day. And we all trailed off towards the eternal coffee ceremony.

Feeling self-conscious, not knowing how I should meet Jean again, I was about to enter the drawingroom with him when suddenly, with a perfectly indifferent look, he slipped a note into my hand. I ran to the cloakroom to read it. The note was very brief, all it said was "Wait for me at the station, as agreed."

I X •

I hurried off, as though expecting him already to be there. It was a lovely day. I sat down on a bench in front of the station, in the sunlight and gave myself over to lethargic daydreaming. Cold as Jean's note was, it had thrilled me. I wondered if we would return to Madame Vaes' and with a kind of passive pleasure visualized the red room, the wood fire . . . These thoughts lulled me, almost putting me to sleep on the bench where I was sitting. What spell held me there in that sunshine which was still not the sunshine of spring, why was I deep in souvenirs that were without sensual delight? Nothing else, perhaps, than the need I felt each spring to rest a little, to close my eyes. A glance at Tamara had twice already checked this need of rest and relaxation; she did nothing but that, now, she concentrated on it. But after all, eclipsing Tamara had not been my only reason for taking a lover, and to let the thought of her spoil my pleasure would really be overdoing it. Thus I made excuses for giving myself over for still another moment to that sunlight and to those thoughts.

I had been waiting for some time when I became aware that I was waiting. What had happened to Jean? Had Tamara noticed my absence and kept him there? Or, in spite of what he had told me the day before about his two-faced behavior with her, had he lingered with her of his own accord? It was ridiculous to get myself upset, and yet I was upset. Certain expressions in Tamara's eyes during lunch had disturbed me. Did she suspect something? If that were the case, she would be unable to resist the pleasure of the contest. And would I be victorious? Nothing was less sure.

"Well, Hélène? Are you dreaming out loud?"

It was Jean's mocking voice.

"I stayed on to chat with your charming stepmother," he explained.

"That's what I supposed," I said, as naturally as I could. But there was nothing to do about it, the sight of Jean's hardened expression gave me a pang of anguish. I expected he would suggest taking me to the red room, but he did not.

"Suppose we take a turn down by the harbor?" he said, without even touching my arm. "They tell me a very picturesque

Fair is going on down there. I could do a few sketches . . ."

I was struck by the coldness of his voice. But I did not want him to think I was disappointed or to imagine that I was dying to be in his arms again. So, a little nervously, I agreed.

"Yes, and it's a very nice Fair. There's a lottery—they raffle off pigs—and a closed carrousel and booths where you buy mulled wine . . . But I didn't know you were interested in such things?"

"I'm interested in everything," he said in the same reserved and laconical way.

I followed him without attempting any more conversation.

We arrived at the harbor, where the pier was cluttered with carnival booths and a milling crowd was making such a noise that the calm lapping of the lake could not be heard. The merry-go-rounds and roller-coasters creaked asthmatically, the crowd was motley, even the fisherwomen, who were dressed as usual in brown or black, were wearing bright colored kerchiefs on their heads. The wind· blew sharp and cold upon all this activity, but with no other result than to increase the excitement. I myself could not keep from sharing in the festive spirit a little, and we plunged into the crowd. From Barfleur, some soldiers had come in great number, and the prostitutes, abandoning indifferent attitudes at their window balustrades, were now covered with cheap jewelry and were openly advertising their wares alongside the booths where the wine merchants were making a fortune selling mulled wine. Perched on high stools, brandishing their pewter ladles like weapons, they proclaimed at the top of their lungs the potency and the bouquet of their vintages, and the odor of cinnamon rose from the big copper cauldrons. The wine merchants did not insult each other as, farther along, the hawkers of roasted chestnuts were doing. They were too sure that their customers would sample the hot wine at all of the booths and by nightfall would be staggering drunk.

On a platform that had been hastily erected, the pigs that

were to be raffled off were grunting and sniffing and stampeding. A goat proudly raised its head, staring at the crowd with the haughty look of a movie star.

"Shall we buy some tickets?" Jean said with what seemed rather forced enthusiasm.

Besides the pigs, there was a display of old feather boas, green and black, two gilt clocks, and some enormous rounds of cheeses to tempt us. Jean bought some tickets and held them out to me. Perhaps I was just imagining it, but I felt there was something hidden and dangerous back of his high spirits.

"This is the kind of lottery I like," he said gaily. "Swear that if you win a feather boa you'll wear it back home! And come, let's have a taste of this hot wine . . ."

Without waiting for a reply, he drew me over to the nearest booth. And we drank in pewter goblets the wine which tasted only of cinnamon and vanilla, but which Jean pronounced exquisite—while insisting upon tasting the wine at other booths. We followed the flood of soldiers which took us from one wine merchant to another. I began to feel a little tipsy and no longer thought about anything, and so when Jean suggested going for a ride on the merry-go-round I enthusiastically agreed to it.

Enormous, with fixedly staring globular eyes, their white manes floating in the wind, their bodies a constellation of mirrors, the wooden horses abandoned by the children who preferred the more modern amusement stands attracted us. And thereupon I was seized with dizziness and a fit of the giggles. Jean was so solemnly seated on one of those fabulous mounts! What would Tamara have said if she saw us? I laughed so much that I would have fallen had not Jean caught me just in time. The merry-go-round slowed down.

Against my will, Jean dragged me off my horse and I remarked once more how he liked to make a show of his strength: he almost carried me. From having clung to the glittering horse I had some long white horse-hairs sticking to my fingers. With complete abandonment I leaned against Jean. After all, it had been a wonderful idea to come to the Fair. I could only have wished that Jean shared my slight tipsiness, but it seemed to me his face was clouded.

I wanted to cheer him up. A little farther along the pier the Waffle Booth raised its white and gilt walls set with shimmering little mirrors. There, in "private rooms"—so-called, for they were merely boarded stalls—all the servant maids of the town were hugging and kissing their boyfriends, while waiting for nightfall when, in the enclosed carrousel, these embraces would become still more intimate. As a child, the Waffle Booth and the closed carrousel had represented to me inaccessible paradises into which there was no least hope of my ever being admitted, and the idea of entering one of them with Jean thrilled me inexplicably. At the entrance to the booth, a waitress greeted us cordially.

"You're in luck!" she said. "There's only two seats left!"

At her heels, we crossed the dubiously white room that was generously decorated in gilt and where the waffles were made, then down a long corridor reeking of hot fat, until we reached one of those "private rooms" so much talked about and which only the absence of doors prevented from being entirely immoral.

"Waffles and beer, yes?" she said in an imperious way.

"Waffles and beer," Jean agreed.

A contemporary of the merry-go-round, the Waffle Booth was in the same style, and the little room, scarcely larger than a beach-hut and furnished simply with a bench and a table, offered such a profusion of gilded wood, of painted landscapes in oval medallions, of mirrors large and small set into the walls, of red silk tassels hung here and there without rhyme or reason that one expected to hear any minute the shrill music of brass cymbals and to feel the hut with its honeycombs full of petting couples begin gently to turn. I had always imagined the Waffle Booth would be like that; despite its stench of frying fat, it was a rather fairy-like place, with its solitude that was no solitude, the laughter of those invisible comrades which the thickness of the partition walls rendered less crude. You almost felt you were inside a music-box or jewel-casket. Something about the mirrors and the paintings gave the Lilliputian impression.

"Well, are you happy?" he asked, rather distantly.

He seemed definitely to have renounced any manifestation of intimacy.

"Oh, you can't imagine! Why, this was the dream of my life. And without you I'd never have come here!"

"Why not?"

"Oh, the people of Gers are so very proper! Why, no one would ever have consented to come here with me!"

"Not even Tamara?"

Something in his voice surprised me. I raised my eyes. He smiled, but his level gaze made me blush.

"Tamara is absolutely opposed to this type of thing," I said with an embarrassment I could not suppress. "And anyway, if she were to visit a carnival, I don't imagine it would be with me."

"Who knows?" he said, smiling.

There was a silence, during which I desperately tried to think up a natural sounding retort. Jean apparently took pity on my confusion.

"For heaven's sake, Hélène! Haven't I already told you I'm not jealous?"

"There's no reason to be jealous," I murmured.

"Nor to feel guilty. Why are you blushing? Or have I made a mistake?"

"No," I said, "you've not made a mistake. Is that of any importance?"

"Not at all, naturally! On the contrary, I think it's rather amusing. And then, that makes one more bond between us, doesn't it?"

The waitress came in, bringing us a stack of waffles and

two enormous glasses of beer. She was a pretty girl, quite young, no doubt one of those farmers' daughters who came from the country to find work in Gers, as waitress in a bar or inn, and glowed for a few years with the freshness of youth, decked out in town clothes that added the weird allure of cheap city finery to their rustic beauty. But the freshness of almost none of them could hold out long against the irrational life they led, with drinking, long nights without sleep, prostitution more or less disguised, and by the time they were eighteen they were faded, had taken jobs as waitresses in small suburban hotels and, having lost hope, became the sweethearts of inconstant soldiers, prostitutes less in demand than the street-walkers of the town, sought after only by the fishermen on Sundays or, if one of them were very clever, she became wife or mistress of a shop-keeper whom she served as cashier.

This girl must have been fourteen or fifteen years old, she had a mop of gleaming black hair that had been waved with a hot iron and was caught back with two rhinestone combs. Her sharp eyes missed nothing of what went on in the "private rooms," and her pretty round face still showed a healthy tan beneath a ridiculously thick layer of powder and rouge. As she went out, she demonstrated that she already knew how to sway her hips to show off the grace of a slender yet well rounded body.

"Pretty girl," said Jean automatically. Then he turned back towards me with a strange smile. "You know, at first I thought you were like that, a not very intelligent, pretty girl, sweet and loving and a little boring. But you're full of pleasant surprises. So then, you and Tamara . . . ? What mistake one makes! I would have sworn that you detested each other."

"But I do detest her!" I said, despondently. "How can I make you understand? That was in the past, but since she married my father . . ."

"It's no go now? Poor Hélène! So that was your great deception! You've certainly revenged yourself. What a manoeuvre!

And I, who took you for a pure, sentimental little creature! I'm certainly no psychologist! But by and large, I prefer you like this. After all, maybe you and I resemble each other a little . . ."

He was holding me close, kissing me from time to time, as if jokingly, and I felt a growing uneasiness. Under his apparent unconcern, I felt he was armed and ready to be dangerous.

"Jean, you don't understand. I assure you, the desire to hurt Tamara had very little to do . . ."

"But, child, what does it matter? You don't have to justify yourself to me. Have I told you about my life? Do you know whether or not I, too, wanted to hurt someone or arouse the jealousy of, say, the Marelli girl, or something like that? Thank God, we don't have to justify ourselves to each other. 'Neither sentiment nor romance,' isn't that what we agreed, darling?"

This reminder of my vehement words of the previous day filled me with shame. I don't know how he managed it, but he had succeeded in making me completely ridiculous in my own eyes. Half-heartedly, I raised my enormous glass of beer.

"It seems to me you're in danger of becoming that melancholy thing, a solitary drinker," he said with sudden sweetness. "Better for us to drink together, don't you think? Mademoiselle, bring us two more beers, please. Now Hélène, make a little effort to be gay!"

The clouded glasses were deposited in front of us. I relaxed a little. The mirrors and the gildings surrounded us; from outside came muffled music. Despite myself, I regretted my confession. Wouldn't it, I wondered, change everything between Jean and me? And I told myself this, as though there had been something between us which was worth the trouble of regretting . . .

"After all, it would be to our advantage to get drunk together," said Jean, with teasing gravity. "We'd forget that little monster Hélène and her complicated intrigues, and that horrible Jean who is always making fun of everything. Let's pretend we're in love and forget them, shall we?"

"Oh yes! Let's forget them!" I cried fervently.

My head was reeling so that I would willingly have forgotten no matter what. This carnival booth charged with magic, the wind, the sun, the wine we had just gulped down in the midst of the milling crowd, the smell of the waffles, the dark and slightly bitter beer, and finally the warmth of that arm around me, everything had succeeded in bringing to a halt the thought that ceaselessly turned and turned in me like a tiresome clock: I must remain on guard.

It stopped turning, and I kissed Jean, and the Waffle Booth became for me, as for all the couples lodged in its honeycombs, just a shelter.

When we left, it was almost night and lanterns were beginning to be lit here and there: the wooden horses of the merry-go-round looked mysterious in the half light in which their mirror spangled bodies and their white manes shimmered; but now, abandoned by the children, they pursued alone their fantastic course. Down there on the pier, the closed carrousel had just lit its lights and promised, with the high pitched voice of a fifteen-year-old spieler, an infinity of pleasures to some soldiers who were hesitating to put down their money.

"I say, what's that?" asked Jean. He seemed terrifically excited.

"Come along, we'll see!"

I hoped that the pleasures of the carrousel would scatter to the winds the last vestige of uneasiness in me.

"Another surprise?" he bantered softly.

The crowd was not very dense around the carrousel. There was no throng until about eleven o'clock, when the girls, warmed up by dancing, would finally consent, after a hundred simpering objections, to go round once or twice. But it was a great thing just to enter it and glimpse the setting of those orgies. In front of the door, a woman cashier with purple hair issued the tickets, with a great air of secret understanding, and we penetrated the mysterious precincts. Within a round-house, rather like a circus tent, revolved, in a propitious semi-darkness, a kind of circular mountainous path to which clung little gondolas. We were standing perilously on a narrow platform of motionless planks, grazed by the passing gondolas and in great danger of being bumped into by one of them. They revolved with a frightening rapidity to the sound of a calliope placed in the motionless wooden shaft around which the machinery turned. The great attraction of the closed carrousel was, everyone said, watching the pictures pass by, the paintings of an unknown artist, but full of life, which depicted, all around, on the wooden wall panels, the various metamorphoses of Jupiter.

The carrousel slowed down. The gondolas passed before us more slowly. Many were empty, others contained couples confusedly entwined, others contained solitary girls, sitting up very straight on the edges of the velvet seats and letting out little cries, presumably joyous, to attract the military who were trying to decide which place to take. From time to time one saw the gleam of a white thigh beneath a skirt quickly pulled down. We installed ourselves in a gondola, a little embarrassed by the too inviting obscurity. Only some spotlights attached to the ceiling lit up the passably obscene metamorphoses of the bearded god: Leda straddling her swan, Danae opening her legs to a rain of gold, Europa surprised at the bath by the bull. Treated with an astonishingly realistic brush, the ensemble was calculated to awaken, in the spectators' minds, an idea eminently moral: in every situation, no matter how incommodious, a god will always find a practical solution for his desires.

"Why, this is a place made for lovers! A veritable trap!" cried Jean with a laugh in which I believed could be discerned a note of defiance.

"There aren't just lovers here," I said. "There are also couples like you and me, neither romantic nor . . ."

"Nor sentimental," he finished. "Decidedly, that will be our motto. What I adore in you, Hélène, is that you never try to be amiable. It's crazy how restful that is!"

And he began again to kiss me. At times the music stopped briefly, they forgot for a few minutes to start it up again, and those minutes during which we slid along in silence to the gentle creaking of the well-oiled machine were curiously peaceful. From time to time the gondolas slowed down, the laughter of the girls rose, and springing from the central column as from infernal depths, an agile gnome leaped from gondola to gondola asking for the price of the next trip, in a low voice. Some girls got in, got out; I recognized the waitress from the Waffle Booth. No doubt she had finished her job for the night and was ready to give herself over to other activities.

"Look, there's the girl we saw just now," said Jean, breaking the silence.

For how long had we been silent, pressed close to each other? I had no idea, but I suffered a little at seeing this felicity broken.

"Oh, yes?" I said languidly.

"You don't recognize her? Yes, yes, it's the girl. She has red earrings, shaped like enormous hearts. Can't you see her?"

Oh yes, I could see her quite well, sitting alone in a gondola, letting out little cries, trying to attract the attention of a young fellow who was mistakenly riding in another gondola, and the spectacle seemed to me without great interest. I said so, but Jean did not appear to be of my opinion.

"What's unheard of," he said warmly, "is that kid's age. She's perhaps not more than fifteen, and she's already come to this! What would you say to it if I went over to sit with her?"

"Nothing at all," I said. But the supposition was disagreeable to me. "Why would you do that?"

"I'm sure I don't know. For fun, that's all. Would you ask me not to do it, if you saw that I wanted to?"

His tone was teasing, but his challenge was again apparent.

"No," I said, without taking him too seriously. "Do you imagine I'd cling to you, imploringly?"

"If I thought that, I'd do it at once!" he said, in the same bantering way.

He was holding my hand, the carrousel was turning, the Leda, the Danae were filing past just as indecently, offering themselves, but I was gradually becoming clear-headed, despite the turning of the machine. Jean seemed to observe with the liveliest interest the acts and gestures of the little waitress, who was getting impatient, alone there in her gondola. The carrousel slowed down and once more stopped.

"Shall we get out?" I said to Jean.

"If you like . . ."

He followed me towards the exit, but stopped just as we were about to go out.

"No," he said, with a kind of laugh, "the poor little thing is bored, all alone! I'm going to take one trip around with her, if you'll allow it?"

"Why, certainly," I murmured, too astounded even to know what I was saying.

I really did not understand what was happening until I saw him jump back, hand the gnome some money, bound off, and settle himself in the gondola beside the little waitress.

He had not asked me to wait for him. I went out.

The pier was still black with people, but it was also dark now. The hawkers of mulled wine were still shouting their spiel. I had some money on me and with it I paid for a glass. I was rather cold. As I passed by the lottery, I had the idea of asking if my ticket had won anything. They gave me an enormous piece of gingerbread. "As for the pig, that will be for next time, my girl!" said the big red-faced man who distributed the prizes. I did not regret the moderateness of my winnings. It would have been the limit to have to go home with a pig under my arm. The evening had been absurd enough as it was.

I went back by trolley car, contrary to my usual habit. Many people were returning from the Fair, the trolley was taken by assault. I slipped into the most crowded part of the car, forcing myself to listen to the conversations going on over my head. The trolley car jogged up the hill, I was half smothering, with my gingerbread in my arms. The heat was intense, one could almost not breathe. I was standing, and the iron bar to which I clung was damp from having been grasped by so many hands. However, as I got out at my stop, I felt a pang at finding myself so deprived of support. The street was silent. Julia opened the door for me.

"Well, well!" she said. "You are certainly not ahead of time, Hélène! Do you know what time it is?"

"No."

"Nine o'clock! What do you say to that? Dinner's almost over. They're at the cheese course now. Oh, anyone can see you've not lost any time."

"What are you talking about?"

"About the Fair, Lena, that's what I'm talking about! About the Fair and the closed carrousel, where Elodie across the street saw you go in! Well, was it nice?"

"If you know everything, what are you asking questions for?"

Offended, she went back to the kitchen, angrily mumbling.

"I'd never have believed that," I heard her say, "I'd never have thought it of you, a well brought up young lady. The closed carrousel! Well, I never!"

I followed her, worried despite everything.

"Julia, you've not told anyone?"

"I'm not a fool, Lena! But you shouldn't have done it, no, you shouldn't have!"

"What? Go out with Monsieur Delfau?"

"No, for Heaven's sake, go into the closed carrousel. You, the daughter of Monsieur Noris, to amuse yourself along with the maids!"

She made a face of disgust.

"Well now, hurry up. They're waiting for you, and Madame doesn't look any too pleased."

I shrugged and entered the diningroom. Tamara and Father were finishing dinner.

"Well, Hélène! This is a strange hour to come home!" said

Father, but without ill-humor. The tone Tamara used was more pointed.

"Just the same," she said, "I hope you're going to tell us where you've been?"

"Can't you see this gingerbread which I am pressing to my heart?" I answered. "To the Fair, of course."

"You'll spoil your appetite with all those nasty things," said Father placidly, as he peeled an orange.

"Day before yesterday, too, you were at the Fair. Do you go there every day now?" said Tamara, with the look of an inquisitor.

But tonight I did not blush, I did not become confused.

"I wanted to see certain things again," I said calmly. And I sat down to eat.

"After all, since your father tolerates your traipsing about in carnivals and allows you to come in at all hours, I don't see what I can do," she concluded. She seemed to be beside herself that evening. Preparations for her trip to Italy were taking up a great deal of time and thought, she was spending her days trying on dresses, making farewell visits, and always with Max trailing after her like a house pet.

"Perhaps it would be better for you to go to bed than to try to eat without appetite," said Father.

"You've been eating all kinds of fried things," she said.

"No, just waffles," I said, for the pleasure of arousing her curiosity.

And obediently I went up to my room. The stairway was long, my shoes were singularly heavy on my feet. As I passed my the little cloakroom I was a bit tempted to turn my head aside, but I made an effort of will and looked in, I even opened the door, out of bravado. Then I continued to climb. The landing, the silent rooms smelling of beeswax, and then another flight of stairs. Tamara's bedroom, opened upon a great disorder of clothes and upon a familiar perfume that was almost intolerable that night . . . Still a flight of stairs before arriving in my room, before sitting down on the bed, pressing my two hands against my thumping heart in a banal gesture, and saying out loud, "How tiring those stairs are!"

A Sunday morning began, like all others, with its sad church-bells, the long sleep of the streets, the cold as pestering as a long sickness. But towards noon, just when the street began to resound like the roar of a seashell with the echoing of hurried footsteps and excited voices, just when the organ music poured out with needless solemnity upon congregations of behatted women and restless children, a pale, convalescent sun appeared above the grey lake. The fisherfolk set out their straw-bottomed chairs on the thresholds of their low houses and sat down on them, pipe in mouth. Bowed women spread out the sails, grey, green, orange, like the wings of dragonflies, to dry. Farther along, the prostitutes must be taking out their oil-cloth market bags to do their hasty shopping, and still but half awake display in the sunlight their dazed night-bird faces.

I was alone in the house, at my bedroom window. And I surveyed the town, lovely this morning, with its glistening pier, its houses with irregular tile roofs climbing the hill, its crooked streets along which the little trolley car inched itself along. And there was the park, with its rockwork, its pond, its closely planted trees, at present black but soon to be green and fresh in the spring. And there was the Plain, back of the town, with its groves, its tall trees, its tall white farms, severe as fortresses . . . All this was beautiful, all this glittering in frost and sunlight, and through the open window I breathed an air so pure that it seemed I was the first to breathe it. Yet despite this brightness and joy, I was overwhelmed and agitated with feverish uneasiness. Constantly I visualized the lottery, the grunting pigs, the trolley car, the people who had talked around me, the big man who had told me, "The pig will be yours next time, my girl." Despite my efforts, I always came back to those hateful images. I could not get out of that Fair, and I knew that without fail, after the lottery, after the Waffle Booth, I would be brought back to that moment when, inside the closed carrousel, Jean had gone over to the little waitress.

I could not draw myself away from that moment, I was still inside the carrousel, still prowled round those gondolas, seeing again the complicated poses of Leda clinging to that swan which looked like a big white calf. What was it he had said? "That poor little thing is alone . . . Excuse me . . ."? Or, "I'm sorry for that poor little thing"? Try as I would to convince myself that this was of no importance, I clung to those details. It seemed to me that I would find peace when I could remember, very precisely, his words.

I went out, crossing the park without hurrying. I had no rendezvous with anyone. The park was full of that same festive noise which filled the streets, echoing footsteps, voices calling, the cries of children. On the miry waters of the pond, some soldiers were manoeuvring a mouldering boat with some difficulty. Several families, dragging youngsters along at a gymnastic pace, were taking the road to the Plain. More and more radiant, this day seemed to be intoxicating the whole town. Through the twisting streets, slowly, automobiles heaved themselves to the top of the hill and, once there, madly drove off across the Plain, glittering in the sunlight. I felt a sudden desperate need to go away. I, too, wanted to leave, I did not want to remain behind in this town everyone was deserting. But go away with whom? Even the little trolley car had the air of fleeing, liberated from its useless rails, and batches of children at the trolley car windows fluttered their gloves and scarves, hallooing as if departing on an immense journey.

Yesterday, still, Jean and I were together, I believed in the possibility of a casual happiness. "That poor little thing . . ." Those words coming back again . . .

I returned home. After all, I asked myself, had anything changed? I was sure I had not been in love with Jean. Why then was I sure, deep down, that the minute I stopped anesthetizing myself with arguments, I would find my chagrin completely intact, like a treasure carefully stowed away? The nearer I got to the house, the more I felt that imminent presence of chagrin, ready to revive, again and again, unflaggingly, like a fountain, the more I felt that it was waiting for me in my room, as tangible, as poignant as the odor of the linden tree in summer.

At least I accepted the idea of never again seeing Jean. I would forget his tender voice, his cold eyes, his arm around my shoulders. My chagrin would not have a name.

X •

Jean was surveying the old-fashioned engravings that hung on the walls of the red room.

"Decidedly, this house is full of surprises. I hadn't noticed these engravings. Well, they're prodigious. Shut the door, will you, Hélène . . ."

Without replying, I went to stand with him in front of those faded pictures, illustrations that no doubt had been taken from an old edition of the Comtesse de Ségur's stories for juveniles. One of them depicted two little girls in wide skirts and lace pantalettes who were rolling hoops; it was entitled "Camille and Madeleine quietly amuse themselves." The other showed a poorly dressed child with downcast eyes standing before two beribboned little boys, and was entitled "Blaise came running at the call of the two little gentlemen of the Château."

"Surely Madame Vaes is a good soul," said Jean. "She must have hung these engravings here to give us a taste for virtue.

'Camille and Madeleine quietly amuse themselves'! Or perhaps she is a humorist."

"She doesn't look like one," I said.

The familiarity with which the proprietress of the house now treated us—had we not become her regular customers?—offended me terribly. It nauseated me, the way she had of escorting us "a bit of the way up the stairs," as if she were participating to a certain extent in a rite preceding the act of love. But how could we revolt? Houses were not numerous in Gers where young girls not of age would be welcomed without checking or registering, and this offensive cordiality was a kind of fee Madame Vaes allowed herself over and above the price we paid for the room, as compensation for her tolerance. I was all the less inclined to be indulgent towards the fat old Madame, since I was not sure that, in returning to the red room, I had done the right thing. Jean's telephone call making the date in the most casual way possible, a few days after that visit to the Fair, had been really a little curt. But had I refused, would that not have been to confess that I was hurt? Would it not have been giving some importance to his escapade? I told myself it was better to meet again quite naturally, and just forget it. In the silence that had fallen between us, Jean suddenly spoke.

"Why in the world did you go away so suddenly the other day? Surely you could have waited a minute for me. Did you mind seeing me take one turn on the carrousel with that kid? I really didn't want to hurt you."

"But I wasn't the least bit hurt, I assure you. I simply wanted to give you a free field, in case you decided to follow up your advantage. You would have been too polite to tell me, I'm sure, and I didn't want to spoil your evening."

"What tact!" he smiled. "Hélène, I repeat, you are the ideal woman. We should have met sooner. I might have married you. But seriously, that girl was charming. Don't you agree?"

"I have no opinion on the subject."

"Oh! Obviously she hasn't Tamara's charm," said he, throwing his coat on a chair. "She barely speaks French, she is from the German part of the country, she has, she told me, quite a talent with the flute . . ."

Was he expecting a question from me? Was he disappointed or pleased at my apparent indifference? Perhaps a little nettled, despite everything.

"And what about you," he went on, "do you play an instrument?"

"No. You're out of luck with me."

"What, don't you even play the piano?"

"Not even the piano."

"You don't sing, you don't embroider, you don't make gloves for poor people, you don't make petit-point bedroom slippers?"

"None of all that. Would you like me to make you a pair of petit-point bedroom slippers?"

"Very much. No one ever made me any. I put my last hope in you! You, who so resemble all the exemplary young girls . . ."

Mechanically, I looked at my face in the mirror, at the too regular features, the neat knot of hair, the white collar of my everyday dress, and I turned away my eyes, displeased.

"One gets tired of looking like all the exemplary young girls," I said. "No matter what I think or do, nothing ever shows on my face! Do you remember telling me the other day that I looked as though half asleep? I often think about that and every time I do, it makes me angry!"

"In short, you are a kind of female Dorian Gray," said Jean negligently, taking off his tie and throwing it on a table.

He seemed happy and was acting naturally. Why was I, too, not happy and natural? He put down his watch carefully on a bedside table. I recalled why I was there and began to undo my blouse, as I went on talking.

"I never envied Dorian Gray," I said. "It seems to me I'd very quickly get tired of always having the same face."

Jean, who had now finished undressing, did not reply, and I

went on talking in the silence, feeling increasingly uncomfortable.

"It's bad enough always to be the same person! I can sympathize with those women who change the color of their hair, for instance. I . . ."

"My God, what a lot of stupid things come out of this child's mouth," sighed Jean, stretching his tanned, naked body. "And how carefully you fold your clothes! You exemplary young girl, you!"

"I don't see why I shouldn't fold my clothes. It would be just as conventional to throw them off in 'passionate disorder' wouldn't it?"

"Perhaps, in your case, it would be more courageous, even so," he said softly.

"What do you mean by that?"

I propped one foot up on a low stool to untie my shoestrings. My hands were trembling a little.

"You know quite well what I mean. It would be more courageous, for instance, if you would stop fiddling with those shoestrings and come over here and kiss me."

"But . . ."

"Oh, without finishing undressing, like that. It's not too hard, is it? There's a way of undressing that's a little more exciting than getting ready to go to the office; there's a way of going to bed that's not like jumping in a river to drown . . ."

I let my shoe drop and approached him. I was in my combination, my ugliest one, dating from pre-Tamara times, a coarse shift of natural linen. I hoped Jean would realize how little importance I attached to our relations when he saw how I refused to go in for the most elementary coquetry. But he seemed not to notice anything, as I went towards him. I hesitated a moment before touching him.

"You're trembling," he said, with a satisfied and completely odious look.

"I'm cold."

"Really!" he bantered. "Then what are you waiting for? Why don't you throw yourself upon my breast?"

I put my arms around him, I pressed myself against his hard body. Never was a kiss given with so much fury. I must have bitten his lips, for I felt his nails drive into my shoulders and tasted blood in my mouth. Finally, when I wanted to draw away, his hands held me, his face remained pressed to mine, and with his whole body he pushed me towards the bed, as if to commit a murder. The struggle was fiercer than it had been before, I forgot that this brutal assailant had a name and a face, I even forgot to defend myself. I scratched and bit until at last I found myself alone, exhausted, more hurt than I had been the first time, and so weak that I felt on the point of bursting into tears. I remained like that for some minutes, sprawled across the bed, my head buried in the embroidered pillow, my aching body inert on the red counterpane.

When I at last raised my head, Jean was coming out of the bathroom, his long hair in his eyes, with a cut lip and his chest scratched as if by briars, all stained with blood. The whole room seemed to reflect the carnage. The counterpane was rolled into a ball under my hips, the sheet was torn, rumpled, and with long bloody streaks as if a wounded animal had taken refuge there, the little table near the bed had been upset and a carafe of water had spilled upon the thick carpet. Clothes were strewn on the floor, clothes that had been torn off in a frenzy, and the only item of clothing that remained to me, my linen shift, was slit wide open.

"This is certainly an example of passionate disarray," said Jean pleasantly. And he drew near and gently stroked my hair. "You'll catch cold. Get under the covers."

I obeyed without a word. I was weary and suffering, my mind was empty of thought. With a bound, Jean reached the other side of the bed and pressed me close, with tender care.

"Feel bad, darling?"

"Yes," I said.

"You see," he said ironically, "I don't do too badly with just one arm. Imagine what it would be like if I had the use of both arms!"

I laid my head on his lacerated chest; it was a sweet, warm shelter. I closed my eyes. I could have been so comfortable. Why did he try to pull me out of that blessed drowsiness which was dimly within reach, like a stretch of cool water in which it would be good to bathe? But he would not let me rest.

"After all," he went on in the same ironical way, "you, who aren't sentimental, it's a wonder you chose a man who can't hold you in his *arms*. Curiosity? No, I forgot, there was Tamara, you wanted to hurt her. But now? Well, you had reached your goal. All you had to do was tell her about it, and you'd accomplished the trick. So why did you come back? Ha, ha," he said playfully, "I'll wager I can guess."

"All right, why?" I murmured.

Why was he dragging me out of that lethargy into which I sporadically sank, a half-dream in which a friendly hand was leading me through summer vistas, leafy shadows, where the sound of tepid, lapping waters lulled my still hurt body . . . That dream even gave me the warmth of a shoulder, the support of a strong arm slipped beneath my neck, the warmth of lips . . . of those lips which were whispering close to my ear.

"I dare you to assert," that teasing voice was saying, almost infantile sounding, but concealing traps and snares, "I dare you to assert that never for a moment did you think, as all women do, 'After all, he's rich.' "

I was torn brutally from my beguiling dream. But what else had I expected? That he would murmur, "I dare you to assert you don't love me?" It had to be admitted, that was the danger for which I was prepared, and the unexpectedness of his question made me gasp.

"You're a very nice girl," murmured the tender and tantalizing voice in my ear. "You have a lucid mind, you don't get indignant, you know how ridiculous that would be. Not a bad calculation, after all."

What could I reply? I opened my eyes and stared up at his face bent over me observantly, the flicker of a smile on his lips.

"Jean, I did not want to revenge myself upon Tamara. I simply wanted to have a lover, that's all. As for whether you're rich or not . . ."

"It's all the same to you, because you adore me?"

And as I remained mute, he burst into the laughter of a child, delighted at having played a good trick on me.

"You see how absolutely it's the same to you! But I've thought of everything, you'll see."

He bounded from the bed into the middle of the room. His naked body was singularly robust, with its large shoulders, hard muscled chest, powerful calves. He must have exercised to acquire such almost abnormal agility. He rummaged in the pocket of his coat, and returned towards me with a small package in his hand.

"Swear you'll not say, 'It's too beautiful!' " he said, holding it out to me.

He had sat down cross legged on the bed and was observing me with a curiously malicious look. I propped myself up on an elbow, and without pleasure undid the paper wrapping and opened a dark red jewel box. It contained a gold bracelet, very plain, very heavy, which I took up in my hands without knowing what to do with it, so disconcerted was I.

"Oh, wonderful!" he exclaimed. And, as I continued holding the bracelet, he went on volubly with his comments. "She doesn't say a word, she weighs the bracelet in her hands! It's almost too good! No, don't say anything, don't spoil it, I beg of you. You can't imagine how you please me by saying nothing. That reflex you had was marvellous, absolutely marvellous! Oh, I know exactly what you want to say, now. 'What kind of a person do you think I am, sir!' Or maybe, 'I'll never accept it,' or 'It's too much, really!' But don't, don't say it. And don't even say, 'I'll give it to the maid'—that's already been said. But your eloquent gesture! Yes, it's quite heavy. I bought only a plain gold one because I was afraid gems would create a scandal, but if your appetite has been whetted, you have only to say the word . . ."

Angrily, I took the bracelet and clasped it around my arm.

"Thank you," I managed to say. "I like it very much."

"And you'll often come back here, won't you?" he said, in a kind of parodied passion. "And you'll tell me you adore me, that you'd dreamed all your life of someone like me, that my strong right arm is enough to make any woman happy?"

"Yes," I said, "I'll say that to you."

But I burst into sobs. Was it love-making that had exhausted me? Jean shrugged impatiently.

"Now, now, don't cry," he said more gently. "There's really no reason to cry. You just don't know how to take a joke, that's all."

And he pulled on his shirt and knotted his tie, using only one hand, with that frightening dexterity of his.

X I ·

What had happened to this intrigue which I had expected would be so trifling, so stripped of everything that gives love its value and importance? How to explain the constantly augmenting bitterness of these encounters which I had wanted to keep on such an ordinary plane? Each morning a curiosity resembling apprehension dragged me out of bed, with the feeling that once I had left my dream-world behind me I would find a solution to the problem. I pressed my hot forehead against the icy windowpanes, I tried once more to find the voluptuous sadness of revery, which everything encouraged. Outside, winter reigned alone over the town white with frost. In the little gardens, the desolate statues each day lost a little more of their concealing lichens and revealed the grey nudity of mummies. The cars moved slowly down the steep streets, their wheels in chains that squeaked, and the baker's trumpet resounded mournfully through the fog. In vain I tried to cling to that misty landscape; already my thoughts were flying off towards the red room.

Jean and I met there almost every day, towards three o'clock in the afternoon. Perhaps he would bring me a far too sumptuous gift, which I would accept without pleasure; perhaps, smiling and relaxed, pretending to drawl out his words as he did in society, he would tell me about his past adventures, affecting to assimilate this one to them; or perhaps his fine face would be set in those hard and almost cruel lines which meant he would goad me into sensual pleasures as if revenging himself upon me. And always I would go away aching in body and soul, without quite knowing why, having fallen into snares that I divined without seeing, having engaged in a contest without knowing what was at stake. Was it his childish vanity, wounded by my indifference, which prompted him to play this far too easy game? Did he take a perverse pleasure in showing me he had only to will it and he could disturb me?

To disturb me . . . a fine result! At least I had managed to interest him or he would not go to such pains. Or was he actuated by that most ordinary reflex of the seducer, whose passions are kindled and maintained by the least physical or moral resistance? He had certainly succeeded pretty well: I knew my hurts, could even count them, they bore his name. Jean. A name I could no longer call to mind without being overcome by the dull, gnawing pain of an invisible bruise, the kind that makes you wonder if, after all, it might not be something serious.

The pleasures of the flesh! No, sensual pleasure was not what drew me, each day, with anguished expectation and the slightest tinge of fear, to the red room. In the beginning I had been afraid of him. I had loved Tamara unrestrainedly, I had felt I knew everything about love, and suddenly I found myself in the unpleasant situation of someone who, well versed in elementary mathematics, discovers algebra and is a little vexed at not having had an inkling of it. I had sufficient inner resources to struggle against this detestable sensation. But who would teach me to fight, who would give me weapons against Jean? It was too late to flee, and anyway I would have been ashamed to retreat: when one has had the smell of blood, even one's own blood, it can never be forgotten. Of all my thoughts, the one I cherished most gladly was the thought of revenge.

Jean was not invulnerable, I was willing to bet. In order to find his vulnerable point and wound him, I had only to understand him. In order to understand him, he must be pinned down. A febrile belligerence—my only reflex which did not have its source in Tamara—goaded me on. If I could manage to triumph over that clever, wily, intelligent man, I would at last be relieved of the doubts that still remained, I would know that all weakness had been banished in me and that henceforth I would not have to depend upon anyone but myself. I would be alone at last.

Max opened the door of his apartment to me—Tamara's apartment, formerly, in the Rempart des Béguines. Since Tamara's marriage I had not been inside it and I was superstitiously fearing this test. But I did not recognize the place, nothing was the same in the two rooms where I had experienced so much. Max had knocked down the partition walls and thrown the two rooms together, and had enlarged the windows, without consideration for the balconies in the form of ships' prows.

The studio was full of canvases in different manners, which

ranged from the most intransigent cubism to an almost naive realism, his last manner of treating the family portrait. A spectacular disorder reigned, calculated to dazzle any respectable bourgeois who might enter the studio of *his* painter for the first time. I had some trouble finding an empty chair.

"I suppose you were expecting someone?" I asked, not without irony, waving at this carefully contrived disorder.

"Yes," he said, with no embarrassment. "A whole family's coming. I'm going to do them in a very amusing group, posing in front of their own house, with the tones very pink, very healthy, very à *la* Henri Rousseau, you see what I mean . . ."

"How charming! But I don't want to waste your time. I didn't come to talk about art. I want to get some information out of you."

"About what, my sweet?"

"About Jean Delfau."

He burst out laughing.

"Oh, so that's it! I was just wondering, myself, if that could last. After all, you see, you're nothing but a sentimentalist, like your old Max. So, the embarkment for Cythera is taking place? All aboard for wedlock? I was expecting this, my child, I can afford to tell you now, it was bound to happen. He's the type destined to suit you, you were made for each other, you . . ."

His loud gaiety, his intentional vulgarity froze me for an instant. This was his revenge, this moment when I needed him.

He had jumped to the conclusion that I was wildly in love and without more ado was taking out his revenge upon me for the contempt with which I had formerly treated him. Had I not criticised him, in a way that must have hurt, for sacrificing his career to Tamara? Had he not felt, deep inside himself, the soundness of those criticisms and therefore held all the more grudge against me for them? By coming here—so he thought—I was proving I had given in to the same weaknesses, which justified him in a way. His jubilation surpassed the bounds of decency, and I tried to bring him back to his senses.

"There's no question of Cythera, as you so elegantly put it. All I wanted was . . . how shall I explain? All I wanted was for you to talk about him, tell me what you know about him and his life, give me your opinion of him, tell me everything, even the things not quite honorable, if they exist. Don't be afraid of hurting me. On the contrary. I want to know everything it's possible to know."

"You're out for revenge? He's jilted you?" he asked, recovering hope.

He was determined to see me as the heroine of a love story, and his eyes already shone with a compassion which was not devoid of spite.

"No, he's not jilted me. Can't you check your melodramatic imagination for a second? I want to know what kind of man I'm up against, period. So don't act like an old Oracle and make me implore you, but get up on your tripod at once. He's a man of talent, that I know. But besides that . . ."

"Oh, a man of talent, that's easy to say," Max remarked grumpily.

"Maybe it's easy to say, but everyone says it," I replied, amused to see him jealous.

"He's the one that says it, especially. And with his father's fortune, naturally, no one denies him anything, while there are people who need work . . ."

"You, for instance?"

"Yes, me, for instance," he blazed. "I don't see why your father had to choose a guy like Delfau, who got round him with pull, instead of choosing me, a local man, with a knowledge of our actors and with something of a reputation, myself. Oh, of course, I'm not Monsieur Jean Delfau, the so-Parisian artist who makes sets for the cinema that are something to weep over. I'm a painter, a real painter, not a mucky stage designer. And just the same, since the stage designer's the only one that's an out-of-towner, it's almost a slap in my face!"

I was surprised to see him so worked up. Formerly, when he

talked about Jean to me, it had been with some evident admiration, if not sympathy. Tamara must have had something to do with this. But I couldn't see what I could get out of all these invectives. Although perhaps . . . That fortune, that dilettantism of Jean's, for which everyone reproached him, perhaps I might find in this a weak point, a flaw, something which would at last allow me, in my turn, to attack? With a patience new to me I waited for Max to vent his spleen. He wiped his face, caught his breath, and again looked like himself—a good fellow, though a little weak and a little damaged by success without honor.

"You know," he said rather awkwardly, "what I've just said was not meant to hurt you. After all, his work isn't so bad."

"As to his work, I don't care a pin," I said. "But there are some things I'd like to know. I mean, real facts about him, Max. For instance, what's all this about a fortune? I thought he made quite a lot of money?"

"Naturally he does," said Max regretfully. "With all that moving picture business, when you once get inside, it's pie in the sky. But just the same, he'd never have succeeded if the firm of Delfau, Gunther and Company hadn't been back of him."

"What is that firm of Delfau, Gunther and Company?"

"Oh a bunch of well-organized thieves. They own antique shops all over the place and think up ways to give a vogue to all the horrors they've paid nothing for, or to fabricate fake antiques which they manage to sell for a higher price than the authentic ones. They do modern stuff, too, wrought iron and plastic things, you know the kind, and they publish a magazine, *Plaisir du Meuble*, which gives them the chance to convince the average man that he can't hope to live happily if he doesn't have his house decorated, arranged, cooked up for him by the firm of Delfau, Gunther and . . ."

"And Company," I finished for him. "I've got the point, thank you. And all this brings in . . . ?"

"Lots of money for Monsieur Jean Delfau, who could afford just to twiddle his thumbs if he was capable of it, instead of barging into a profession which is already crowded enough!"

In his voice could be sensed the quivering rancor that must be shared by many of his colleagues. Did Jean suffer from this rancor? Did it arouse in him a doubt, a remorse? It did not show at first sight, but I must try this means. If I managed, even for once, to be aware of any vulnerability in him, I believed I would feel liberated.

"And so," I said patiently, "he could afford not to work?"

"And how! And plenty of people think he'd do much better. I certainly know he has offers galore, but it's due to the snobbishness of the stage managers when it's not due to a hope that he might put money in a show."

Once more, he was overcome with bitterness. I cut him short.

"He's not married, is he?"

"No, my pet. You'd like to offer yourself the Delfau firm and him to boot, would you? Well, except for a fluke, I don't believe you'll succeed. He lives in Paris with a very pretty gal, I've heard her name but I've forgotten it, wait a minute . . . And then, there's Sandra Marelli, who's also staying at the Carlton, she's one of your most dangerous rivals, and then . . . Listen, as a matter of fact I know someone who could give you plenty of information—if you hanker that much for information—she's a funny little thing, Spanish, who was with him for a year or two, he introduced me to her and I saw her land in Lausanne one fine day without a *sou*, and with an orchestra director or something of the kind trailing after her, I'll only say that much. Well, that young lady, Manuela Gonzalez or Ramirez or something like that is now working in Varfleur, in a movie house. If you like, I could try to find out which theatre, you could talk to her, though I don't see where that would get you."

"I don't either," I said thoughtfully. "But just the same, try to get in touch with her. And I'll come back to see you."

So there I was, awkwardly confronting him, armed with a weapon I did not know how to use. I was waiting for him to lower his guard, even just a little, but his smiling face indicated no tension, no abandonment of reserve that would be favorable to me since it would expose the tender spot where I must strike. It was an afternoon like all the others in front of the station. His smile made his face look agreeably ordinary, it was the face of any man who, after a day's work, longs for rest, relaxation, simplicity. And it took a great deal of attention and that kind of wisdom given us by the approach of danger, to perceive in his eyes, very blue that day, an amused gleam which had no kindliness in it.

"Oh, I really don't feel like shutting myself in, today," he said. "The air is so pure! Do you have any suggestions?"

He had spoken naturally, but his expression had become more attentive, his eyes were searching my face for the least sign of disappointment. However, I was by then accustomed to these duels, and I was able to reply without any sadness.

"You're absolutely right! It's such a lovely day, perhaps you'd like to go for a walk? Or perhaps you might like to take me to a movie?"

He seemed to be put off a little by so much amiability on my part. How could he have guessed that in my modest fashion I was weaving a plot against him, on which I pinned high hopes?

"How about taking a taxi to Barfleur?"

I acquiesced. Nothing could suit me better.

"Max told me 'Gentlemen Prefer Blondes' is being shown at the Empyrean," I said. "I'd like to see that film, if it wouldn't bore you."

"Not at all. A tour of the country and some mechanical art—that's an excellent program. So, come along, let's jump into a taxi."

Despite everything, he seemed a little astonished at my desire for a movie. No doubt he took it as a challenge. In fact, I was not quite sure what prompted me to get Jean to take me to the Empyrean where, as I knew, the Manuela girl was exhibiting herself in a stage appearance. I expected only that it would give him a shock, which would enable me to see him in a new and perhaps less favorable light than the one in which he usually showed himself to me.

We took a taxi. The air was glacial, a pale sun did not even manage to melt the frost on the trees. On how many afternoons had we gone, like this, to some sham-elegant bar or other, or into some stifling moving picture theatre, fleeing that red room which was waiting for us and where each of us longed to be with the other . . . The taxi drove slowly and cautiously across the denuded plain; the bare trees, the farms as enclosed as fortresses, from which only a line of smoke escaped, the ponds where children were skating, the occasional pedestrians passing by, smothered in furs, everything inclined one to sadness, or at least to gravity. But we seemed to be filled with a feverish gaiety, and kept up an almost insane chatter.

"Have you known Max for a long time?" I asked, not without design, as he spoke of his Parisian life.

"For a long time, yes, but in fact not very well. I didn't know he was from Gers, and when your father chose him as intermediary, I was amazed to learn that he lived here half the year."

"Oh, he's in very good standing here," I said, without looking at him. "He comes from a very poor family, as you perhaps know, and has had no one to give him a leg-up. He really deserves a lot!"

I tried to put into my voice an enthusiasm I only half felt for Max's supposed courage. But the "Oh! Really?" a little too exaggeratedly inattentive with which Jean greeted this was my only recompense. Was I on the right track?

"And don't you think," I went on, "that he's very talented? Everyone here says so, although the people of Gers do not usually cry up people like Max, for he has no social position or fortune. He's an exception . . ."

The expression in Jean's eyes, which were gazing steadily at me, made it impossible for me to finish my sentence. While his face remained smiling, his eyes had hardened, glazed, like water freezing. I was almost afraid. But immediately his look softened and when he spoke it was laughingly.

"Oh, come, come, Hélène, what's the meaning of this pompous eulogy? Are you, by any chance, trying to make me jealous of Max?"

"No," I said, trying to sound indifferent. "If I wanted to do that, I'd go about it another way. I merely thought that Max was your friend and that you would enjoy talking about him."

He did not labor the point, and we talked about other things.

But for a brief moment I had trembled. I had the feeling of having glimpsed a disquieting certainty opening up like an abyss at my feet, of having just missed glimpsing a different face. Had I trembled with pleasure or anxiety? I could not say.

In front of the imposing, gilded façade of the cinema, we waited to go in.

"I find this life extraordinarily restful," said Jean. "It's all so calm!"

"To much so, perhaps?"

"Not at all. This winter, this calm winter in a little town, the snow, the trolley car—I hadn't seen a trolley for years—an interesting setting, a nice girl, healthy amusements . . . I'm turning into a woodchuck."

"And like the woodchucks, you'll wake up in the spring," I said, thoughtlessly.

He gave me an inquiring look.

"As a matter of fact, that's true, I'd not thought any more

about it. You see how sluggish I've become! I'd quite forgotten that I'm not in Gers forever. After all, I'm rather fond of the little town . . ."

For a moment we remained silent, thinking of that departure. The temptation was there between us, almost tangible, to go back to Gers and to the red room that was waiting for us. What were we doing, standing there in front of that cinema which, with its enormous entrance and its lurid posters, seemed to be a gaping mouth of Hell? For a moment I felt like taking him by the arm and suggesting that we leave. Then I remembered his cold opening remarks, how he had said, "I really don't feel like shutting myself in today," and I hesitated. I was still hesitating when I heard an irritable voice behind us.

"Well, are you going to step up or not?"

It was the cashier, who was becoming impatient.

"Well, what will you have, orchestra or balcony?"

"Two orchestras," said Jean.

A surging and tumultuous crowd filled the theatre to bursting. The Empyrean looked something like a transformed hangar or garage. Formerly, these walls must have been painted a pleasant color, the plaster mouldings must have reflected a soft light. But so many children's hands, black and sticky, had left their marks on the walls, the mouldings had become so filled with detritus—apple cores, old caramels, gobs of chewing-gum— that all effort at embellishment or even cleanliness had been abandoned. The theatre was glaringly lit by three enormous light bulbs, swinging at the end of a wire, and in the brutal light the plush seats, the curtain fringed with tarnished gold, the draperies of the boxes where amorous couples found concealment, were shown up with all their stains and holes and badly mended scars. It was a complete and unblushing indigence, this grinning parody of luxury. Some urchins were throwing paper wads at the stage with sling-shots concocted out of elastic bands. In front of us, a row of young fellows in dungarees were laughing loudly. Jean consulted the program with a smile. He seemed contented, relaxed, remote. I wondered if this confrontation I had planned would lead to anything. My imagination had evidently carried me too far. And yet, I waited impatiently the appearance, among the other numbers, of Manuela Lopez.

"Well, Jean? What's on the program?"

"Oh, they promise us some unheard-of things: 'A series of choice numbers'—chosen by whom, one would like to know—'will, this month, delight the eyes and ears of the Empyrean's faithful public.' What will enchant the ears is, I imagine, the promised Organ Festival, unless perhaps the reference is to some sentimental ballads sung by Mademoiselle Ida Saloma, who won the first prize at the Conservatory of Geneva? True, she received that high recompense quite some time ago . . ."

"And what will enchant our eyes?" I asked, laughing a little constrainedly.

"Why, of course, Miss Saint-Gall and Miss Winterthur, two beauty queens, between whom the management will ask us to choose, to find out if, as the film title affirms, gentlemen do prefer blondes. And we are asked kindly to detach the green page from our program and to hand it, either entire, if we prefer the blonde, or torn in two, if we prefer the brunette. 'Les Misses'—as they are referred to on the program—'will take pleasure'—I quote!—'in passing down the aisles to collect the votes.' Well, Hélène, if you dare to maintain that there's no fun to be had in your country, after such merrymakings as this!"

I was about to reply, when the cinema organ drowned us in its mawkish bellowings; and at the same time, the theatre was plunged in colored light, first blood-red, then greenish. Shouts of satisfaction rose among the urchins. In the boxes, the couples became sentimental. Then a stout woman, who seemed capable of raising weights at a Fair but who was made up for the rôle of the delicate Athalia, stepped forward on the stage and in a thin little saucy child's voice sang: "*Le rossignol m'a a dit.*" Apparently the ballad about the night bird was very popular.

The extreme poverty of these numbers united us momentarily in an infantile glee. The wind was howling outside, you could hear its roar above the glass roof. In the sordid theatre there sprang up a kind of fraternity, favored by the warmth and the foul air. We bought some peanuts, we acclaimed the withdrawal of Madame Ida Saloma with frenzied applause. Once more, I was on the point of talking about leaving. I was filled with doubts. After all, wasn't it more dangerous than useful to penetrate the hidden universe of Jean? There still remained some innocent pleasures in our affair—for instance, that very moment, sitting side by side, laughing heartily at the repeated curtain calls being taken by Madame Ida Saloma. Might not all this be spoilt, in a second, by the appearance of Manuela Lopez? After the stories Jean had told about his conquests, I could imagine that he would find it very unpleasant to reencounter this one, devoid of grandeur.

I had wanted to enjoy his embarrassment; but now that the moment was approaching, when this flimsy plan was on the point of succeeding, I was worried. Supposing he guessed that I had something to do with the encounter? Supposing he were to react in an unexpected way, turn the tables on me? He had underestimated me in treating me like a little girl who could easily be put out of countenance; was I not going to commit the same mistake in believing that all I had to do to upset him was to confront him with his past? And if my calculations were right, if it needed only this flaw in the edifice of our relations to make it crumble, would it not have been better for me to . . .

A greasy little man in a dinner jacket far too big for him and with the woeful look of Levantine rug merchants, came to clutch the micro. His falsetto voice bounced round the auditorium in weird little chortles that made the children rejoice.

"Men prefer blondes!" he yapped, comically hugging the metal stem. "At least, that is the assertion made by the film we are about to present before our esteemed public! Well now, before seeing it, the spectators are going to have the great, the inimitable privilege of participating in a Referendum! By that I mean to say they will have the right to affirm their opinion, to tell us if they, too, prefer blondes. And for this reason, at the cost of immense sacrifices, the management is going to present two queens of beauty, two glamorous creatures, one a brunette, the other a blonde. All you have to do is choose between them!"

Applause burst out, along with shouts and smutty jokes. Turning towards the wings, the little man summoned the actresses on stage with a great waving of the hands, pretending to be struck with admiration, and again jumped towards the micro which he embraced, yelling the remainder of his speech in the voice of a drowning person.

"Attention! Lights! Spots! And here, here at last is the blonde, Miss Saint-Gall, the newly elected and ravishing Miss Saint-Gall of this year, but whom we know by her real name as Josette Burger. Miss Saint-Gall, give the audience a little smile, will you? And to the left, here's Miss Winterthur, elected only three weeks ago, the dazzling but shy Miss Winterthur, the brunette, whose name—remember it well—is Manuelita Valency. Now, smile, ladies. Look at your judges. And now, gentlemen, make your decisions without asking the advice of your wives. Do you prefer blondes?"

On the stage, the two beauties had stepped forward, wagging their hips a little, affecting a charming embarrassment until, the front of the stage being reached, they stripped off their long and just a bit shabby fur coats, no doubt lent to them by some furrier badly in need of publicity, and whose name must figure on the program. As the electric organ ululated a parody of admiration, they appeared in very reduced bathing suits. There were shouts, yells of joy, the shrill laughter of children, comments more or less flattering. Jean laughed and applauded along with the others. Hadn't he recognized her, then? Or else, had Max been mistaken?

"Extraordinary, these exhibitions!" he said enthusiastically. "And what an audience! You'd say they were tigers being thrown red meat!"

In effect, the sailors in the first row and the young people around us and the invisible spectators in the balcony were all stamping and shouting loudly at the beauty queens, who were still simpering on the stage. The blonde one was too fat, with a little-girl face like a mask, and short, fair hair. The brunette's legs were too thin and her shoulders were rather hunched, but she had a pretty enough face, with a pert little nose and sparkling eyes.

"For whom are you going to vote?" I asked Jean, a trifle nervously.

"Let's see. The blonde is too fat, the brunette is too thin," he said pensively. He was frankly enjoying himself. "Well, shall we say the brunette? Since you're not my wife, I've the right to consult you. And then, she reminds me, somehow, of a girl I used to know . . ." He stopped, as if struck by a sudden idea. "What did he say she was called?"

"Valency, I believe, or Valençay . . ."

"Then it can't be she. The one I knew had a Spanish name. And anyway, she was better looking than that. I say, here they are. Let's hope there'll be some papers left for us."

The two girls, in their skintight bathing suits, were threading their way among the young fellows, doing their best to obtain the green ballots, putting forth all their charms, letting out little cries, and here and there creating veritable small-scale riots.

"Gentlemen, gentlemen! A little moderation," intoned the man in the dinner jacket, gripping the micro. "Let the young ladies pass! Don't frighten them, they are so timid and shy!"

This assertion provoked a torrent of laughter, not very flattering to the young ladies; but they did not seem to mind. As they approached us, Jean rose from his seat.

"No, it's not possible," he murmured. Then he broke into a laugh. "Why, it is she! I say, this is extraordinary! Manuela!"

The brunette turned her head, widened her eyes, stared into the obscurity, then she, too, began to laugh.

"Johnny! Why, what are you doing here? You're going to vote for me, I hope?"

"And how! It's absolutely amazing, our meeting here in Barfleur! What was it they called you? Miss Winterthur?"

"Exactly," she said, with dignity. She leaned her aggressively pointed bosom over towards us, while cries of ironic protest arose from the group of young fellows.

"I'll explain this later on, if you'll meet me at the exit in half an hour?"

"Unfortunately, my child, that's impossible. I have a rehearsal, yes, I'm doing the sets for the theatre in Gers, and then, you may have noticed that I'm with a young friend, Mademoiselle Hélène Noris, whose parents are waiting in agony for her return, with no idea that she is attending this depraved show."

I intervened, with slightly forced enthusiasm.

"My parents don't expect me home before seven, Jean, and I'd like very much to make the acquaintance of Miss Winterthur."

"All right, all right," said Jean, who did not seem delighted at my taking the initiative like that. "Then, 'Lita, we'll meet you at the exit in a half hour."

She left us, to the applause of some half ironically impassioned young fellows, and went on with her harvesting of votes, swaying her slender hips.

"What's all this about wanting to know Manuelita?" he asked, when she was barely out of hearing. "She's an old friend of mine, true, but I don't have the least yearning to endure her chatter."

"I thought it would make you happy," I said innocently. "I thought you were turning her down for my sake, so as not to leave me alone . . ."

"You're very kind and thoughtful, today. Max, Manuelita . . . Is there anything you'd like to ask me?"

"Always, of course," I said with a laugh.

Meanwhile, the triumph of Miss Winterthur had been announced.

A half hour afterwards, leaving the seductive technicolor sirens to their evolutions, we rejoined, at the entrance to the Empyrean, Miss Winterthur, stripped of her furs and buttoned into a little black tailored suit, very neat, which made her look like a piano teacher with just a trifle too much makeup.

"Oh, it's swell to see you again, Johnny!" she called out, with an exuberance that made two or three people turn to look. "What do you say to a drink at the Sandoz restaurant on the square? That's where Bruno's working, he'd be so glad to see you."

"I don't know who Bruno is," said Jean rather shortly, "and I'm not keen to know."

Miss Winterthur, apparently unhurt by this, dragged us away towards the square.

"Johnny, you've not forgotten Bruno, it's impossible! Bruno, he's the one who played the hermit in *Rome est àtoi*, you put him in pants that were too short, you could see his calves."

Jean gave a rather forced laugh.

"Oh, yes! My hermit. What's he doing in this restaurant?"

"Why, what he *does*, Johnny! He played the hermit because he was out of work, but he's really an orchestra conductor!"

We entered the Sandoz restaurant, where a great many respectable ladies were drinking tea to the sound of gypsy music, and sat down at the far end of the big room.

"I only have a minute," said Jean, who seemed to be ill at ease. "I didn't count on seeing the picture to the end, I've an enormous amount of work to do in Gers. Tell me in three words what brings you here, and explain Winterthur and, above all, that other grotesque name the announcer gave you? Tracy?"

"Valency," said Miss Winterthur.

In the warmth of the room, she had relaxed, and her face, looking a little pinched without the pert stage-smile, avowed the menacing approach of the thirties. I examined her eagerly. Hadn't she, too, been Jean's mistress? A rival, in a way? The word amused me. Jean pronounced it sometimes, that word, with an intonation that evoked elegant, well dressed women, very superior to poor me, and before whose shadowy figures I could only humbly efface myself. He had told me about his affair with Jacqueline Thor, the well known actress of the angelic face, he had talked about Sandra Marelli. I was not at all sorry to find myself confronted by this one, of whom he had not talked and who seemed to know him well. So I looked at Manuela Lopez. Her frizzy permanent, her cheap, flashy earrings, her well cut suit which was shiny from use, the superfluous little scarf knotted around her far too thin neck, and especially her shoes with cracks no amount of shoe-polish could disguise—all this denoted a poverty that could assume a bohemian air. The same determination to make the best of things could be read on her worn face. Already too set in the mold of professional allure, that determination showed in the stubborn little forehead, the fixed smile; but one could also read there a deeper courage, which almost gaily accepted this misery in masquerade. On the whole, Manuela Lopez, alias Miss Winterthur, was rather likeable.

It was a long and complicated story she was telling us. Bruno, seeing her without an engagement in Paris, had had the idea of entering her in the "Miss Winterthur" beauty contest. He had some friends on the Winterthur jury. But in order to win that glorious title, she would have to take out naturalization papers. A friend of Bruno's, also an orchestra conductor, had spared her this trouble by consenting to marry her, with the understanding that he would have his share in the profits. But once the title had been captured, he had managed to pocket the receipts—she had been singing in his orchestra. From then on, she had been overwhelmed by a run of bad luck. She had been artist's model (I imagined that was how Max had met her), had sung in a nightclub, and then had secured this engagement at the Empyrean, but she did not like the place at all, for the manager, who was the "protector" of Miss Saint-Gall, made her life a misery every time the vote went to her.

"Oh, I was sure," she went on, putting her hand on Jean's, "that all I had to do was to write you and you'd have given me a lift. But I had my pride . . ."

"Fortunately!" said Jean nastily.

She appeared to take no notice, but I searched the familiar face for that harsh expression which I had thought was reserved for me.

"And I went on, telling myself that if ever things got completely bad there'd always be time to write to Jean. I remembered how you had helped out Anne-Marie, Gaby . . ."

"Why not give a complete list of my intimates to this young lady? I see you've become dangerously talkative, Manuelita. I believe we'd do well, Hélène, to get out of here."

He had already stood up to get his overcoat.

"Speak for yourself, Jean," I said, "As for me, I have plenty of time. I'll take the six o'clock train. I'm staying on here for a while with Miss . . . Valency."

If my daring displeased him, he showed no sign of it.

"In that case, I'll leave you two to your gossip. By the way, Manuelita, where did you get the name Valency? If I'm not mistaken, when you were singing at the *Veau Mairn*, you were called Gomez?"

"Lopez," she corrected, flushing slightly. "And it wasn't the *Veau*, it was the *Triton*."

"Oh yes, that old Triton," he sighed, lingering. "And how you vamped the Americans! It's true you had a slight Spanish accent in those days, you pulled off those '*Hombres!*' very well, and you had a nice little story of how you happened to leave Spain. . . . Goodbye, now. I'll drop a word to you one of these days. Can I address you at the Empyrean?"

"Yes," she murmured, "I'll be here for another two weeks."

But something in her, in her blush, her constrained smile,

left me with the feeling that Jean's recollections represented nothing pleasant to her. Already he was going off, with rapid step, his overcoat thrown over his shoulders.

She at once drew near me. As all women do when left to themselves by a man, we assumed the air of conspirators.

"There now, he's furious," she said in a warm voice. "I'll bet it's because you said you'd stay. Maybe you ought to have gone away with him?"

"I'm not very worried about his ill humor," I said resolutely.

"Oh, good. But aren't you engaged?"

Her effort at being tactful made me smile.

"For the duration of his stay in Gers, no doubt."

"Oh! I suppose you're acting in the play?"

"No," I said, a little surprised. "I simply happen to live in Gers. Has Jean a special fondness for actresses?"

"I suppose he thinks they're easier than the others, and since he doesn't like to take a risk except on a sure thing . . ."

Suddenly she smiled in a charming way, rather sad, rather tender, which was more becoming to her than her assumed hoydenish air.

"Perhaps I'm boring you with all this. I always talk too much about Jean, Bruno's always telling me I do. 'Say right out that you're in love with him,' that's what I hear every time I open my mouth. And of course that's not true. To begin with, you'd have to be an angel to be in love with that kind of guy—I hope at least I'm not shocking you?"

"No," I said, smiling. "I'm not an angel."

But nevertheless I was disconcerted by Manuelita's chatter. After all, what I had wanted to hear, what Max had not ceased hoping for, were recriminations, anecdotes I could use, a fund of slimy rancor which would disclose Jean in a light similar to that under which I saw Tamara. The almost indulgent tone used by Manuelita disappointed me. However, despite the secret instinct which put me on guard, I wanted to hear more.

"Of course," Manuelita said, "It's not entirely his fault.

There's that arm of his. And then, all that money. It's hard for a fellow like Jean, a serious type like there aren't many of, to hear himself treated like an upstart by a whole bunch of poeple who aren't a patch on him, and all that just because his father left him a little too much money."

"I thought he was so proud of his money? So glad to live in luxury and not have to work at anything if he doesn't want to, so glad he can choose?"

"What would you do, if you were cross-eyed?" asked Manuelita, with an astute air. "You'd try to make everyone believe that cross-eyes are the prettiest, and that only ugly women's eyes are straight, wouldn't you?"

I was decidedly beginning to learn a great deal from Miss Winterthur, alias Valency, alias Lopez: among other things, the falsity of the prejudice which gives beauty queens a reputation for stupidity.

"Look, a hard blow for him, for instance, was when they wouldn't have him design the sets for the *Populiste* theatre, because he was only an amateur—that was their excuse. Just some jealousies, you can take it from me. Of course—it was when we were together—he pretended he wouldn't for the world want to work with . . . what did he call it? I can't remember, but . . . Oh, yes, with prophets . . ."

That word reminded me of something.

"And God knows he's not an amateur! Lots of people don't work like he works. Two days before the opening, two days, I'm telling you, I've seen him stay all night at the theatre to finish some screens that hadn't been done right. Himself! But what a devil he is, too! What a devil! You heard what he said just now, to make me mad? Naturally, you can't know what the 'Triton' was like, if you live here; well, it was a bum little night-club, something like those dives down by the harbor in Gers. Only more chic, of course. Well, I left all that, I'm an actress now. Anyway, I adore the theatre, I'd have done anything to go on the stage. So I meet Monsieur, and what does he tell me?

That I don't have any talent, that I wouldn't even be able to walk on, that I don't know how to hold myself, that I'd better just throw myself at the first guy that came along, because that's the only thing I have a talent for, and I'll spare you the rest. What a life! What a hell! That's why I don't laugh except a little when Bruno tells me I was in love with Jean. Oh, it's quite a change, since I'm with Bruno!"

Her eyes turned affectionately towards the orchestra, resting caressingly upon the bald pate of a big man in gypsy costume who was sweating over his violin.

"Is that he?" I asked, out of politeness.

"Yes," she sighed. "He's good, isn't he? What was I saying? Oh, yes. Jean. Well! It's not generosity that he lacks. Take this, take that . . . You don't lack anything while you're with him."

Mechanically, I touched the heavy bracelet that weighed down my left arm. Alert, Manuelita's eyes followed my movement.

"And when you come to it, all those gifts, do they make us happy? I'd rather have a little bouquet from my Bruno . . ."

I had been on the point of feeling tender pity; now a slight nausea saved me. Perhaps, after all, there was something of the beauty queen in Manuelita.

"And I know some girls," she went on, "who've been driven crazy! Always the gifts, but if they tried to say one slightly nice word, he put on his big 'lucid' act. That's the word he uses, believe it or not: I am lucid. I can't be caught, it's on account of my money, it's on account of my reputation, so shut up—that's that. God knows it's not such a terrible thing, that arm of his. I know guys with faces that disgust me more than his arm. But his father was a little crazy, a widower, you know. He brought up the kid separated from other kids, thinking he'd be happier that way, so what could you expect? You can't stay all by yourself forever, you notice there are other people in the world, and you're humiliated . . . You've noticed how he uses his right arm? He must have exercised and exercised to do that! Especially when you realize he began when he was sixteen. Before that, the servants always helped him. Then, suddenly, he didn't want that any more."

"You certainly know a lot about Jean!" I smiled. "Are you sure Bruno's not right?"

She shrugged, perhaps a little nervously.

"He's rotten, I tell you. And do you realize he's thirty-two years old? You can't change a man at that age, believe you me. But as for you, you should worry, since you only have him for the duration of the play. So just don't pay any attention if he puts on the lucid act. Say 'Yes, yes,' don't listen to a thing, and get yourself paid in some jewelry that lasts."

Upon these disenchanted words, her eyes dimmed once more and she began to look tenderly at the violinist who was directing with one hand, mopping his brow, and then once more going back to drawing from his violin threads of music so fine that they tore cries of admiration from some of the rapturous old females.

"He's too good a violinist for a joint like this," she sighed. "He could give concerts, I assure you."

Her eyes met the violinist's languishing big eyes and she smiled, with that half-conscious mooncalf look on her face that all women in love try to imitate. I judged it the moment to begin the ceremony of adieux. Miss Winterthur was demonstrative. I had to endure several embraces quite respectably perfumed with lavender, and unblinkingly I heard myself called "my pet" "my treasure" and even "kitten." Manuelita was evidently capable of subtle discernment only when it came to Jean. She seemed to imagine that it would give me infinite pleasure to see her again, she gave me her address, told me I must absolutely make Bruno's acquaintance, that he would charm me, and she exacted my address in return, writing it in a tiny notebook bound in oxidized silver, a souvenir of her beauty contest splendors.

At the door of the Sandoz restaurant I turned back and saw that, taking advantage of an interval, the gypsy violinist had gone to sit beside Manuelita who, with her head resting on his shoulder, seemed to be enjoying the utmost bliss. A huge mirror behind them displayed its elaborately carved gold frame, which made them look like a wedding photograph, the very ugliness of which rendered it all the more touching.

I just barely caught the 6.05 train.

X I I I ·

This was nothing but a trap—a trap of pity, comprehension, and affection. But I refused to let myself be caught. It had been unwise of me to force my way into Jean's life, instead of remaining outside these secret complications. Violence had been done me; I must react with corresponding violence. I did not want to share the fate of the unfortunate Manuelita, who had made the mistake of feeling pity for a creature as dangerous as Jean. I must see someone else, interest myself in someone else—that was my only way of getting out of this, the only way to shut out Manuelita's voice repeating, "Of course, it's not entirely his fault . . ."

I decided to go see Stani. Since the beginning of my affair with Jean, I had gone to the Academy not more than twice, and I had not had time to ask my Polish friend for news of Odette Périer. By chance, I knew the address of the Mierowicz family. It had made an impression on me when I first heard it: Rue d'Ecosse, behind the station. That was certainly one of the narrowest, shabbiest, and most disreputable streets in Gers. No wonder Stani was dying to get out of it. Had he gone to see

Madame Périer? Had he succeeded in capturing her interest? I was asking myself these questions as I rang at the low door in the Rue d'Ecosse. No matter what, his gossip would be a welcome change.

The door half opened slowly. A woman's head, covered with tight little grey curls, looked out cautiously. As soon as she perceived me, the little lady's expression of mistrust turned into one of smiling compassion and she opened the door wide for me.

"Why, how do you do, Mademoiselle?" the lady asked, almost in a bass voice. She was wearing a plushy, mauve-colored dressing gown and talked with a short bone cigarette holder stuck in the corner of her mouth. Her accent was foreign and I imagined she must be Madame Mierowicz.

"Be so kind as to enter. Careful, there are two steps to go down . . . Yes, we are very temporarily settled here, while waiting for my husband to find a big studio . . ."

Her tone was so mournfully compassionate that I wondered if something had happened. It would have been pure tragicomedy to hear just then of Stani's death. Without daring to put the question, I followed her down a long, dark corridor, keeping just behind the mauve dressing gown which trotted ahead, and at last I was introduced into a long room, where two small windows let in almost no daylight but provided a view at sidewalk-level of a procession of legs and feet.

In the middle of this room, of which I could scarcely see anything except a great disorder, was a table covered with papers. Sitting behind it was a kind of ogre, red faced, wide shouldered, large mouthed, big nosed, and with a black beard; his fat hands rested on the arms of a Henry III armchair as if it were a throne. The ogre had evidently found too many trustful little boys on his road, for when he stood up to greet me, I saw with stupefaction that his enormous paunch and thick legs formed a mis-shapen, formless block, giving him the look of a statue of Atlas, only half disengaged from the stone.

"This is Monsieur Mierowicz," said Stani's mother, in the mournful low voice that had already surprised me, since it did not seem to go with her singularly lively big black eyes.

"Sit down, Mademoiselle—or perhaps Madame?" said the ogre, sinking back into his chair, and with a royal gesture of his gigantic arm, indicating a chair on the other side of the table.

"Mademoiselle," I said. "I'm Hélène Noris. Excuse me for coming unexpectedly like this, I only wanted to see Stani . . ."

Had Monsieur and Madame Mierowicz burst into sobs at these words and handed me Stani's obituary, I would have been less surprised than I was at the explosion of laughter that followed my words, particularly since it came from a couple who, a minute before, had appeared so solemn and afflicted.

Monsieur Mierowicz' laughter corresponded to his appearance: it was gargantuan. It so filled the room with its loud thundering that one expected the walls to crumble under its blast. As for Madame Mierowicz, her laughter was shriller, more metallic; tears came to her eyes and the bone cigarette holder fell out of her mouth to the floor.

I was still waiting patiently for this hilarity to spend itself, when a door at the end of the room opened and Stani appeared. He was in shirtsleeves, one of his cheeks was covered with lather, and he held a razor in his hand. This apparition seemed to raise his family's merriment to the highest pitch. As for Stani, he had recoiled, at sight of me, as if from a serpent; then he checked himself, and came forward, flushing deeply.

"Hélène! How nice! If I'd known, I'd have . . . Well, please excuse me, I was not expecting . . ."

He stopped his stammering excuses, put down his razor on a piece of paper, and began to scold his parents, whose hilarity had diminished a little.

"So that's the way you welcome my friends when they come to visit me? Can't I have a girl here to see me without you two giggling like idiots?"

"But can't you realize, Stani, my precious?" Madame Miero-

wicz groaned, still panting with laughter and wiping away the
tears that had streamed down her wrinkled cheeks. "I'm the
one, poor stupid creature, who mistook your friend for one of
your father's customers—the one who lost a little daughter and
wants to have such a pretty tombstone made. I must tell you,
Mademoiselle, that my husband is an artist, a real artist,
Stani takes after him. All you have to do is look around you and
you'll see you are in an artistic home!"

With a wide wave of the arms, she embraced the room where
the walls were, in fact, covered with designs of a funereal appearance. Monsieur Mierowicz, as I later learned, worked in a firm
of stone cutters specializing in sumptuous tombstones. The designs were sketches of his most successful works.

I tried in vain to make them see that the misunderstanding
was of no importance. Madame Mierowicz was determined to
overwhelm me in a torrent of excuses; while Monsieur Mierowicz blasted his son for having insulted him, and Stani de-
fended himself shrilly.

"Now, that's enough," said Madame Mierowicz, and the tu-
mult subsided a little.

"Yossip," she went on, "let these children go off to themselves and have a talk together. They'd much rather do that than
listen to your idiotic jabber." After which, she once more
screwed the short cigarette holder into a corner of her mouth.

"You take sides with this degenerate boy," roared Monsieur
Mierowicz, "who's not even my son."

"If he was yours, he'd not be so beautiful!" retorted Madame
Mierowicz, with reason.

Stani drew me away into the adjoining bedroom. No sooner
was the door shut than the voice of Monsieur Mierowicz became completely extinguished.

"Cork," said Stani with satisfaction. "The walls are cork-lined.
Mamma's the one that put it in, to give me more peace. I hope
they didn't scare you too much? You know, they're always argu-

ing like that, but they're angels! Especially mamma, of course, but papa's a wonderful guy, when he wants to be. And they both sleep in the diningroom so as to leave me a room where I can see my friends. Angels, I tell you . . ."

I had a strange vision of Madame Mierowicz, her cigarette holder clenched in her equine jaws, soaring towards Heaven. As for Monsieur Mierowicz, I gave up trying to imagine the dimensions of the wings that could lift his terrestrial form. I sat down on the bed and Stani drew near.

"I was so surprised to see you that I did not even thank you for coming. I'm so glad to see you, Hélène."

"No need for effusions," I cut in rather shortly. "I didn't come here for that. Wipe off your cheek and tell me how things are going with you."

"What things?" he asked, wiping off his face with a handkerchief.

"Your affair with the gorgeous Odette."

"Oh that, well, not bad," he sighed. "I mean, I showed her my drawings."

"Which she declared sensational, of course?"

"She liked them a lot," he said haughtily. "And she asked me if I would decorate the two drawingroom doors, she wants to change the decorations there. I did some sketches—girls dancing in a rustic scene of love—and she approved. I began painting two days ago."

"Is she paying you?"

"Very well," he said cautiously.

"And aside from your painting, what else has she asked of you?"

"Nothing. That is to say, she asked me to dinner twice."

"Without Fontanas?"

"Yes."

"It's clear. But what are you waiting for? For her to change her mind?"

"That's just what bothers me. You see, what I want is something lasting, like marriage, like . . ."

"A steady income, in fact."

"Yes, that's it. But you can't ask for that sort of thing right away, can you?"

I liked his frankness, and the meditative look on his frowning brow. That was what I had come there to find. Obscurely, I must have felt that I would find again the sweet savor of disdain and thus forget a wound that my pride was seeking to minimize.

"You'll get it, you'll have your income, if you know how to go about it," I said, almost affectionately. "After all, perhaps you were not so wrong to pretend not to understand. That will make her go for you seriously. Keep on painting and don't worry about anything—it may work."

"I'll try. But there's one fly in the ointment."

"What is it? Is she that unattractive to you?"

"No, no, that's got nothing to do with it. I'm worried about the ladders," he said darkly.

"What ladders?"

"Well, to paint the panels above the doors, I'll have to use a ladder, see? And I can't stay on a ladder, I get dizzy."

Despite myself, I burst out laughing.

"Oh, poor Stani! How typical!"

"Yes," he sighed, "I'm unlucky. But say, have a look at this?"

On the wall in a corner of the room could be seen a number of quite academic sketches of languorous nymphs.

"Not bad," said I, perfidiously.

At once, he was radiant.

"You think so? And that's not all. Behind the group, there'll be a nymph, I mean a sylphid, a Maenad . . . What the hell, I've forgotten the word . . . a dryad, that's it, coming out from behind a tree, you'll only see her profile, see, like this . . ."

Impulsively he sped up the ladder, and with a piece of charcoal traced a few lines on the wall.

"And there, see, will be a musician holding some kind of rustic musical instrument, a shepherd's pipe or something, and here there'll be groves of trees, and here, another nymph . . . So far, I've only sketched the central group, see."

"Yes, yes, I see. The central group . . ." I murmured, suddenly overcome with mirth at the aspect of those spiritless nymphs, and, seizing a leg of the ladder, I gave it a shake.

"Hélène! You're crazy!" he cried, clutching at the upper rung.

He had become livid in a second. His wild expression struck me as funny, and I gave the ladder another shake.

"Let go! You're going to kill me!" he whimpered, so pitiably that I stopped.

But he remained seated on his perch, with one hand over his eyes.

"That's clever of you! Now I'll never be able to come down, my head's spinning so!"

I went up two or three rungs and held out my hand to him. As he came down I noticed that his legs were trembling. He went and flung himself on the bed, his face glowering.

"Really, you're not nice. I'd practiced for three days staying up there, and now I'll never even be able to climb it again."

"Oh, of course you will."

He looked very upset. His long, slender body remained sprawled across the bed. I kissed his pale lips. He gave a long, happy sigh. If he had tried to draw me towards him I would have fled, perhaps, overcome by a recent memory; but he only half opened his slanting golden eyes, and was so visibly waiting upon my desire that I was the one to hold out my arms.

No one interrupted us. The Mierowicz couple seemed to be very busy when we came out of the bedroom. Monsieur Mierowicz was feverishly designing a tombstone on which two angels were in an embrace.

"It's for a couple who were killed in an automobile accident," he said, with a gentle smile. The eyes that sparkled lazily in his

117

puffy face, were, I noticed, handsome and golden, exactly like those upon which, only a moment before, I had been pressing my lips.

Madame Mierowicz was lounging on a couch in the midst of the strangest assortment of things—boxes of all sizes, books, piles of clothing, an impressive series of buttons, a very attractive Negro fetich, junk jewelry, a Russian doll—and was smoking cigarette after cigarette, grinding out the butts on the uncarpeted floor, and reading a novel.

"Everything all right, my little angels?" she said, in an absent-minded way. "Is the new girl friend going to stay to dinner? We're having pancakes and onions . . ."

I declined with thanks. The menu did not at all tempt me, nor did the prospect of an evening in the company of the Miero-wicz couple. Stani directed me to the door, by way of the dark corridor.

"So you think that's what I've got to do, for Madame Périer?"

"Absolutely," I said, in a firm voice. "But in the meantime you must be very nice, you know. Always accept her invitations, give her fond looks, but behave decently. That's your only way to cut out Fontanas, who is rather too obviously grasping."

"All the same, he got a car out of her," pouted Stani, obviously afraid that an exaggerated pose of disinterestedness would make Odette think she was loved for herself alone and would cause her to abandon her generous habits.

"You'll get a car, too. Don't be in too big a hurry, and you'll get far more out of her than Fontanas has."

Spontaneously he kissed me on the cheek.

"How kind you are, Hélène! Without you, I'd never have been able to manage. Well, I shall always remember, I swear it."

"All right, I'm not asking for a percentage," I cut in.

That his gratitude was more for my advice than for the gift of my body highly amused me. After all, he was the one I should have taken as a lover, right from the start. He was always talking about his feelings, but you had only to mention money and his fiery passions were extinguished. There was something of Tamara in him: all the noble reasons he gave himself for courting Odette Périer's fortune were just about as genuine as Tamara's attitudes towards Father.

Why had I so stupidly thrown myself at Jean Delfau's head? Never had he given me this exhilarating sensation which Stani had given me by letting me use him like an instrument that I could take up again whenever I liked and without any least problem arising.

"You'll come back? Say you will," he murmured.

"Yes. I'll warn you by telephone next time, so I won't be mistaken for a desolate widow."

"And may I telephone you? Supposing your system doesn't work?"

"Of course," I said, smiling at this strange way of managing Madame Périer's love-life.

"Well, so long, Hélène. Thanks again, thanks a lot. You don't know how you've cheered me up," he said with an air of sincerity.

I feared a sentimental effusion of some sort.

"Cheered? Really?"

"Yes. What you said about my painting. That it was good. You know, I'm glad to think that, after all, it's not just because she likes me that she asked me to do the decorations."

And as if bashfully, after a final smile, he quickly shut the door.

In the street once more, I shrugged. Poor Stani, with his filial devotion and his taste for money, his laziness and his timid self-esteem as a painter, and the strange way he had of managing his contradictory feelings in order to persuade himself that he was a remarkable fellow with a bright future.

But was I also going to try to comprehend Stani?

Father was leaving for Italy, to settle some mysterious cotton business, not to mention a still more important affair he only referred to in disguised terms as "my trump card." I imagined it had something to do with a new setup for the Zoological Gardens, perhaps a shipment of animals which would arrive on the eve of elections. But I did not try to discover the reason for his great show of secret bliss. I thought of the two weeks of solitude his absence would give me, and the thought filled me with a kind of sad, sensual lethargy. I had not tried to penetrate further into Jean's life. I had recoiled in fear before the image which emerged from Manuelita's tales, for I could regard it neither which indifference nor contempt. I therefore took refuge in an assumed frivolity that was just a bit wild-eyed and light-headed, an attitude disrupted only by sudden rages. But more than ever I was dreading those encounters with Jean. His sarcasms and ruthlessness still hurt me, but my chief dread came from another cause: the pang of comprehension, almost of pity, which I occasionally felt. By listening to Manuelita, I had crossed over into a terrain of tempting pitfalls: of comprehension, indulgence, compromise. If I succeeded in understanding Jean, I would also have to understand my father, Tamara, Julia, everyone. And I did not want that. So I managed, for the most part, to turn my back on these vain and alluring mirages.

"My boy, I count on you as upon a second self," Father said to Jean, as the chauffeur brought up the car for him. "I'll not be back here until about three weeks from now—that is to say, practically on the eve of the opening, so you see how much confidence I have in you. I dare say my election rests in part with you. So, if the least difficulty arises, don't hesitate to let me know— send me a wire. I left orders with my secretary to give you all my addresses. And as to the financial question, she also has orders to give you carte blanche . . . So then, my boy, we'll say au revoir and good luck . . ."

But the cordial slaps on Jean's back were less cordial than formerly. For some time he had been acting a little jealous, irrelevantly enough.

Tamara coldly surveyed these adieux.

"Hadn't you better hurry up, René? If we expect to cover the first stage . . ."

She kissed me sweetly. Ever since I had been absorbed with other cares, we had got along well together. However, her aversion for Jean had increased, perhaps because she had still not found anyone to soothe her wounded self-esteem. Before getting into the car, she gave him a long and meaningful look. Then her eyes turned towards me and perhaps, at seeing us standing like that side by side, waiting for their departure, a suspicion of the truth crossed her mind. She made as if to get out to say a few words to me, but Father had at last come to the end of his instructions and rejoined her in the car, and the chauffeur had shut the door with a bang. So she said nothing, merely giving me a friendly wave of the hand, and sank back into her furs. The car drove off.

"Won't you come in a moment, sir?" said Julia, who had watched the departure. She could never restrain her desire to play the go-between, and her grief over the departure of Maurice, the chauffeur, did not keep her from taking a benevolent interest in what she called my romance.

"I'll bring you some coffee in the library, if you will permit, sir, for everything is topsyturvy in the drawingrooms, on account of the big housecleaning."

"You're very kind, Julia," he said in his most drawling, society voice. These mannerisms impressed the cook, who thought him very distinguished. As for me, his mannerisms were sometimes exasperating. Without a word, we went up to the library.

It was dark there; the small, bluish, leaded windowpanes of

the long dark room barely let in the yellow light of this foggy day. The leather bindings of the books which crowded the shelves, the green-shaded lamps placed here and there, contributed to darkening the atmosphere still more. Jean said nothing. He seemed to be expecting some spontaneous gesture from me. But after all, just because Tamara had gone away and because we were free, I was not going to throw myself on his breast! The weather was humid, all the woodwork of the house was creaking, and if you listened, you could hear the foghorns of the boats on the distant river. Nothing could have been better than to sit down in the leather armchairs and talk calmly, in subdued, low voices, as mysterious as the yellow light and the fog outside, discussing superlative things, the sea voyages we would never take, journeys to places which existed only today, within the bounds of the fog . . . I would have liked to tell my thoughts to Jean, but he was leaning against the bookshelves in an attitude of idle waiting, affecting such a look of being at loose ends that I should have been offended. I, too, remained silent. I, too, just looked at him. There were such moments between us when we struggled against each other like wrestlers, shoulder to shoulder, in silence. Jean had the advantage of an impassive face, to which some deep lines, carved by time, readily gave a look of weary indifference. For my part, I had an infinite reserve of silence, accumulated over a period of years, but I knew my eyes betrayed my troubled conscience, that the savage resolution I had made could easily be read in them, and I was embarrassed. I accepted the struggle too openly not to be overwhelmed with shame at any weakening; whereas Jean knew how to give a great air of elegance to his concessions, as though he were playing a game that had suddenly become a bore.

Julia knocked very distinctly at the door, waited quite a while, then entered, loaded down with gleaming silverware. She obviously wanted to please Jean with this display, which she did not make for all our guests. And what a wealth of precautions! Surely, in her mind, the car had barely left when we had thrown ourselves recklessly into each other's arms, crying, "Alone at last!" What a simple-minded conception! When I visualized ourselves as Julia imagined us I wondered, not without melancholy, if I would ever know an affair as simple as all that.

"Why, what are you thinking about, Hélène?" said Julia, with a hint of malice, as she set down the coffee tray on the big table. "You should have turned on the light, Monsieur Delfau is in the dark!" And she busied herself around the brass lamps.

"How right you are, Julia! What's this child got on her mind?" said Jean, pouring himself some coffee.

"You may know better than I do, sir," Julia laughed. And she went out, quickly, noiselessly, offensively discreet.

A gentle glow was shed by the thick green paper lampshades. I was reminded of ships' lanterns. Outside, the light was becoming still yellower, a storm was brewing, and the long dark room with its vaulted ceiling, with the bay windows at each end set with small leaded panes of glass, looked like the interior of a ship lost in the fog, a ship in distress, which we alone inhabited.

"Julia's amiability is something!" said Jean, breaking the heavy silence.

"It's too much," I said. "She reminds me strangely of Clara Vaes this afternoon. It's a wonder she didn't suggest some clean sheets."

"I adore procuresses," sighed Jean. "But I find your language very coarse for a nice young girl."

"I am not a nice young girl."

"That's true, I forgot. But you are not a woman either, or not much of a one!"

"What do you call a woman?" I asked irritatedly, thinking he was alluding to my relative ignorance.

"What I call a woman? Why, for heaven's sake . . . a repose, a sweetness, a comprehension, something peaceable and agreeable . . . in short, just the opposite of what you are, little serpent."

"Thank God!" I said. "I wouldn't like at all to be your ideal woman. In fact, what you're describing is a kind of pillow."

"Don't brag," he said, drinking down his coffee. "More than one serpent has been seen to turn into a pillow. It's a very ordinary metamorphosis, no one's astonished at it any more."

"Never!" I said furiously. It was all I could do to keep from throwing my cup, still full of coffee, at his head.

"That's what it is to live far from Paris," he said, smiling at the way I had shouted that word. "One loses all sense of proportion and, I must say, of the ridiculous. But I don't want to be unjust, my dear; the word you just shouted had beauty in it. Or rather, would have, if it were followed by an end-of-the-act kiss. But since no curtain is going to fall, I think you will have some trouble maintaining the conversation at that level."

Although almost trembling with anger, what impartiality still remained in me admitted he was right. I had gone too far, I had committed a considerable blunder, and he had at once and pitilessly taken advantage of it. To have my revenge, I needed to recover my self-possession. I walked over to the bay window overlooking the street. The rain was now beating against the panes; the street was gradually becoming wet. Some drainage work was in progress and from a hole in the sidewalk a man came out, muddy, black, looking like a deep sea diver. The seagulls were screaming, circling endlessly in the darkened air, grazing the rooftops with a clapping of wings. Noiselessly, Jean had come to stand behind me, and without a word he drew me close. As long as he said nothing, I accepted his warmth, his comforting embrace.

"Shall we go there? Do you want to?" he asked softly.

Yes, I wanted it, I wanted to leave the long sad room, I wanted to stop hearing the seagulls' screams, and to find again that red room; even so, it held enough souvenirs to make it *our* room, the centre of my life . . . I suddenly felt weak, and if desire had been enough to operate a miracle, we would already have been there, protected by the red plush canopy and by those gilded caryatids of the indecent postures. There we would have been silent, there, without apparent defeat, I could rest my secret weariness on Jean's breast.

But was not that weariness the very sign of my dwindling power? Beneath a mask of pity, I seemed to feel a suspicious tenderness, a carnal weakening which, since Tamara, I had not known. I recalled his cutting words: "It's such an ordinary metamorphosis . . ." I was closer than he thought to a shameful femininity. What would he have said, he who called me his little serpent, if he had known how burningly I longed for oblivion, for forgetfulness, and how keen was the horror of my solitude in the midst of this town that had been taken over by the wind and the rain. What would he have said had he known that the weight of his arm around my waist was, just then, a support which my body required and without which it seemed to me I would suddenly fall down, deprived of all strength? He would have laughed, no doubt; he would have rejoiced at this victory which was not his first one; he would have congratulated himself on knowing women so well; he would even, perhaps, have felt a passing tenderness for this poor little Hélène, so easily vanquished. "Such an ordinary metamorphosis . . ." No, I would still defend myself.

"This afternoon I have to go to the Academy."

I did not fall down when Jean gently released me and thrust his hand deeply into his pocket.

"As you like, my dear. I'm going to have a look at the theatre. I swear, it's worth looking at. What a shambles!"

Well, had I expected him to respond otherwise? Why had his voice, which had again become drawling, suddenly lacerated me? But I certainly did not expect what followed. Abruptly he turned away, went towards the table, gathered up his raincoat which he had thrown there. I followed him reluctantly towards the door, which opened out upon the landing.

"Au revoir, my dear," he said smilingly.

It was his old game of appearing not to be hurt by anything, of acting as though, wilfully, I were hurting only myself. That minute I doubted Manuelita's information. I would have given anything to feel, if only for a second, that I had hurt him. At the bottom of the stairs he kissed me. That was a part of his pretense. Why should he not have kissed me, since he had not even remarked that I had perhaps said something unpleasant? I forced myself to adopt the same attitude.

"So, until tomorrow, Jean?"

He smiled sweetly at me.

"Oh, not tomorrow, dear. Sandra's arriving tomorrow . . ."

I went down to the kitchen. To the sound of the radio, Julia was furiously stoking the stove. I sat down on the stool, right up against the heat of the fire.

"Well, Lena? You didn't go out with your admirer?"

Since I did not reply, she put down the poker.

"No doubt he has some work to do. That's Maurice all over, and if I may say so, I miss that rascal. It's the truth, nothing can replace a man! But don't you mourn, Hélène. If you don't go out with him this afternoon, it'll be for tonight."

"No," I said, despite myself.

"Tomorrow, then."

"Not tomorrow, either."

"Oh, so you've had a quarrel. That happens, yes, that happens. Do you imagine I never have a quarrel with Maurice? Such quarrels don't last, when you're in love."

"I'm not in love."

Julia burst out laughing.

"Not today, maybe, but what about tomorrow?"

I shrugged.

"Tomorrow, it will be the same thing," I said with irritation. And I drew still nearer the fire, for I was cold.

The days that followed were beautiful. The town recovered from the storms of the night, the wet streets gleamed under a hard, bright sun. In the puddles of tepid water lay scattered the tree branches that had been broken. The old spinsters, sitting at their windows, were decorating their wide black straw hats with an assortment of artificial flowers, and behind every spying window with its artfully placed mirror and its crocheted lace curtains—which were all too much like the curtains of the red room—flourished the violent colors of that genteel and imitation spring; a touching sight, all the same, for it proclaimed the desire for a real spring.

During the afternoons in the red room, Jean was as thoughtfully attentive as if I had been a convalescent. Was Sandra Marelli using up all his harshness? That was the only thing, then, of which I might be jealous, and Jean's new gentleness troubled and obsessed me like a regret. Anyway, the opening night was drawing nearer all the time. Was his sweetness perhaps an autumn sweetness?

Disturbed, restless, unable to concentrate my thoughts or my desires, I occasionally went in the evenings to Stani's, seeking to renew my strength.

My arrival on this particular evening was greeted by Madame Mierowicz as usual: she was always frizzed like a poodle, always attired in her mauve-colored plush dressing gown, always with the cigarette holder stuck between her long, nicotine-stained teeth, and constantly more ebullient.

"My dear! What a pleasure it is to open the door and see your sweet face!" she exclaimed. "Stani has been waiting hours and hours for you."

She willfully made up these polite lies, convinced in her ingenuous pander's soul that I adored Stani and that, unable to marry him, I had sufficient greatness of soul to hand him over to Madame Périer. With a great ceremony of exclamations, she led me into the main room where Monsieur Mierowicz, sunk in his fat, was designing tombstones. He painfully got up to greet me, despite my protestations. The Mierowicz's called me their guardian angel ever since Odette had spoken of giving them an apartment she owned and from which she was now actively engaged in dislodging a helpless old man, living in retirement.

In the midst of this almost respectful consideration, I felt revived. Two hours before, in the red room, I had felt so unsafe! Here, I recovered all my integrity.

"Where's Stani?" I asked.

They indicated his bedroom, I entered it in a proprietary way, and shut the door behind me. For nothing in the world would the Mierowicz's have disturbed us. For nothing in the world would Stani have omitted to rise from his chair with every sign of tender eagerness on his handsome tanned face as he exclaimed about my tardiness.

"How late you are, Hélène! I was beginning to be afraid you'd not come!"

He then recounted how his adventure with the beautiful Odette was progressing. Unprecedented phenomenon, even before having assured herself of Stani's feelings, she had given Fontanas his walking papers. At present she spent her free time exhausting every imaginable means to expel the unfortunate old pensioner from the apartment in the Rue de l'Anneau, where he continued to hang on. Following my advice, Stani was not indulging in any other demonstration besides passionate kisses deposited on his patroness' hands, and puzzled by such delicate restraint, the poor Odette was beginning to think of herself as the heroine of a great romance. I liked to hear Stani's tales, and enjoyed their innocent scurviness. To feel that I was managing this pitiable intrigue strengthened me in my pride; I felt protected again, for a second, and I could envisage with the same disdain my relations with Jean. I was less fond of Stani's occasional and tardy scruples.

"That poor woman, she devours me with her eyes! Isn't it mean to make her think I secretly adore her? She'd have a terrible shock if she found out . . . And then, it's rather disgusting for a man to make a woman coax him like that, don't you think?"

I detested the gleam of humanity, of understanding, which blemished his handsome face. I detested everything that resembled pity. In such moments, I would have liked to slap him. Instead, I continued gently to advise him.

"Oh, see here, Stani, after all, you have a perfectly good reason to act as you do. You can't let your mother go on perishing in this basement . . . And besides, you're an artist, you need security. I'm sure you'll manage to get that apartment, she'll make a gift of it to you. Think about all she spent on Fontanas. For you, if you know how to manage it, she'll do ten times more."

"You think so?" he said, pensively.

Pity and humanity had disappeared, like will-o'-the-wisps before these glowing prospects. His face was the very face of cowardice and falsity, of self-satisfaction. And upon that face I pressed my lips slowly, joyfully.

X V •

Mustering all my forces, feeling them disperse an hour afterwards, I waited for the passing days to produce a miracle. Did not spring also prepare itself in silence? I waited for a burgeoning, an Easter. And with joy I fled the sombre familial house. Once upon a time, when Jean had first entered it, I had believed he would exorcise the spell which had made the house Tamara's fief. "The mirrors are waking up," I had thought, "the portraits are peering out again, the partition walls are snapping and cracking as they stretch themselves." But now I was afraid that the premonition of evil concerned me alone, and I waited—perhaps with secret impatience—for it to overwhelm me.

Tamara's letter struck me like a bolt from the blue. My father was not returning, she said, until a fortnight afterwards, but she would be home in two days, to perform the supreme acts of pre-elections politeness. While I had counted on having almost two more weeks of freedom, I suddenly found myself reduced to two days. "It's unfair," I raged inwardly, "it's terribly unfair!" Just when there was to have occurred, during those two weeks, so many things. Just when those two weeks were in a way due me, and I had counted on them to regulate my conduct with Jean. Just when, if I had had those two weeks, I would have been able to separate myself from him almost without regret, I was sure of it now. Those two weeks were being stolen from me by Tamara. I detested her more that minute than ever before. I could not throw off the idea that she knew what she was doing and was deliberately depriving me, out of pure meanness, of those two weeks that belonged to me.

I received that letter in the morning mail and spent the morning in a state of complete panic, my only hope being that Jean would find a solution, hesitating for two hours whether to telephone him and at last bringing myself to do it.

He was not at the hotel, they replied, but at the theatre, directing a rehearsal. How could I reach him there? I gave up and, very upset, waited for him to come. What did I expect of him? That he would make Tamara stay in Italy? That he would abduct me? That he would make time stand still? From where did my absurd conviction come that he would do something? Quite evidently, there was nothing to do. But all the same I waited, watching the clock, and when he arrived an hour earlier than usual, I flung myself upon him with desperate confidence.

"What's up, child? They told me just now that you telephoned, and I came right away."

Now that he was there, I no longer knew what to say to him. Silently, I pulled the letter out of my pocket and held it out to him.

"And you're sad? And you called me?" he said slowly, without changing expression. "What in the world do you expect of me?"

Already I no longer expected anything, I was frozen by his caution, his slowness. Could I, without making myself laughable, tell him I'd hoped for him to perform a miracle?

"Nothing," I said. "I desire nothing and I expect nothing of you."

"Obviously," he said ironically. "You called me, quite wildly, on the telephone, but all you wanted was just to chat. You hold out a letter to me melodramatically, but it's only to have me admire Tamara's style. Oh, you're really a funny little person!"

He softened a little and lightly pressed me to him.

"Come now, what upsets you in this letter? You've always known your father would return, haven't you? You've always known I'd go back to Paris the day after the opening, that this adventure of ours was without issue and without consequence, haven't you? Well then, what's two weeks more or less? This is an inconvenience, at the most. A tiny little inconvenience. Unless, that is . . . unless you've changed your point of view, of course. Perhaps you . . ."

Was it a trap? Beneath that indulgent and condescending voice was there a secret and almost imperceptible tenderness? I was carried away too quickly by fear and could not check my hurried and anxious words.

"You're right. There's nothing to get upset about. I don't know why I was so silly . . . Forgive me, I'm sorry I bothered you. I'm so nervous nowadays . . ."

Suddenly he began to laugh, in an unexpected way.

"You certainly can make a quick come-back! But how childish you are! You'd do better to think a little before giving in to your impulses. Quite understandably, you're upset over Tamara's return, for she'll keep you from seeing me as often as you want to, and when I come here . . ."

"That's not true," I said angrily.

I no longer knew why I had called him, but I was very sure it was not for the reason he ironically implied.

"That's not true! You have the bad side of all Don Juans,

which is to imagine that no one can look at you without falling in love. I am not in love with you and never will be. I like you, I like to be with you, and that's all."

"And you hang on to the telephone because you don't want to lose my companionship? That's just what I said."

"So you're going to be patronizing, Jean?" I demanded, trying to sound playful. "I was annoyed over losing these two weeks, that's true. But there's quite a margin between annoyance and despair. Certainly, Tamara's unexpected return is disagreeable, and I wouldn't dream of hiding the fact from you."

Yes, that was the tone I should always have adopted with him: calm, smiling, restrained. And not those childish rages of mine. I imagined a look of uncertainty floated in Jean's eyes, and was about to go back on my words, but he left me no time.

"Then, my dear, there's only one thing to do: tell her everything."

"Tell Tamara?"

"Quite. I'm sure she'll not find a thing to say against a little affair that only has two more weeks to go. She is so understanding. And I'm persuaded she'll let you have all the freedom you could wish . . . for two weeks . . ."

With a satisfied air, he took out a cigarette and snapped on his lighter. He must be satisfied with himself. How could I not take up the challenge? And yet, there was always the chance that Tamara would immediately forbid me to see Jean again. What did it matter to him, not ever to see me again? Sandra Marelli would more than replace me. Deliberately, I forgot the tenderness I thought I had felt in him just now. Before everything, I must show him that I did not fear him.

"I'll speak to Tamara," I said resolutely. "It might be rather amusing. You're right."

I expected at least to have his admiration. But he replied only by humming a snatch of a popular love-song in his agreeable low voice and continued placidly smoking his cigarette.

As usual, an interminable afternoon of fighting began. We went into the big white drawingroom where we found the glass objects dear to Tamara, the mahogany furniture, the elegant sofa, the little writing desk where the fine old books that had belonged to my mother were shut up forever, never being opened by anyone now, and exhaling their strange odor of gilt and humidity. The sunlight, the oppressive boredom, and my desire impelled us towards the red room, towards it through the echoing little streets, as tortuously winding as the inner convolutions of a shell. But we were in the cold white drawingroom and we remained there.

Julia, disapproving and uncomprehending, brought coffee. The sounds changed with the hours. Jean at last emptied his cup, and the bicycles carrying the factory hands to work passed with a soft sound of wings; later on, it was the schoolchildren singing on their way to the municipal swimming pool. The afternoon slipped through our fingers like cool sand, and there would remain nothing of it, not even a memory.

Sitting at the piano, Jean softly hummed a tune and played with one hand, sketching out a familiar theme. He had been sitting only three steps away. How easy it would have been to take those three steps and to say quite simply, "Shall we go, Jean?" But I had waited another minute, I had thought I saw on his lips and in his eyes the words ready to be pronounced. "Say them, say them," I had inwardly implored. And I had thought, "If he takes only one step towards me, I will never again struggle against him, never!" But he had stood up, had gone over to the piano and had begun to sing, as if for himself alone, waiting so visibly for me to make a movement towards him that I could not do it. I continued to sit there, not far from him, agitated by a kind of inner trembling, with the idiotic desire to touch his hand, just his hand, so as to feel less alone. And I could not do it.

The afternoon passed. The sunlight dimmed on the stone balcony. Jean was now puzzling out some old sheet-music that had belonged to my mother and he seemed to be quite absorbed in the melodies. The bells of the church nearby rang, as they ring on Sunday, for a long time and sadly, and time passed, as it does on Sunday, a day which could have been beautiful and which, inexplicably, had not been. Again, after the oasis of silence that had marked the middle of the afternoon, the sound of footsteps filled the street. But those footsteps, which not long before had sounded, if not gay, at least lively, hurried, active, were now dragging, as if weary of everything, and were not even hurrying towards the evening meal. It was a great wave of harassed footsteps, which evoked so clearly the bowed shoulders, the weary faces of those men returning home; and Jean's face was also weary. Even if I had wanted to, we no longer had time to go to the red room. Anyway, did I still want to? I, too, was weary, exhausted by this afternoon which was apparently so calm. In a few minutes, the last sound of footsteps would die out and Jean would suddenly stand up, saying, "You're not very talkative tonight, Hélène. See you soon!"

He was about to go. He had gone. I remained alone, condemned to maintain my defiance, condemned not to weaken. And in my sadness and weariness, I called out "Jean!" As if, had he been present, everything would not have begun all over again.

Tamara arrived in a great commotion, a great confusion of parcels and suitcases, as if she had been away for months and months. She hugged me, with touching effusions. No, she was not disappointed at having to return so soon. My father had heard about some complicated plots being laid between old Maalens, who was trying his best to be reelected, and the city councillor, Haberlin, and had immediately delegated Tamara to clear up that mystery. But they would go back to Italy later on, after the elections, for they already had many friends down there.

"Have you had lunch, Hélène? No? Then let's have lunch together, I have such a lot to tell you. Julia can finish unpacking, later on. I've brought back some dresses. Well, you'll see. Just imagine, when we reached Genoa, your father told me . . ."

I followed her into the diningroom. She chatted interminably and I observed this person who would soon, perhaps, be threatening me. She had tanned a little and her wrinkles showed up more. She was wearing a grey linen dress, with a square-cut neckline, revealing a neck reddened by the sun.

Everything about her, from her full chin to her loquacity was flabby. Revolting animal, eating in front of me, totting up her supposed triumphs in Milan! I could just imagine her using her charm, holding out her hand to the fat, oily-looking and talkative cotton merchants in Genoa, in Milan, who congratulated my father on his young wife.

Outside, the weather was beautiful. I detested the lovely weather which was warming the garden. Through the French window I could see the lilac bushes, already covered with tiny buds, the linden tree which would soon spread its warm, acrid odor of honey. And there she was in front of me, this Tamara I had loved, and for whom, however, I had never suffered this anguish.

Tamara then proceeded to ask questions, and I had to reply. What had I done during her absence? Had I done much drawing? No, very little, I had not had the time. Had I enjoyed myself? I replied yes. Had I seen Jean often?

"Very often," I replied coldly. She seemed astonished.

"I hope he didn't flirt with you, at any rate?"

"Well, he certainly flirted with you."

"Hélène! You're joking, I hope. There are certain things a man can permit himself with a married woman without impropriety, but which . . . Why, he could not have had the audacity . . ."

"Oh, he didn't need much audacity . . ."

She straightened up in a melodramatic attitude that amused me.

"What are you implying, Hélène? Did he . . . No, it's impossible, he isn't . . ."

"Why yes, of course, of course . . ." I said warily.

This vulgar scene was dragging out far too slowly, it seemed to me; I was vaguely amused, but intermixed with that amusement was a slight feeling of nausea. Tamara went on melodramatically delivering the monologue of the Offended Mother. Her face had assumed an expression of outraged dignity that was rather comical, and she threw out wild interjections, without taking very much account of me.

"How is it possible? When did it happen? What did he promise you? I'll bet, I'll . . . Hélène, tell me you're joking!"

"You're the one that's joking, it seems to me," I said softly. "The fact that I've taken a lover, at the age of eighteen, does not justify your throwing such a fit. Please control yourself a little."

"My poor child," she groaned, "my poor dear little Hélène."

Her voice was strange, and as I raised my eyes towards her, I saw that a tear was running down her cheek. I laughed a little, but without putting much heart into it.

"Oh come, Tam, you're not the one that's lost her virginity," I said. "After all, there's no reason to make such a terrible fuss."

She stood up, came round the table, and sat down beside me. I was a little annoyed at this display of affection, for I felt that it might be transformed into fury any minute. Her arm was around me, and she tried to draw me to her breast. Clearly, she would have liked for us to weep together.

"All this is my fault," she murmured in a voice drowned in tears. "I should never have left you alone, my poor little unfortunate . . . You're not the guilty one, my poor child, it wasn't wrong to search for a little love around you. He's the one that's to blame. I should never have received such a person be-

neath my roof. He took advantage of the situation, of your be-
wilderment . . . I'll tell him . . ."

She was shedding tears abundantly.

"Why not say, 'vile seducer,' while you're about it?" I said,
shaking off her embrace.

A few of her tears had run down my neck, wetting it. I had not
expected this serial-story despair, but rather had expected the
fury of an offended rival.

"How hard that man has made you, Hélène!" she sighed.

There was a moment of silence while she tried to think up
something appropriate to say after such an emotional exhibition. I longed to go and lie down, sleep was overpowering me.
Suddenly, something in her seemed to stiffen and she bruskly
asked, "Did he propose marriage?"

This time I frankly laughed. This was too utterly banal!

"No, he did not propose marriage, my poor Tam. What are
you thinking of? Why should he have suggested marriage when
I did not ask for it? All this is so silly!"

She seemed to be consoled by this declaration.

"In short," she said in a voice which forgot all affliction,
"immediately after the opening night of the play, everything
will be over between you?"

"Apparently," I said lightly. She sighed and seemed inclined
to drop the conversation.

"All I can say is this, Hélène: I feel very sorry. I could have
wished something else for you than this lamentable initia-
tion . . ."

The expression aggravated me. What did she know? How
could she judge?

"Why 'lamentable'?" I asked. "What else would you have
wished for me?"

"Why . . . love, Hélène!" she said in such a sentimental way
that I laughed in spite of myself. "And just think," she added
softly, "just think how your father is going to suffer when he

hears of this affair—for of course I shall tell him, it's my duty."

"Where would we be if we all did our duty?" I murmured.

And that was that. Tamara had exhausted the charms of pathos, and no doubt was glad to think that Jean had consoled himself with me for her hard treatment. Would she have dismissed so lightly a lasting affair? The question was irrelevant, I told myself, and I managed not to think any more about it. Had I not taken up Jean's challenge?

From then on there was no question of anything but the elections, the theatre, and about my father and the Griselidis in Milan. Tamara finally told me what the famous bomb was that my father was keeping to explode over the town after the theatre opening. From an Italian exporter of colonial products, he had bought a consignment of wild animals that had been ordered by a circus which had gone bankrupt and could not accept delivery. He proposed making a gift of these to our unfortunate Zoological Gardens, which would open their doors, entirely renovated, at the time of the great Carnival. These two surprises, one after the other, should win all hearts. And what an affront to Maalens, who in his last electoral speech had also talked about the disintegration of "our fine Zoo!" Not words, but acts, seemed to be my father's retort. The gift of those three or four wild beasts, no doubt moth-eaten and tame from their long wait in the hold of the vessel—they were still waiting for the moment of their apparition—would silence Maalens, once and for all. Tamara seemed terribly thrilled over this bright idea, and I must admit that it rather pleased me. Little by little, Father was becoming a master in this game of swaying public opinion. Miniature Machiavelli, he had found a town cut to his size, so why not profit by it?

"And we have on our side all the hotel-keepers, restaurant and café owners, all the little shopkeepers, right down to the newspaper vendors! Can you imagine how many votes that represents? And your father has written a speech which will create a sensation, announcing the arrival of serpents, crocodiles, and

Heaven only knows what else. It's almost a certainty, now, that he'll be elected."

The radiant prospect of so many banquets, receptions, long dresses, had quite excited her. Of what account, beside that, was my adventure with Jean? Her recent virtuous indignation had already been forgotten. There was no question of stopping me from going out, of revealing my infamy to Father, of creating catastrophes. Counting the votes acquired by my father occupied her far more than that.

"I'm going to have such a quantity of calls to make! It's an atrocious bore. And by the way, you'll have to accompany me on half the calls, at least. It would look very bad if you didn't go with me."

"You think so?"

"Indeed I do. I've already had a 'phone call from the Brennendoncks, asking why you weren't at the last meeting of the 'Lady-Birds.' Your absence was very remarked."

The "Lady-Birds" was the charming name given to a group of young girls who were ardent propagandists for Father. Every Sunday they held pompous little reunions called 'meetings,' during which the young and very emancipated ladies gave themselves the pleasure, while drinking tea, of enouncing their political ideas. These meetings tempted me all the less since, if I did not want to compromise Father's future chances, I would not be able to express the slightest personal opinion on anything political.

"Long-suffering as you are, you'll not be able to stand the 'Lady-Birds'," I said.

"In any case, you must call on the Maalens, not to do so would look too obvious. And on the Van Becks, naturally; and on Madame Périer. Oh, did you know she has a new admirer? But of course, how stupid of me, you would have heard about it since he's a friend of yours, you know, the Polish boy . . ."

"Stani? I certainly knew there was a possibility of it, but I didn't know it was official."

"As official as possible, my dear. And poor Fontanas, riding around in his new Jaguar, let himself be evicted before he knew what had happened. And Odette is setting up her new love in her little apartment near the Post Office, along with his entire impossible family. Oh, you have friends who know how to get on in the world!"

I felt a flicker of pride, but it was immediately extinguished by an incomprehensible sadness.

"Don't you want to come with me and have a look at that?" Tamara pursued. "I'm going to Odette's this afternoon for tea."

"No," I murmured listlessly. "I have something to do."

"To do with Monsieur Delfau, no doubt?" she asked quickly. There was a malicious gleam in her eyes, but she quickly controlled herself. "Oh well," she sighed, "take advantage of these last days . . ."

Leaving her, I rushed to the Theatre. Jean must be there, directing the rehearsal. If I told him I had picked up his challenge, wouldn't he show some feeling towards me, of tenderness, of admiration, or even of anger? I had reached the point of wanting anything from him that would bring us nearer each other.

As I crossed the little elm-planted green, my heart was pounding as though it would break. Would I even manage to talk to him alone? Wouldn't he be all taken up with his work—and with Sandra Marelli? I had never seen her, but I had heard she was very pretty. I wanted to compare my looks with hers, as much as I wanted to talk to Jean.

With no trouble I entered the little baroque building which resembled some kind of immense and hideous bonbon box. The lobby and corridors were empty, but from the auditorium came the sound of voices. I went in, with some hesitation.

The auditorium was plunged in darkness, and the actors were walking about on the stage in a lackadaisical way. For a long while I could not distinguish anything around me. Then I heard Jean's voice.

"Come on, now," it shouted joyously. "We'll run through that scene once more. Lievens, stand a little more to the right, please. You walk round the throne, you stop near the window, and you begin after a pause . . . No, no, for the Lord's sake! Berthe is not at your right!"

From the first row of the orchestra he bounded upon the stage, shoved a sullen young man aside, grabbed a young woman by the arm—was it Sandra Marelli?—and led her to the middle of the scene.

"You, my dear, stand there. How many times do I have to tell you? And when he begins his monologue, you turn towards him, registering surprise—no, it's not necessary to open your eyes that wide, we're not doing a pantomime! You step forward on 'I, too, would have preferred wild gallops . . .' Then, intimidated, you step back towards the open fire. Where the devil is it, the open fire?"

An aerial voice, which could have passed for that of a sylph except for the German accent, replied.

"The fireplace isn't finished yet, Monsieur Delfau . . ."

"Well then, put something there, no matter what, a chair or table . . . Look, Lievens, stand over there a minute and make like an open fire. That's a perfect rôle for you. I'm going to go through the scene with Berthe myself."

He fluttered about on the stage, pushing the actors here and there like pieces of furniture, dancing about like a thin and frisky demon. I watched him from a distance. No doubt I would not find the courage to interrupt him. But I no longer dreamed of doing so; I was completely enthralled at seeing him so energetic, without a trace of nonchalance, his voice nervous, his gestures abrupt, and on his animated face an expression that was more than pleasure, almost of happiness.

I jumped with surprise as a hand was laid on my shoulder.

141

"What are you doing here?" a voice nearby whispered.

I turned round and perceived behind me a vague feminine form which, to my great surprise, immediately reached out and grasped my hand.

"Come into the lobby," the mysterious voice whispered. "Spectators are not allowed at rehearsals."

Obediently I followed, expecting to be thrown out of the theatre without ceremony. But the girl who was leading me did not seem to be in a bellicose mood, her dark eyes sparkled mischievously.

"Whom are you looking for?" she asked kindly. "I warned you about the ruling because from time to time the stage manager goes through the auditorium and throws out curious people. But if you're in love with Lievens, maybe I could do something for you?"

Without waiting for a reply, she burst out laughing. It was a pretty laugh, like a tinkling bell.

"No," I murmured, "that is to say, what I wanted was to have a word with Monsieur Delfau, but seeing that he's very busy, I . . ."

The tinkling bells multiplied, and she held me as though I were about to escape.

"No, no, don't run away! I'll tell him, he'll manage, he'll be very glad to see you. You're Hélène, aren't you?"

"Why, yes," I said, disconcerted. "I don't know . . ."

"Don't be so shy!" She threw back her head and laughed again. "There's no reason for you to blush, I assure you. Oh, I see. You're surprised that I know your name. Well, he's told me all about you, about your love affair, I adore such romantic stories. And he must have told you about me, too? I'm Sandra, Sandra Marelli. I'm playing the part of the Sarrazin girl, you know the play, I imagine. And . . ."

She went on gaily talking in a strange, husky voice, like that of a boy whose voice is changing, now deep and grave, now clear and shrill, rising to the bell-like laugh, trembling and pure, almost inhuman. Scarcely comprehending, I let myself be drawn towards a velvet covered bench, on which we sat down. I could not stop looking at her, trying to convince myself of her reality. Sandra was not the very pretty girl the people of Gers said she was. Her round, deep-set eyes were not big, her lips were too full, and they opened over square teeth which were white but uneven, and her little nose, which had started out as a snub-nose, had an unfinished look. But her eyes sparkled so gaily, her lips smiled so continually, that nose of hers was so expressive, Sandra's personality emitted such a lively brilliance that I felt as if annihilated, and was incapable of comprehending her outpourings. I was even wondering if I were not being treated to a cruel practical joke. Everything about her was in movement: her arms, head, nose, the dark bun of hair, an abundance of little stray curls that tumbled over her forehead and temples, and each part of her seemed ready to assume its own distinct personality and join it with her laughter. This young Folly, who only lacked cap and bells, was wearing rather ugly earrings, a red sweater, a skirt of grey wool—quite ordinary clothes, in which her lithe body moved about so continually and vivaciously that it seemed something other than a human body submitted to the laws of gravity. As in a dream, I saw these minute details without grasping the essential, which was the repeated offer she was making to go find Jean for me. But finally this did reach my ears, and I trembled a little with anger. Had I come to this, to have to be led to him by this rival, who was sorry for me? I had strength enough to draw away, and I started to leave. But a sudden weakness in my legs made me sit down again on the velvet bench beside the surprised Sandra.

"What's wrong with you, for goodness sake? You're so pale! Stay here, I'll go find Jean. Don't budge."

"No, not Jean, not you . . ." I said faintly.

All I wanted was to pull myself together and go back home, as a wounded animal tries to drag itself to its hole. At the sight of Sandra, I had a sudden revelation of the importance I attached to my place beside Jean, no matter how uncomfortable and rude that place might be.

"Why not me?" asked Sandra quickly, noticing my reticence. "Why don't you want me to bring him?"

"I don't like pity," I said, with what strength remained. "Aren't you even jealous?"

"Jealous? Why, for goodness sake . . . Oh!"—she let out a real cry—"They've told you I was his mistress!"

"He told me . . ."

"He did? What a monster! But it's not true, it's a dreadful lie, a trick to make you suffer, to arouse your own jealousy! Why, he's a sadist, a frightful sadist! Oh, my poor dear! Sure, I've slept with Jean, but it was centuries ago, at least eight months ago, and only once. He was never my lover, for goodness sake! I laughed too much, it seems . . . Look here . . ."

While I pulled myself together after her storm of indignation, she feverishly rummaged in a little suède handbag.

"Look here. This is the man I'm in love with. Oh, no, wait, that's Roger's assistant—Roger's a doctor, a darling, I don't ever have to pay him, he can cure anything, it's very convenient. Oh! Here's Philippe!"

She handed me the photograph of a fair-haired young man which I took mechanically without looking at it.

"He's a sweetheart!" said Sandra, taking back the photograph at once and pressing it to her lips tenderly. "He's good-looking, don't you think? I hope he'll not be unfaithful, he's on the road now, in Morocco, and if his plane crashes, he'll die all alone, without me . . . I forgot, he's already there. But you never know what will happen."

With tender care she replaced the photograph in her bag. Her dazzling sincerity had convinced me, but still I did not understand, and I wondered . . . I felt a rush of warm blood: strength was flowing back into my body, made aware, before I was, that all was well.

"He's just a monster, that's all," she kept reiterating. "You've had a quarrel, probably. Love's a terrible thing. I was in love once with a boy, he was a bookkeeper, an . . . But I don't want to bore you, I'm going to find Jean for you, it's so nice to make up after a quarrel. Oh, what a monster! I'll give him a piece of my mind. No, you're right, I'll not say a thing, better for him not to know that I've squealed on him! Don't you worry, I'll send him to you, I'm off now, I'll hurry . . ."

The tinkling laughter died down in the auditorium. After a brief pause, Jean appeared.

"Hélène! Why, this is the first time you've come here! What an event! Has anything happened?"

"No," I said, "nothing's happened at all. I just wanted to see you. Is that so surprising?"

I tried to act playful, but the vivid emotions I had just experienced still lingered in a slight trembling, a barely perceptible breathlessness.

"I'm astonished. Sandra told me a veiled woman was waiting for me in the lobby, but she wouldn't tell me who. I believed it was a bad joke."

"I'm your bad joke. Are you disappointed?"

"Not in the least, you goose! It's a wonderful idea. Has Tamara come home?"

"Yes."

I sensed that a question hovered on his lips, which he held back with difficulty. I was touched by his kindness, and felt very near him that moment.

"She's come home," I said softly, "but I've not talked about anything to her."

XVI ·

The box where we sat was one of the best in the Grand Theatre of Gers, but I noticed that Tamara was casting fond glances at the box of honor where, for the first time, amidst the gold and the crimson, old Maalens, mayor of the town for eighteen days more, sat in state. The house was extraordinarily crowded and the toilettes of the ladies were no less extraordinary, for they were determined to dazzle the Parisian critics who were there, thanks to some complicated scheming on the part of Father, seconded by Jean to the best of his ability. And so, adorned in a way they believed would outshine the most brilliant social events of Paris, the ladies all seemed to be in high good humor. Tamara was the only exception in this joyous excitement and, despite my father's encouragements, she remained silent in the uproar. No doubt she found it unpleasant to attend an evening performance which was to be a kind of triumph for Jean. Another frequent cause of moodiness with her was the sight of other women wearing sumptuous jewels, while she herself had none. She surveyed the lady in the neighboring box, Bertha van Scherp, a forty-year-old little hunchback, covered with lace and displaying upon her shrunken bosom a splendid amount of gold and pearls.

"You see," she murmured to my father, "she's put on that necklace again. I'm ashamed to be seen sitting beside her with my ridiculous pearls. And look at Madame Diricks, have you noticed her amethysts?"

In effect, the beautiful Jewess was wearing a kind of choker of enormous stones, a princely adornment that was attracting all eyes.

"And to think that I," Tamara went on, nervously tapping

the edge of the box with her fan, "if you're elected, I'll not even have a decent necklace to wear at the ball!"

Beneath the eyes of the audience, she kept a strained smile on her face, holding out her hand to be kissed by passing acquaintances but from time to time turning upon my father to shower him with reproaches.

"Why, my dearest, all those ladies are wearing heirloom jewels which they'd never be able to buy! Mademoiselle van Scherp's necklace was worn by her grandmother. The amethysts Madame Diricks is wearing were given an ancestress by a minister of Napoleon III, as everyone knows!"

During this family wrangle I could not keep from smiling, not unaware that it was premeditated. Had not Tamara told me her plan as she helped fasten my gown? "I'll get my emeralds tonight or never!" was what she had said.

So I did not intervene in the discussion, though I felt rather sorry for my unfortunate father. But of what good would it have been to bring him my useless support? And, too, for the past few days I had been on rather good terms with Tamara, who gave me a quizzical look when I went out to meet Jean, but who put up no obstacle to those meetings. The only thing I could reproach her was the conclusion she had reached a little too quickly that this evening marked the final point in my relations with Jean. After all, he had not shown the least desire to break off and I was certainly not going to take the initiative. I was even sure that during the reception after the performance, he would talk about coming back. During these last feverish days, I had seen little of him and when we had met he had mostly talked about the uncooperativeness of the actors, the objections van Beck made to any cuts in his text. But a new peace reigned between us.

I looked for him in the auditorium, but he was not there. He must be occupied in the wings, I thought, giving the actors some of those instructions they took so unwillingly. At last, from what he had told me that very morning, everything would go off pretty well. He had stayed at the theatre throughout the entire previous day and I had not seen him until that morning.

The morning had been singularly calm, we had talked about his work in Paris and about my drawings. He had asked me why I didn't go to Paris to study at the Beaux-Arts, and I had promised to mention it to Father. Nothing could have resembled a break less, I told myself, smiling inwardly at Tamara's confidence.

The theatre was now full; I caught a glimpse of Madame Périer with Stani. He was wearing a new dinner jacket with magnificent ease and was casting a bored look over the audience with his beautiful eyes. Behind them appeared the tiny and venomous Alexis Freud, whose head popped up from time to time between them like the head of a serpent, to whisper something spiteful in their ears. Not far off, Fontanas, the lover in disgrace, was unhappily contemplating Stani—not Madame Périer, but Stani in his new clothes, Stani triumphant. The sculptor, Rodière, and his disciple were in the second row of the orchestra, beside some critics upon whom they were showering compliments and tags of gossip.

At last the curtain rose on *La Reine Berthe*, while the unhappy van Beck writhed with anguish in his stage box. I listened absent-mindedly to the first bits of dialogue, for I was thinking about something else. If Jean did not mention another rendezvous, shortly, how should I behave? Again, that morning, we had not talked about anything and he had treated me as though we would be seeing each other again, soon. It did not seem possible that tonight, from one minute to another, I might be seeing him for the last time. After all, had I ever seriously envisaged ending our relations with this opening of the show? Absorbed in these thoughts, I was listening with only half a mind to the play, when a curious sensation made me more attentive. I felt I had already heard a line that Lievens was saying, and saying badly. Sure enough, as I gave all my attention to the play, I heard the line repeated by Lievens for a third time! He must be having a black-out, I thought. But why didn't the prompter help him? Just then Lievens stopped completely and his partner on stage began a line which he left unfinished.

After this, the play continued somehow or other, but whether it was this incident or stage-fright, all the actors seemed to be getting out of hand, running hither and yon, acting without cohesion, giving to the boring tragedy the aspect of vaudeville. The Parisian critics seemed very surprised and moved restlessly in their seats—all, with the exception of the eldest who, completely deaf, remained motionless with an ecstatic smile on his lips, no doubt already composing, from the program, his article for next day. Father also seemed very disturbed. He should have foreseen, though, these little drawbacks of the local actors. That gang of unfortunate tame cats and society comedians could not, even under the aegis of Jean, compose a serious theatrical company.

For the moment, the unhappy Lievens was getting entangled for the third time with his sword. The first act ended in the midst of polite applause, but everyone was amazed. Father hurried out to mingle with the crowd and spread the rumor that only the heat had upset the actors, that the heating system was going to be regulated—the auditorium had, indeed, been much too warm. Some people charitably accepted the excuse; others, partisans of old Maalens, smiled knowingly and insinuated that Father had economized on the rehearsals, for which the actors were paid. The ladies minimized the affair, saying that in the second act, when Sandra would come on, everything would be all right. They were grateful to Father for having provided them with an occasion to exhibit their diamonds. I prowled through the crowd, catching a tag of conversation here and there, vaguely hoping to find Jean. As I passed Madame Périer and Stani, she tapped my cheek with a royal gesture.

"Don't you worry, child," she said in her beautiful tragedienne's voice. "No matter what happens, your father shall have my support."

I thanked her, a little taken aback, for it mattered very little to me whether or not my father became mayor of Gers. Stani leaned towards me, as she passed on.

"Well!" he muttered spitefully, "Your friend Delfau is certainly taking a beating!"

"Oh," I said, forcing myself to appear indifferent, "what's happening isn't his fault at all, it's those idiots who've lost their heads."

"Possibly, but no one will ever admit that the people of Gers have made a mistake. Odette is telling everyone that if it hadn't been for him everything would have been perfect."

"Good night," I said, irritated and indignant at his imbecile spitefulness. For goodness sake, what reason had he to show such ill will towards Jean, whom he barely knew? He was incapable of jealousy, I was sure, and anyway, I had never told him about my affair with Jean. But I remembered having sometimes praised Jean's talent as a decorator and this had probably wounded his self-esteem as an artist, so that now he was not incapable of taking a paltry revenge.

I finally saw Jean in Van Beck's box, half hidden in the shadows.

"Jean?"

He turned a disgruntled face towards me.

"Oh, it's you, dear? Van Beck, will you excuse me?"

"Yes, yes," replied the unhappy man in a weak voice. He was wiping his forehead with a big purple handkerchief and seemed to be very upset. Jean, too, must be upset, for he had addressed me affectionately in public. He drew me backstage to the stairs leading up to the dressingrooms.

"Well, you've seen," he said darkly. "The rotters!"

"They must have been specially surprised at Lievens' muffing his lines. But when Sandra comes on stage they'll surely make a real effort."

"Why, you've not understood a thing, my poor dear Hélène.

All this is no accident, that's a sure thing. Only yesterday they knew their lines perfectly, Lievens better than any!"

"You mean, they're muffing it on purpose?"

"They most certainly are doing it on purpose, little idiot, it hits you in the eye!"

"But why, Jean?"

"Why? What the devil do I know about the why and wherefore? To revenge themselves on me and my advice, I suppose, to get me to beg them to play well, or what have you. But they can get themselves hissed and have rotten tomatoes thrown at them, for all I care. To be hissed in Gers—you can imagine how much that means to me! This disgusting hole of a town, what an imbecile I was to think I could create a theatre here! Create a theatre! With those stage-struck salesmen. The old hams have put the others up to it because I criticized their accents!"

He calmed down a little.

"My dear Hélène, I'm shouting at you as if you were to blame. Go back to your seat, run along. What's your father saying?"

"He looks worried. He's trying to pretend that what upset the troup was the heat, but . . ."

"The heat! That's a good one! Just wait till he sees what the heat does in the second act. The rotters! But they'll not get me to budge from here, now."

I wished I could have given him some kind of comfort. He seemed to be more affected than he would admit, but he gave me a gentle shove towards the exit.

"Run along, have fun, child."

I returned to my seat, heavy-hearted at the thought that he believed me capable of enjoying the spitefulness of those people. Couldn't he feel how much I was on his side, tonight more than ever?

The atmosphere was tense as the curtain rose on the second act. It began with a monologue by Sandra, alone in the forest, dressed in the rags of the little Sarrazin slave. Her clear voice and diction brought forth a big sigh of relief from the house. The Parisian critics seemed to calm down and to observe Sandra's graceful figure, the deafest of them approvingly nodding his head.

I relaxed a little, in the obscurity of the box, and had just noticed a smile on Father's face, when the premature entrance of Lievens cut short Sandra's lines. I was really alarmed. This time there could be no question of a slip. Sandra's clear voice would be distinctly heard off-stage, and anyway, Lievens could have consulted the printed lines for his cue. I felt sick, there was a burning sensation in my stomach. Jean must be suffering a thousand deaths, there in Van Beck's box. I tried to get a glimpse of him, managing badly to see his profile which showed only dimly in the shadows but enough to make my heart throb. Sandra, to the best of her ability, had got on top of the situation. For a moment, the play seemed to be unfolding normally. Lievens—in the rôle of knight-errant, at first moved by the unhappy slave's beauty then touched by her innocence and gaiety—was boldly delivering his lines. Then, suddenly, he could be seen to hesitate, turn towards the wings as if for encouragement, and the mother of the slave appeared, cutting short a scene which monopolized three quarters of the act. She stammered a few words, muffed her lines as Lievens had done, burst out laughing, gave Sandra a reply that belonged in the third act, then went off stage.

I wrung my hands. Jean's profile had disappeared from Van Beck's box. Had he run away? Or had he felt obliged to harangue the disorganized actors back stage? Van Beck's head was bowed, his face was buried in his hands. His beautiful scene of love and of medieval poesy was being slaughtered. Sandra was desperately struggling to go on with her part, and without the proper replies to her lines she was brilliantly ad-libbing. But meanwhile Lievens, as if completely drunk, came and went and brandished his sword, counter to the most elementary good sense.

For a long time the audience remained astounded, not knowing whether to laugh or applaud, doubting its own judgment before the absurdity of that dialogue. Then suddenly, to one side of me, laughter broke out, loud, irresistible, perhaps a little forced. It was Tamara who was laughing. Then immediately, a little farther off, could be recognized the shrill laughter of Stani, soon to be followed by the whole house, at first stifled, then irresistibly growing, expanding, becoming immense, infecting myself, even, until I was laughing nervously, ready to burst into sobs. For a few more minutes the form of Sandra moved about on the stage, still trying to hold out against the storm of laughter. But when there suddenly entered the hermit who was supposed to deliver the epilogue in the fifth act, and when she saw her partners on stage laughing as hard as the audience at her efforts, Sandra, courageous Sandra, shrugged her shoulders, turned on her heels, and strode off stage, her face covered with tears.

The house was in a complete uproar, thundering with laughter, the kind of laughter that cannot be stopped. The curtain was brought down, amidst shouts and hisses. It went up again and an actor stepped forward as if to make an announcement, but the crowd booed, and no one could hear his voice. This audience, which had been so stiff and proper a few minutes before, was letting itself go like an obstreperous child suddenly turned loose and drunk with newfound freedom. Some matrons who, a moment before, had been stiffly formal, were laughing till they cried, screaming with joy. Madame Diricks had leaned back in her seat to laugh with greater freedom, and her handsome white bosom had partly slipped out of her crimson bodice. The little hunchbacked woman beside us was gasping with delighted laughter. My father was very red. Tamara surveyed this confusion in a satisfied and distinguished sort of way. I noticed that Madame Périer was booing the stage-manager who had come before the curtain and was attempting to establish a little order. Stani had his neck stretched out like a serpent and was hissing with all the strength of his lungs. Never, in the memory of man, had such a scandalous thing occurred in Gers. The Parisian critics had got up and left with dignity, explaining with great gesticulations to the unfortunate deaf man what had happened. But no one followed them. The town, that night, was making up for twenty years of restraint. An ironic voice calling for the author brought the audience to a pitch of delirium. Van Beck had fortunately disappeared. The crowd would have been capable of carrying him off in mock triumph. And Jean? I did not see him. Had he, too, left the theatre? Would he leave for Paris next day without having seen me again?

Seized with a wild anguish, I dashed out of the box and down the corridors where some of the more self-controlled spectators were reclaiming their coats from the cloak-room. Jean was not there.

The Van Beck box, to which I ran, was empty. The corridors were full of noise and movement, but Jean could not be there, I had hurried down them without thinking. Would he be in the lobby, or outside? I ran down the stairs, jostling the people who were leaving and who must be looking at me in stupefaction, and ran outside, holding my long dress up to the knees.

It was raining, I splattered my dress with mud as I crossed the street between the automobiles, hurrying, panting, and at last reaching the other sidewalk. There I caught a glimpse of Jean, who was tranquilly walking in the direction of his hotel.

"Jean!"

I called so loudly that passers-by within a hundred yards turned to look, but little did I care. The important thing was to catch him, tell him, oh Heavens, tell him no matter what, so that he would understand that I was with him, that I was not a part of that insulting crowd, he must understand it before going away . . .

"Jean!"

I reached him at last, I saw him again. He turned round, surprised, and I threw myself into his arms.

"Why, Hélène! You are crying?"

I had not noticed it, I must not know how to cry. Now that I was near him, I could not think of anything to say. I could only press myself, trembling, against him, and wait for him to make a decision. I had completely lost my head. A crowd was gathering; he wanted to get away from the theatre district, so I followed. I had forgotten to put on my coat. It was raining on my white dress, my slippers were all out of shape, but I did not think of asking him to find shelter for us. All that was quite secondary. We went down towards the harbor, without a word. The air freshened as we approached the water. I slipped a little on the wet sidewalk, with my uncomfortable dancing pumps, and Jean held me. The electric signs of the little cafés blazed orange and green. The street became more and more narrow, and more animated. From time to time a door opened to let out a staggering sailor and simultaneously a flood of discordant music. Suddenly we came out upon the pier. Under the white light of an arc lamp, a crowd of people milled about in the mud and the rain.

They were sailors newly disembarked, who were looking for a noisy place to relax in, fishermen who wanted to celebrate Saturday night properly, street-walkers who were bravely looking for customers, despite the gluey humidity rising from the docks.

All along the quays the little taverns had their doors open, and a great roar of music, shouting, clinking of glasses engulfed the crowds of people on the sidewalk who did not move ahead. For a long time we remained a part of this confused mass of people, pushed this way and that, accosted by convivial strangers smelling of alcohol. Under the white light of the high projector, faces were greenish, ghostlike, and their joyous or drunken expressions appeared all the more extraordinary.

"Suppose we go in here?" said Jean.

I assented. The rain on my bare shoulders was beginning to make me shiver, and my slippers were hurting me. I only thought about these very simple things. As for the rest, I had no worries, feeling peaceful as one feels on a train riding to a known destination.

Our entrance was hailed with shouts and whistles, largely thanks to my long dress. We sat down at one of the little wooden tables, where, without our ordering it, we were brought two mugs of beer, huge porcelain mugs with pewter lids. The curiosity around us died down. Jean was dressed quite simply, and the bedraggled hem of my dress made the sailors think—as I saw from their dumb-show—that Jean had picked me up in the street, where my costume served to attract customers. Consequently, after a minute, no one paid any attention to us.

"A strange night!" said Jean. "Begun at the Grand Theatre of Gers, and ending here!"

He handed me his comb, and in my pocket looking-glass I saw with astonishment my dishevelled hair, my face disfigured by unashamed tears. I tidied myself up as best I could, without succeeding any too well.

"Don't bother," he said. "What does it matter?"

His arm encircled my shoulders. We were sitting on a wooden bench against the wall. The room was square and small; a stairway led up to a small overhanging gallery where some peasants and servant girls were dancing and singing in chorus, to the music of a lovely, bright accordion. Near us, a stout woman, very powdered and rouged, wearing a transparent blouse and a skirt short enough to give glimpses of her thighs, had put an old beige-colored shawl round her bare shoulders and was coughing dreadfully. On the benches against the wall, couples were embracing, and men's hands could be seen pawing half drunken girls. More than one blouse was unbuttoned, and I could even catch sight of more than one opulent and sun browned breast. The peasants stopped singing only to kiss, placing resounding kisses on the cheeks and plump shoulders of their partners. There was a great deal of laughter and everyone seemed to be in a seventh heaven of bliss.

"They must be pretty sore, down there, at not finding me," said Jean. He looked relaxed, his anger had died down, and he was again wearing his ironic smile.

"Why?"

"Why, because they were dying to gloat over me, make hypocritical excuses, have a little more fun at my expense. Not to mention the ironical compliments and not to mention the expression on your poor father's face. I'm certainly not sorry to escape that. And think of all the good-fellowship one would have to endure at the little theatre party after the show! But perhaps your father will decide not to answer the doorbell, which would be the wise thing to do. The poor soul, I'm pretty sure he's sunk as far as the elections go. Not counting that, obviously, he and I are at daggers' drawn now, for the rest of our lives."

"Why, Jean? It's not your fault, he must have realized that, and . . ."

"Child, whether it's my fault or not is of absolutely no consequence. I will always be an unpleasant reminder, and if I know your father as I think I do, he'll much prefer never to see me again rather than have to admit that he made a mistake in putting any hopes in that incredible troup of actors. But what does it matter?"

"You'll not be able to come to the house any more," I said.

It seemed natural to say those words, although only a week before I would not have let them be wrung out of me for anything in the world.

"In any case, I had no intention of making many polite calls on you," he smiled, and I felt a kind of hollow feeling in my stomach. "We can meet elsewhere, don't you think?"

"Yes," I said. "wherever you like, and as you like!"

I was happy. I could have stayed there forever beside him, looking at his poor tired face, almost ugly that night, shamming gaiety and unconcern. He was so different from his usual self that I was not ashamed to talk to him without pride or to lay my head affectionately on his shoulder. He had dressed almost negligently, no doubt on purpose, so as to appear to be caught unawares by the applause, interrupted in the middle of his work: the thought was touching, somehow.

"Suppose we go up and dance a little," I said, seeing that he was starting to think again, no doubt to relive that hateful evening.

"You want to?" he said, without much enthusiasm.

"Very much," I said, taking him by the hand. He consented, with a condescending smile.

In a kind of rapture, I told myself, "That was the right thing to do. Let him think he's making me happy and forget his disappointment that way. Let him think only of me and not of those imbeciles." I felt closer to him than ever before, as we climbed the little wooden stairs and mingled with the couples who were dancing between the tables. The accordion player was a big fair-haired boy with shining red cheeks. Everyone was singing and waltzing, and I, too, began to sing.

"You seem to be in high spirits, Hélène," said Jean. He did not seem to be very comfortable in the midst of these jubilations of the common people.

"It's because I'm glad to be with you," I said.

The couples turned and turned, joyously and loudly singing, bumping into the tables, snatching up big mugs of beer in passing, and taking a gulp without interrupting their dance. Jean must, absolutely must, become like all the others, he must amuse himself, drink, and forget everything except that he was dancing with a not unattractive girl. It was difficult. He held me close, no doubt intrigued at my unaccustomed sweetness, but still anxious and not at all stirred by the atmosphere of merrymaking. I would have to think up something else. I noticed that Jean was looking admiringly at the barmaid, who happened to be the daughter of the café proprietor. She was very young, plump, tanned, a real peasant girl, and perhaps on account of the approaching Carnival season, she was got up in a Harlequin costume, which was very becoming.

"Wait for me, I'm going to comb my hair," I said, and approached the girl.

"Is there a place where I can comb my hair?"

"Why yes," the girl said in an embarrassed way, "in the cloakroom. But there are already lots of sailors there. Maybe you would like to use my room?"

Just what I was hoping for! No sooner was I in the little bedroom, a rather prettily furnished place under the eaves, than I put a five hundred franc note—my entire fortune—in her hand.

"I've splattered my dress coming here from the theatre," I said, as naturally as I could. "Would you mind lending me one of your dresses?"

I clearly saw by her expression that she took me for a respectable middle-class girl who had come to this cabaret to hide her love affair with some sailor or other—Jean's careless attire gave grounds for the supposition—and who was afraid of being recognized. The charming little Harlequiness, a little too plump, but with the plumpness of a child and the attractiveness of a young animal, refused my banknote and gave me a kiss on the cheek.

"I understand," she said knowingly. "Choose whichever one of my dresses you like and leave your beautiful outfit here, you can take it with you when you leave."

And with a royal gesture she opened a wardrobe where three or four very neat dresses hung. We argued for a second, since she was determined to have me put on her Sunday dress, a full-skirted lilac-colored one, but I was finally allowed to put on a pleated brown skirt, typical of the provinces, and a white linen blouse. Swiftly I rearranged my hair, which was drawn back into a rather ugly bun, plaiting it in a thick braid which I tied up with a ribbon in the fashion of peasant women, fastening it at the back of the neck. In our country they often call young girls "little pitchers" because of this way of dressing the hair in a loop that resembles the handle of a jug. Then I went down into the restaurant where Jean was gloomily waiting for me with a stein of beer before him. He did not recognize me at first, but then he burst out laughing.

"What a transformation! All you lack are wooden shoes."

"I almost have them," I said, showing him the heavy iron-tipped shoes of the Harlequiness. "And now, will you dare to dance with me?"

"Why not?" he said, standing up, apparently amused at my changed appearance.

"But now that I've changed shoes, we'll have to dance like the others . . ."

Indeed, it was impossible with those shoes to go on waltzing a trifle stiffly as we had done awhile ago. We were now obliged to jump noisily, like everyone, and I saw with pleasure that after a minute Jean seemed to enjoy it. Warmed by the dance, we drank great draughts from the blue and white faience mugs, and we sang louder and louder.

Down below, the fishermen who were not dancing were laughing boisterously, with the cool beer before them, and the smoke from their long porcelain pipes came up to us on the gallery, surrounding us in thick clouds. From time to time, the accordion-player stopped and we collapsed, breathless, on the wooden benches, where strangers linked arms with us or slapped us on the shoulder; and always the beer came from the cellar in the big mugs dewy with coolness, and the laughter and the singing went on, the loud kisses continued to be exchanged. And Jean ended up by smiling.

I was surprised at my own happiness. "If only it could last forever," I said to myself, and did not even notice how cliché was the wish. The beer and the noisy accordion contributed no doubt to this kind of anesthesia. At that moment I felt I had always known that happiness with Jean, and I tenderly surveyed the cabaret that was our shelter. "What joy," I inwardly exalted, "what a piece of good luck that the play tonight was a fiasco! At last we have come together."

I felt as though we had reached a goal towards which we had been journeying forever. We had almost missed it, but at last, I told myself, we had arrived.

XVII ·

Madame Périer's little Moroccan reception room was jammed with potted palms, flower-trimmed hats, and grey heads. The elder people were discussing the approaching elections, while the others were far more interested in the buffet or had gathered in a corner of the room around Stani, who was letting himself be stared at with barbarous self-possession.

"When Odette first took notice of my painting," he was saying, blandly, "my manner was not at all the same. The line was more studied, less nervous, see what I mean?"

I could not keep from smiling. After all, Stani, too, had reached a terminus. He was as cut out to be the lover of Odette as I was to love Jean. At least, so I told myself.

Tamara was sitting beside Madame Périer who, in her exotic veils, was radiating satisfaction. Madame Mierowicz, in the next room, dressed in a sumptuous gown of black silk which I had not seen before, was endlessly perorating, at the height of a happiness to which it would seem an exaggerated absorption of cocktails somewhat contributed.

"Hélène, my child!" she called, at sight of me. "Why, it's you, our guardian angel!" And she drew me into a corner, murmuring rapturously, "You're a saint, Lena, a saint. Your love for him is not egotistic, you wanted his true happiness. Come to see him tonight, he'll be there for dinner. Doesn't he look like a god in his new suit?"

I politely declined the offers of that naive procuress, but acquiesced in her admiration. More than one of the ladies present seemed to be thrilled by Stani's face, with its high cheekbones and its expression of noble indifference. Stani was at ease in his new, well cut clothes, his gleaming white shirt, his tie—just a little too loud. There was something just a little too strained and slightly vulgar in his elegance. Madame Mierowicz could not leave off admiring him.

"I was so anxious over that boy! Oh, Hélène, the day you came to see us for the first time, I should have realized at once that you were an angel in disguise. And to think, you haven't seen the apartment. You must, must come to see it. Such luxury. There is an enormous sunken bathtub—three steps down, like a swimming pool. There's a big room for each of us, you can see the lake as far as the river, it's an absolute paradise. And Stani's room—impossible to describe. Come next week, if you can't come tonight."

Pink-cheeked, excited, with her cigarette holder still, despite everything, in the corner of her mouth, Madame Mierowicz seemed rejuvenated by twenty years. And even Monsieur Mierowicz was there, I suddenly noticed, having managed by some miracle to transport his imposing mass of flesh to Odette's second floor apartment. There he was, a peaceful smile now flickering on his lips that were so fertile in maledictions. He was squeezed into an armchair, a glass of champagne was in his hand, and his great golden eyes roved over the crowd with no least trace, now, of melancholy. The entire family radiated an immoral but complete happiness.

"Hello, Hélène," said Stani, coming up to join us. "Have you seen what I did on the side panels? I finally managed, in spite of the ladder."

I had avoided till then raising my eyes to the conventional

and uninspired rustic scenes which would henceforth inhabit Madame Périer's salon.

"Very nice," I said without exaggerated enthusiasm. "If you'll allow me, I'll go back to Tamara now, I have to."

"Oh, surely you needn't hurry? She seems to be well occupied. I say, is it true, that story about Delfau?"

I was about to go, but stopped short.

"What story?"

"Oh, I just thought it was one of your stepmother's jokes. But she certainly has a nerve! I heard her talking about Delfau. Of course, everyone's down on him since the *Reine Berthe* flop, which was a little her fault, I must say. I wanted to find out how she was taking it, so I joined the crowd around her to listen, just in time to hear her say, 'It's lucky he's disappeared since the fiasco, for I was going to be obliged to make him realize he was not wanted in a respectable home.' Everyone was as astonished as I was, and expected to hear her say he'd tried to rape her, but instead, in that calm little way of hers, you know what I mean, she said, 'Yes, in a home where there's a young girl to whom he paid a little too marked attention . . .' We were dumb-founded, I can tell you! Naturally, nobody believed it, but she acted it out so well that everyone pretended to believe her. What do you say to that?"

I said nothing, but left him, to plough through the crowd and rejoin Tamara, to hear what she was saying. In the crowd around her, they were talking about nothing but the opening night fiasco. It hadn't hurt my father as much as could have been expected. Once Jean had left, the actors had gone on with the play, invitations had been sent out, the following production had gone off quite well, and everyone had quickly calmed down. A very simple explanation of the whole thing was the intense boredom which usually reigned in Gers. Well, plenty of people frankly confessed that in their whole life they had not had as much fun as at the scandalous and from then on famous opening night of *La Reine Berthe*. From this fact arose a kind of grateful feeling towards Father who had, though quite involuntarily, provided them with this entertainment. A few days before, the Parisian critics who had taken the trouble to attend had published their articles and on the theme of "Let us honor futile courage" they had covered Jean and Sandra with bouquets for being the unfortunate victims of the bad taste and ill will of the people of Gers. A great wave of indignation had risen at this time on the subject of these articles, in the Périer salon. Vainly, the languorous voice of Odette tried to pacify the arguments. Out of a strange reaction of national pride, everyone agreed in maintaining that the catastrophe of the first night was entirely due to the stupid staging of Jean and the capricious behavior of Sandra.

"The minute they were left to themselves, the actors kept to their lines marvellously," said little Van Beck, the most rabid attacker of Jean, who had had the misfortune of asking the author to make a few cuts. Naturally, the day after the opening, the text had been restored and Van Beck was not far from attributing to this the satisfactory performances that had followed.

"Anyway, it was badly staged, you felt the hand of a novice in it. Although, really, the sets weren't too bad."

It was Joris, the sculptor, who spoke with a self-satisfied air. His mitigated praise aroused indignation. There was no question, now, of giving even reserved praise to the least thing Jean might have done.

"Well, I always loathed those sets. And you realize, of course, that the costumes were not at all historical. I was told they were anachronistic to a degree."

Tamara's calm voice was raised, as if to put a period to these venomous exclamations.

"After all," she said, "poor Delfau didn't have much luck in Gers. He took two terrible beatings—*La Reine Berthe*, and Hélène."

This nasty remark, which sounded sincere, caused a great deal of laughter.

"Monsieur Delfau was never in love with me, Tamara," I said in a voice that trembled a little, but which could be clearly heard. "And you well know it."

"Did he fail less completely than I thought, Hélène?" she smilingly retorted.

At my embarrassment, additional laughter broke out. It would have been silly to say more, so I fell silent, raging inwardly at Tamara's rehabilitation. On the eve of elections, she had managed to erase what may have been the only black mark against her since her marriage. What she had just said was not absolutely false, it could not even seriously damage my reputation, but there was something that worried me a trifle in the way she was putting my confidences to use. It was not for the first time that I regretted the confession I had made to her during the final phase of my stormy affair with Jean.

Since the scene at the theatre, we had not talked of anything important, and she seemed to have concluded that everything was over between Jean and me. However, there had been a coolness between us ever since that night, when I had behaved with complete recklessness and when she had had to come downstairs at three in the morning to open the door for me. She had asked no question, and my father had been much too busy that evening being sorry for himself and cancelling the little supper party to pay the least attention to my tardy return. As to my flight from the theatre, he had seen in it a touching gesture of filial despair. During the following days, his serenity was restored by the numerous expressions of sympathy that had reached him and by the success of the second "opening" organized five days later. Finally, the arrival of the wild animals ordered in Italy amply compensated his sufferings. In honor of those poor beasts, which arrived exhausted by the journey, the buildings of the Zoological Gardens were repainted, an orchestra was set up in the kiosk that had lost its gilding, and on the following Sunday the populace had been invited to look at the unfortunate carnivora which, frightened by the throng, were roaring in a satisfying way. The news had spread like wildfire, and towards five o'clock, when we—my father, Tamara, and I—went to judge what effect the "trump card" was having, families that wanted to instruct their progeny were taking the gardens by assault. They were regaled by a concert, a seedy old camel carried the children in a kind of palanquin, and we walked slowly in the midst of the excited crowd, Father assuming a studied air of benevolence, Tamara and I affecting the distinction suitable to the wife and daughter of a full-fledged burgomaster.

Old Maalens' henchmen were almost the only ones that day not to shake hands with Father, so grateful were the people of Gers to the man who was restoring their past splendors. The elders recalled having taken their first steps in those Zoological Gardens, which had been flourishing then; the children's nurses applauded the orchestra frenziedly, the hawkers of lemonade, peanuts, and coconuts did a thriving trade, the babies, stunned by the banging cymbals, dozed lethargically. In brief, everyone was contented except the lions and me: the lions, because they were being fed far too much, the keepers having long since forgotten the diet suitable to them, and I, well, I was waiting for a letter from Jean.

That Sunday was Father's day of triumph. Next day, old Maalens took steps to minimize it. Being informed by official reports of the effect produced on the populace by Father's stratagem and likewise informed that on account of the general satisfaction the municipal councillors were considering awarding him a decoration, old Maalens let it be known that, suddenly stricken with a weirdly named malady of the stomach, he would be unable to run for reelection. This deprived my father of the triumph of winning the elections and practically amounted to appointing him to the highest municipal office.

No other serious candidate could be seriously imagined; it required too much money and pull to represent the municipality with the desired ostentation. In fact, then, Father only had to await the formal consecration of office, while receiving the innumerable ceremonial calls which in Gers were customarily made upon a new burgomaster; calls which, significantly enough, had already begun ten days before the elections. The entire house was in a state of hectic agitation. And in the midst of all this, Tamara moved with the dignity of a queen, receiving the whole town in her drawingrooms.

Father had taken a very benevolent attitude towards me. "My child," he had said, "you were right not to decide to marry sooner. With what I now represent, you can have the pick of the town. That young Baron Frederick isn't bad. What do you think about him? Or else Van Beck's son, he'll come into a tremendous fortune, that boy. Think it over, child, think it over. You're no longer the daughter of a nobody!"

It mattered very little to me whether or not I was the mayor's daughter. I was waiting for a letter from Jean. Twelve days had already gone by since his departure, since that night which had seemed miraculous. I suffered at the idea of his having resumed his old habits and amusements in Paris, doubting that the memory of Gers could put up much resistance against them. I suffered at the thought of the mistress he had there, the girl Max had told me about, and I suffered with shame at having to admit I was a victim of anything as banal as jealousy.

And then, I suffered from something else. In vain did I try to reconstitute myself as I had formerly been, and to make this love an additional feature of the personality I had wanted to acquire. Each day I discovered in myself new flaws which love had made.

One day I went out for an early walk in those streets where Jean had once accosted me. On that distant day, how indifferent I had been to everything, how well-armed I had supposed myself to be! What remained of that protective carapace now?

Those streets which I had formerly thought so deserted were now swarming with a multitude of beings I would not even have seen, then. They were no longer just a group of women, a postman, some children, a baker: each one suddenly had an individuality, a name, chapped hands, a wound—what had caused that wound? The baby with bleary eyes, crying in its mother's arms, looked like no other baby in the world, and each one of those seedy old men, looking for a job as dishwasher in a hotel or as a mender of nets, each one touched a suddenly bared sensitive place in my heart. I went down a miserable street, where a woman, still young, with the wretched kind of blond hair produced by cheap dyes, gave me a toothless smile. She talked to me for a moment about her troubles, about the fish she was having a hard time selling although they were not abundant that year; then, noticing that while I replied to her I could not take my eyes away from the gaping holes in that young mouth, she lightly mentioned the subject. "You're looking at my snags?" she said. "Oh, it's just from having kids, I've had two, and that's fatal. All the women I know have bad teeth like this, it's always the same when you have kids, on account of the decalcification."

I would have liked to reply in the same calm tone, or go off and leave her, or at least turn my eyes away from that pathetic jaw with its pale gums, but I was unable to budge. A sickening feeling of pity welled up in me, a kind of nausea, and suddenly I burst into tears. At first the woman stared at me in stupefaction, but then, as if offended, she turned on her heel and went into her house, banging the door.

I had gone home, still dazed and sick over these revelations but refusing to admit it, blaming my upset on fatigue, the nervous tension over that letter I was waiting for and which did not come. . . .

The letter finally came, after more than a fortnight of waiting. It brought little comfort. I had hoped to find in it something of the peace we had finally attained that night at the

Petit Matelot café. Jean did not allude to that night. He addressed me as though I were just anybody to whom he had momentarily been attracted, with a light-hearted gallantry that astounded me, after those serious hours. Without appearing to attach much importance to it, he announced, at the end of the letter, that he was planning to come to Gers a little later on, for a couple of days, on his way to London, where a contract of long-standing date obliged him to go. Perhaps he was ashamed of those instants when I had given him comfort, perhaps he hated the memory which represented no more than a weak moment in his life. Formerly, I would have flown into a rage. Now, I tried to understand, was ready to forgive. Clearly, I was no longer myself.

And that love continued to live in me, ravage me. I had been alone and free; now, I allowed Jean to exercise rights over me, and not only Jean, but the others—the old man wanting to chat, the woman asking me to hold her baby, even the mangy dog, coming shamelessly to beg. You would say they sensed the presence of love, that they scented it on me like a perfume and, recognizing me as inoffensive and disarmed, they demanded their portion. The beggar with the alert eyes almost hidden under pitiful eyebrows, the bold beggar "from the orphanage" who held out his hand authoritatively to take what I gave him, the half of my savings, for he well knew I could *not* refuse that money to him any more than I could refuse to give him my cloak if he asked for it. Through the breach in my defences opened by love, the entire world might enter, and everywhere I seemed to see the hand and the eyes of Jean. Fearful and withdrawn, I remained motionless in that domain of love where I had scarcely set foot and already was losing my equilibrium. And I was determined to maintain that immobility.

So I did not write to Jean the words of love which sprang to my lips whenever I found myself alone, nor express that cry which despite all my efforts threatened to burst from me, imploring Jean to be there at my side and give me peace. But there was no defiance, either, in my letters. I knew him too well now, knew too well how he suffered from wounded pride to dare try his patience. I waited. And Max did not even succeed in making me cross when, happening to drop in to see me, and being confronted with a portrait of Jean I had sketched during these days, he muttered with a grimace, "Being in love doesn't suit you, Hélène." He was right, and I knew it. Because of affectionate scruples, I had refrained from emphasizing the lines on that face, or the bitterness, and the portrait had bogged down in insipidity. I could have done a better portrait of Jean had I not been in love with him; but with a love as clear-sighted and hard as hatred, I could have drawn in the lines, marked the bitterness of the mouth, the weary eyelids, and could also have captured the rare light that suddenly illumined that face during music and after the act of love. Would I ever achieve that kind of love? I preferred not to think about it.

Jean finally arrived, during the preparations for the Carnival, always grandiose in Gers, but which, thanks to Father, was going to be even more brilliant that year. I had been solemnly appointed by him to supervise the floral decorations. Max was responsible for the floats and for the traditional costumes that needed to be replaced.

And so it was that I met Jean at the station bursting with talk, gossip, futilities, which had the supreme advantage of bridging the first difficult moments.

As for Jean himself, he smiled gaily and seemed overflowing with projects. Thanks to the generous notices his work in Gers had received, he had been entrusted with an important theatrical assignment in Nancy, where the government was beginning a campaign of decentralisation. There was going to be a gala performance, with the President of the Republic in attendance. Jean would go to Nancy immediately upon his return from London. When would he come back to Gers? He did not say.

There was no question of our going to the red room: too many memories lurked there. The porter of the Carlton hotel, who knew me well, surveyed me with astonishment as I accompanied Jean up to his room. But what did I care? In that little nile-green room, so clean and modern and impersonal, I experienced a kind of relief. Jean unpacked his bags without haste, while talking about the film for which he was going to do the sets in London.

"It's one of those big, rather Victorian productions, but with three hundred actors, you see what I mean. As for the costumes, it's going to be quite interesting. I'm going to try for ensemble effects, rather hard to manage, for even when all the costumes are effective, separately, they can clash in a group. And since it's going to be slightly parodied, working on it may be rather fun, don't you think?"

I agreed. Sitting on the bed, listening to this easy, relaxed, everyday chatter, so unusual between us, I almost had the impression that we were two travellers who had just arrived in this hotel in an unknown town. We interrupted each other's anecdotes, we did not wait to finish laughing at one before telling another.

When Jean could not go on any longer pretending to unpack his bag, he turned towards me, and silence fell. I was afraid, more afraid than ever before in my life. And yet, we looked so foolishly abashed as we faced each other, that I was seized with an inner trembling, as if shaken by prolonged and very gentle laughter. As he drew near me, I noticed his face looked wearier than I had ever seen it, as if a trifle aged by a secret emotion. Tears of unexpected tenderness sprang to my eyes. He was going to say, "After all, you do love me," and I was going to reply, after all, "Yes." But all he said was "Hélène . . ." and it was only to myself that I said the words he had not asked me to say.

We lay down together on the bed, without undressing. Perhaps we were afraid of our naked bodies; they were still enemies, they must be given more time than we had had to pass from combat to confidence. We did not even kiss each other. There was plenty of time ahead for that: were we not together for always?

"I've not been so happy," I said despite myself, "since I was twelve."

"Your mother wasn't dead, when you were twelve?"

"Yes. But I scarcely knew her at all . . . What about you?"

He frowned slightly, but replied without apparent sadness.

"I was eight years old when my mother died. It was afterwards that my father and I went to Paris to live."

And as if carried away he went on, without my having asked a question.

"She went for a walk, they brought her back home on a stretcher. I believe a snake had bitten her."

"You believe? Why . . ."

"I saw them bringing her, pale as a corpse, perhaps already dead. That night they came to tell me—it was, I recall, a little fifteen-year-old servant girl, since my father had not wanted me to see his face ravaged with tears—to tell me that my mother had gone away on a very long journey. And I, already suspecting the truth, I cried out that it wasn't true, that I wanted to know. But when I saw, by the girl's expression, for she could not hide her feelings and they showed in her reddened eyes, that the terrible truth was approaching, was about to be *said*, I threw myself upon her, screaming and crying, 'Don't say anything, I believe it! I believe it!' And isn't it strange, I kept up that fiction for years, I persistently talked about her return, although people averted their eyes, and I was already thirteen when a schoolmate, talking about me to someone in front of me said, without intending to hurt, 'His mother is dead.' So then, since she was dead, I very quickly forgot her."

"And then?"

"Why, child, there isn't any 'and then.' I'm not telling you the story of my life."

"Too bad! I wish you would tell me the story of your life."

"You'd be very disappointed. It seems to me I once told you there's nothing interesting in it. My mother's death was the one real grief of my life. The rest is happier and completely uninteresting. You surely don't want me to tell you about all the stage-sets I've made, the women I've—more or less—loved . . ."

"No, I'm not asking that. It's not your present life that interests me. It's your childhood."

"But there's nothing to tell about my childhood."

"Oh, but I'm sure there is. You went to Paris to live with your father. Was he nice, your father?"

"Oh, Lord . . . not exactly nice, but very kind, certainly. We lived very much alone together."

Jean's father, of Spanish and Jewish origins, already owned several stores which sold "modern and antique furniture" when they moved to Paris to live in a house that was gloomy and full of treasures. Jean was nine years old. Because of his infirmity he had to live apart from other children—at least so his father believed. In addition, there were the usual barriers set up by wealth. Jean's father was very wealthy, and Jean was very much alone.

"Fortunately," he said, "I've never much liked contact with my own kind—with my own kind of men, at least—and I was very happy. When I got bored, Father sent me to the Opera, to his box there, with my nurse. I was in love with the actresses, with the red velvet, and even with the dust. Thank God, my love for actresses did not survive after I was fifteen. But my love for the theatre remained a little and perhaps that's why I began to make a career in it. I could not hope to act, I did not like to write, so I began to design sets and costumes."

Was he as happy as all that, I wondered, the little boy sent with his nurse to sit among the dusty velvets of the theatre? Was he as happy as all that, the little boy with the inert arm who had chosen, as if defiantly, to learn to draw?

His father, who was already sixty when he was twelve, was

from that time on his sole companion. They went out together and the old man talked to the boy as if they were the same age. In this way he communicated to him his experience, which was that of a sensitive man who had often been hurt, a man conscious of his origins and of his wealth, not, certainly, as a blemish but as a condition which set him apart from the common run of mankind and who, for all the more reason, secluded his crippled son from the world. I had a feeling that this good man, rather skeptical, and with his fortune made and not seeing much sense in the whole immense effort, had had an enormous influence over his son. Listening to him, Jean received all his father's hurts and was cured of them with him. Thus, he learned not to give much credit to life. And when he reached the age of eighteen, it was still worse. Monsieur Delfau was then sixty-six and had reverted to the faith of his ancestors, having always observed certain practices, not so much out of routine as out of a kind of pride in not abjuring his race.

Restored to his God, he began, with the patience and attention to detail which had won him his fortune, to prepare for his death. Moreover, he felt an increasing horror at any human contacts. Little by little, with singular pleasure, he stripped the big apartment of its multitude of precious furnishings, now banishing one piece, which went to his stores, now another, which he gave to his son. And one after another the great rooms were shut, the guest rooms were emptied, all the rooms, less and less used, ceased to exist, extinguished like candles blown out after a party, when the guests have gone and only the master of the house remains, and he goes to bed. With his friends it was the same thing. The old friend who formerly lunched every Monday with the antiquarian must accustom himself to coming only every two weeks, then once a month, then not at all. An employee, with whom he had the habit of chatting for an hour after shutting up shop, saw the time allotted to him reduced more and more, without his even being able to notice anything strange in his employer's attitude. Jean himself saw less and less of his father. Each time the old man was with his son, he took care to be less expansive, as if to prepare him little by little to be definitely separated by death from this father who had held such a big place in his life. It was as though Monsieur Delfau enjoyed the subtle pleasure of seeing himself disappear. His hair slowly whitened—he had dyed it from the age of fifty, and did not want to confess this innocent piece of deceit—he let his beard grow, and began more and more to resemble the Wandering Jew of the picture-books, as if he had wanted to facilitate God's task and to be recognized straight away for what he was.

That tactful man died at last during one of Jean's absences, and without any alarming signs having been noted, except a considerable exhaustion of long date. And so he disturbed no one, not even the doctor, for he died in the daytime just when the doctor paid his daily visit. He left Jean at the head of a perfectly well-ordered business, which was ably administered by his friend and co-religionist Gunther, whose honesty could not be questioned, since he had managed the business for the last ten years of Monsieur Delfau's life and had not grown one penny richer by it. So the old man, upon dying, had bequeathed to this old bachelor a rather important part of his interests, knowing that Jean would not oppose it and under condition that Gunther should continue, for the rest of his life, to manage the whole affair.

"So you don't even need to work?" I asked thoughtlessly.

"That's just what they've reproached me for all my life," said Jean, not without a certain bitterness. "My father thought he was assuring me an ideal existence, relieved of all cares, and in fact he only bequeathed me a rather heavy burden that I never wanted, not for a single day. Just imagine . . . I've never told this to anyone before, you see how I trust you . . . just imagine, I swore, when I was twenty, that I would never touch that fortune but that I would earn my living, and earn enough to live very well."

"And have you done it?"

"Only partly. I soon earned enough to live well; but since I'd proved to myself that I could do it, why continue to refuse a fortune which permitted additional pleasures? Perhaps I was wrong, after all. Wouldn't it have been worth more . . . What are you making me say? Stupidities. That's what happens when one calls up childhood memories. Regrets. And God knows I'm not in the habit of having regrets."

"Maybe it would have been better if your father had brought you into contact with life a little sooner?" I asked, not quite knowing how to deal with this situation.

"That's it," he said sarcastically. "I was so well equipped to cut out a place for myself in the world, wasn't I? No, my father acted wisely. And I would act still more wisely by not talking about myself any more."

"But please go on, I'm not bored," I warmly protested. "On the contrary, I would so like to help you, you who . . ."

"I have a horror of sisters of charity," he said in his old tone of voice, dry, cold, detestable.

And I suddenly remembered with a strange uneasiness the almost forgotten words of that girl, Manuelita: "In order to love that man, you must be an angel . . ."

Night was falling when we separated. He left me not far from home, I promised to return next day after lunch. No really tender words were said—we did not feel they were necessary. Next morning I would go to the Academy, I had to put in an occasional appearance there, and anyway, Jean always slept late. Then, at two o'clock, I would see him. That well-ordered day seemed to me to be life.

X V I I I ·

Next morning, towards ten o'clock, I was about to leave the house, my portfolio under my arm, when Tamara sharply detained me. I had barely noticed her during lunch and as I glanced at her now I saw with astonishment the distracted look on her face.

"Where are you going?" she asked, almost choking with wrath.

"Why, to the Academy," I said, astonished to see her like this. And I started to pass by.

"You shall not go out of here!" she shouted, holding me by the wrist. I stopped, dumbfounded.

"Tamara, are you insane?"

"Insane or not, you shall not go out of here," she said through clenched teeth. She was quivering with such rage that she could barely speak. I made an effort to free my wrist, but she held on to it firmly.

"If you try to leave in spite of me, I'll call your father, who's in the next room, and I'll tell him right here and now where you intend to go."

"Well, where do I intend to go, please?" I shouted in my turn, exasperated at her strange conduct.

"For heaven's sake, you little fool, do you suppose I don't know? Why, to the Carlton hotel, of course, to meet Jean. Isn't that so?"

My heart pounded deafeningly, but I replied as calmly as I could.

"Why, Tam, I was going to the Academy this morning. I don't have a date with Jean until this afternoon. Now, will you kindly let me pass?"

"You shan't set foot outside this house without my permission, and I forbid it at the moment. Go back to your room and stay there till I call you!"

"I'm going to see what papa has to say about this," I said, going towards his room.

"If you go in there to speak to your father," she screamed, "I'll ask him what he thinks of a girl who goes brazenly into the Carlton with Delfau and stays three hours with him, to the knowledge of everyone in town. No doubt you forget that the elections take place in three days and that such a thing would be enough to make him lose! And all the calls are paid, the invitations to the ball are ready to be sent out—not to mention all the money spent on the Carnival. Yes, I really think your father would be glad to hear all this!"

I calmed down a trifle. So that was what she feared!

"Tamara, there's no reason to get yourself so worked up. I'll admit, the Carlton is a little too public a place for such meetings. If someone's seen me there, I'll explain that I went to ask Jean's advice about the Carnival decorations, and that's that. And I'll arrange by telephone to meet him somewhere else."

My voice was more assured than I myself was. Tamara's violence had pretty thoroughly frightened me; she had so sharply disrupted my peace.

"You're not going to meet him at the Carlton or anywhere else," she said shortly. "I shall notify that gentleman that he should return to Paris as soon as possible, and that until he leaves Gers, you're not going to set foot outside this house."

Her voice was so firm that I went all too pieces.

"What's it to you, Tam, if I see Jean? I've never hidden my affair with him from you, why, you and I even joked about it . . ."

The sneering look she gave me reminded me of the Rempart des Béguines. No doubt of it, she was enjoying my discomfiture. But her face quickly composed itself and she continued with great dignity.

"I've been able to tolerate your foolishness, Hélène, but I won't tolerate your having a serious affair—you shan't have that with my permission. Please remember that I always made my silence conditional upon your breaking off with him after the opening of *La Reine Berthe.*"

This crass deformation of the truth shocked me.

"There was never a question of conditions!" I said. "I told you I counted on breaking off with Jean, but . . ."

"I kept quiet on that condition, I was counting on that. You intended to break off; well, you shall break off now, once and for all."

"But I don't want to!" I wailed.

Of course it would have been better for me to have pretended a certain indifference as to the outcome of my relations with Jean, and to appear indignant only at the violence of her intervention, but I was incapable of pretending, for I was beside myself with rage at the protective attitude she was so cleverly taking. And so I threw myself blindly against the obstacle, without seeing that the obstacle existed only because of my efforts.

"Ah, so our dear little Hélène is in love now?" she said with a hateful smile, the same smile I had seen on Max's face several weeks before. "My poor child," she went on in a wheedling voice, "you should not have slept with him. I could have tolerated a sentimental affair, but this serious one, never. My responsibility towards you and towards your father prevents me even from dreaming of allowing you to go out. The only thing I can grant you is my silence. Tomorrow Jean will have left, we'll drop the subject, I'll not mention it again. Now, go up to your room."

This way of ending the discussion drove me wild.

"You have not right to forbid me anything, no matter what,"

I cried. "I'll not break off with Jean. I'll see him whenever I like. Let me go, now!"

I was now the wrathful one, while she was the one who remained calm.

"There's no question of rights," she said coldly, her back to the diningroom door to keep me from going. "If you want me to use such language, you're the one who hasn't the right to protest, you, an eighteen-year-old girl, not yet of age! If you don't go this instant to your room, where I intend to lock you up, your father shall be told everything. And do you believe he'll listen only to you when he realizes his chances of winning the elections are threatened, just when he is already visualizing himself in the burgomaster's chair? I don't think you have much chance of persuading him to let you go out, Hélène! But perhaps you'd like to try?"

She half opened the door, now, and waved towards my father's study. I hesitated. He was very occupied with callers, he was being showered with congratulations; could I burst in there to announce that the post he so firmly counted upon might be lost through my fault? I would be committing the worst possible blunder at the moment. Even if I succeeded in making him consider Tamara's attitude strange, he would nonetheless be mortally offended with me. I knew it, and Tamara knew it.

"Well, aren't you going?" she sneered.

"It's not exactly the moment," I said as calmly as I could.

"If it's not the moment to talk to him, it is the moment to go up to your room. Choose. But if you try to leave the house, I'll call him."

She seemed capable of it, so I had to obey. If I had resisted as courageously the temptation to take up Jean's challenge, I bitterly reflected, I would not have reached this point. She shut and locked the door of my room upon me. I shed only a few tears, for I was filled with rage. Somehow I must let Jean know.

Feverishly I paced the room. I opened the window, which was about ten yards above the ground. And suddenly, I had an idea. Quite near my window ran a rain gutter, very wide, which went round the entire house and must go past the attic window. If that were open, it would be easy to make an escape, at least from this part of the house. It would still be necessary to go downstairs without running into Tamara. But with a little luck, it could be done. I must leave immediately. Tamara might already have told some clever fib or other to Jean. And supposing he left without waiting? That idea made me tremble so that I had to lie down a moment. I would have to take care not to fall as I climbed out the window. I was no longer young enough to think of rejoicing in advance at Tamara's remorse; and anyway, I was almost sure she would have very little.

Her voice could be heard in various parts of the house, giving orders, bustling about. I ran no risk of being caught at that moment. So I drew near the window. Was it the scene I had just gone through that had deprived me of strength? Every time I started to climb out of the window, the thought of Jean, who had perhaps already gone away, made me so weak that I had to sit down again, trembling, on the bed. The worst of it was that I had climbed out on the roof hundreds of times in the past, either to read a forbidden book in peace or to take a sun bath. Was I to be incapable of doing anything for Jean? I was in despair. Incapable of avowing my love for him, incapable of not picking up his challenge, was I now incapable of making this tiny physical effort? If I were this despicable, how could I ever hope to be loved? This final reflection whipped up my courage. With a lunge, I pulled myself up, climbed over the windowsill and, hanging on to it, set foot in the rain gutter. I did all this with an extreme sensation of physical weakness, expecting any moment to pitch down into empty space. When, finally, I straightened up on the narrow ledge, my head swam, and I clung to the tiles for a second, without moving. Then I recovered my wits and realized I must hurry. If Tamara found my room empty, wouldn't she have the house searched first? Cautiously, then, I advanced along the edge of the roof. The first dormer window was shut. I considered breaking the windowpanes with one of my shoes, but was afraid of making a noise. I went on, rounded a corner, and arrived at Julia's room. There the window was open and Julia could be seen sitting on her bed, sewing. She had neither seen nor heard me. I hesitated to return to the other attic window and break it. But Julia, no doubt, would run at the sound and would be less well-disposed towards me than if I were to take her into my confidence . . .

"Julia!" I called softly.

She looked up, startled at seeing me leaning against her window.

"Why, Lena, what in the world are you doing out there?" she cried, hurrying to help me climb down into her room.

"You must help me," I said rapidly, as soon as this was done. "Tamara locked me in my room, she's found out everything and wants to keep me from seeing Monsieur Delfau."

"Jealousy!" said Julia, with a knowing look.

"It's possible. But I want to get out of the house without running into her. What shall I do?"

Julia thought it over for a minute.

"Easy," she said. "I'll go down first, making a lot of noise, and I'll ask for Madame. You—you'll take your time following me. If she's there, she'll come upstairs. If that happens, you mustn't move, I'll tell her something or other, she'll go into one of the bedrooms with me to talk, I'll shut the door, and then you can pass by."

The simple plan seemed brilliant to me. Upset as I was over the possibility of Tamara's appearing suddenly, I would not have been capable of thinking it up myself. Julia, on the other hand, seemed to be hugely enjoying herself.

"I'm off," she said, with a warlike air. "Don't keep too near behind me, Madame might see you."

She went down to the first landing, the one on which were Tamara's and Father's rooms.

"Is Madame there?" she clamored. There was no reply, so I began to go down. Tamara's door opened and she came out.

"What do you want, Julia?"

I had beaten a hasty retreat and now listened anxiously.

"I must really have a talk with you, Madame!" said Julia, in a perfectly imitated tone of fury. "That cleaning-woman, she's impossible now, she . . ."

"Later, Julia. Wait for me in my room. I want to say a word or two to Mademoiselle Hélène, then I'll come back to you."

At these words I retreated quickly into Julia's room, utterly bewildered. There was the sound of footsteps on the stairs. I saw her pass in front of me, two yards away, down the little corridor which led to my room. Then I realized the stairs were free and, without more precautions, I ran downstairs, bumping into Julia on the first landing, continuing to run until I reached the ground floor at last, and was out in the street. All the way to the hotel I ran, without stopping. Supposing Tamara jumped into the car and tried to catch up with me? She must know that I would go straight to the Carlton . . .

I was completely out of breath when I reached the hotel, red-eyed, looking very strange, no doubt, for the porter and the page boy surveyed me in a more stupefied way than they had done the day before.

"Is Monsieur Delfau in?"

"Yes, Mademoiselle, he's in his room, but . . ."

I did not stop to hear more, but dashed up the stairs. Yes, he was there, standing near the window, pensively smoking. I fell into his arms, sobbing with emotion and relief. For a moment he held me close, then, as I couldn't stop sobbing, he began questioning me.

"Hélène, Hélène! Why, what's wrong? What's happened? Tamara told me . . ."

"Tamara," I said between sobs, "has Tamara told you something? She wanted to keep me from leaving the house, she . . ."

He shook me roughly, almost angrily.

"You told her, little stupid?"

"Yes," I sobbed. "Yes, but I didn't want this."

"What did you want, then?" he asked, icily, letting go of me. "Did you expect congratulations?"

I saw that he did not understand, and tried to compose myself.

"Why, Jean, it wasn't just now, it was three weeks ago that I told her, long before the opening, and I didn't want to tell you because it wouldn't seem nice and . . ."

He was generous enough to interrupt my confused explanations.

"Oh! If you begin thinking, now, of being nice . . . Anyway, it's really of no importance. Come, stop crying, you're getting my shirt damp . . ."

We sat down together on the bed. I had no thought at all, except that I was saved, since I was near him.

"What a little stupid you are!" he said, almost tenderly. "Everything would have been so easy if you hadn't been idiotic. Come, tell me about what's happened."

I told him, as exactly as possible. He laughed a great deal over my romantic escape, but seemed unexpectedly anxious over Tamara's threats.

"We mustn't make light of this, child. She's quite capable of putting you into a convent or into a reform school for three years until you come of age," he said, frowning. "We must not let things get to that point . . . When she telephoned me . . ."

"Did she telephone you this morning?"

"I do nothing but keep on repeating it. She telephoned me perhaps a half hour ago to say that you had just confessed about our affair, that you had shut yourself into your room, that you wanted to break off with me and dared not, and heaven only knows what else. In short, she said she was acting for you in telling me that you would not come either this afternoon or ever."

"Oh!" I exclaimed. "And she knows that . . ."

I stopped and Jean burst out laughing.

"Still being a little stupid, eh? Yes, she knows that . . . and she did not hesitate to say it to me. And she added that you had decided not to leave your room until the break with me had been made, and by her. The last words being said in a reflective and gentle way calculated to give me food for thought."

"And . . . did you believe her?"

"Strangely enough, I did not. I'm quite aware that your little brain is devilishly tortuous, but from that to imagining your delegating Tamara to break off with me—no. You would have had enough courage to do it yourself, if you'd wanted to."

"But you did think I might have wanted to?" I cried, dumbfounded at his apparently not having grasped all the tenderness I had thought I had expressed the night before.

"Good Lord, how do I know?" he said lightly. I saw that he was determined to prevent us from becoming emotional. And so I said nothing more.

"Now," he added more seriously, "let's take a few necessary steps."

He picked up the telephone near his bed and called the porter.

"If I'm asked for," he said, "tell them I've gone out, with a young girl, and that I will not be back until tonight, understand? But you will notify me when I'm asked for . . . Thank you."

"Do you think she'll telephone here?" I asked, as he hung up.

"I think she'll come here and that she's probably already on the way, hoping for a great heart-rending three-character scene with cries, tears, mutual reproaches, confessions, and so on. It's insane the way you go in for complications, here in Gers."

185

With a sigh, he sat down once more beside me.

"Well, my child, we must draw up our plan of attack. It's a two to one chance that, when she saw you'd gone out, Tamara had a talk with your father. When I'm gone, tonight . . ."

"What, you're going away tonight?"

I was frightened at my own perturbation. I had almost shouted the words.

"I can't stay, child, it's impossible. I have some absolutely necessary appointments, some things to prepare for my trip to London. But I'll come back here in two weeks, don't you worry."

I was not to worry! When I felt so vulnerable, and when he was abandoning me to Tamara's anger, and perhaps my father's, too! Did he think I was that strong?

"Now then, you will go to your father," said Jean in a perfectly calm tone of voice. "You will tell him you had lunch with me—which is what we are about to have—he will immediately make a scene about the indecency of your lunching alone with me. You will reply that during lunch I had the honor to ask your hand in marriage, which will give said luncheon a perfectly decent character. And you will add that . . ."

"Jean!" I interrupted. But he waved me to silence and went on.

"You will add that I plan to call upon him, during my next visit to Gers, to make this serious request officially. Now, Hélène! Don't put on that tragic face! Isn't this what is usually called a 'happy ending'? You see how I come to the rescue of young ladies in distress!"

I scarcely heard his words. A long silence hovered, the silence that follows the fall of a bomb, when, overwhelmed by the explosion, one does not yet dream of wondering whether or not one is living or dead.

"Tamara's going to get a weird shock!" Jean was saying with a smile. How right he was to joke and smile! But how incapable I was of replying. A prey to the most absolute be-wilderment, I was still completely absorbed in wondering whether or not I was really there, really alive. And Jean was looking at me with a kind of gentle irony, tapping his cigarette on the edge of a dreadful little lacquered table. How I struggled not to burst into sobs! And how I struggled against a frightful thought that had flashed like lightning through my mind! "Now that he's given me this proof of confidence, now that he assuredly loves me, I must tell him everything, he has to know."

Why had that thought come to me? Even to myself it seemed absurd, ridiculous. Of what interest to Jean could my brief little affair with Stani be? Did Jean tell me about his life since he had left me? Did he not try to minimize as much as possible even this moment of time we were living? And ought I not to help him do this? I managed to smile briefly and I heard a few of his words.

"Naturally, it won't go off without some trouble. I'll write a letter . . . astonishment of my friends . . . ceremony full of ostentation, that will be more amusing . . ."

He must be joking again. He seemed to be enjoying himself a great deal. "You're right," I murmured to myself, in a kind of exorcism or prayer. "You know what must be done, you're right, I'll leave it all to you." But despite myself, my soul rebelled, demanding something else, something more than this satisfaction at a happily concluded affair, more even than the secret tenderness he did not express. My soul wanted words, perhaps ridiculous but true, wanted kisses, confessions and, yes, tears. In secret my soul implored Jean to say one word, make one gesture which would finally cast down all the barriers so cleverly erected between us, implored me to make that confession which would destroy our anguish and our shame. Suddenly we were no longer alone; between us had slipped a redoubtable power to which it was enough to yield only once for it to carry us away. Quickly, quickly I must conceal this lightheadedness of mine. Already a dangerous silence was settling down between us. Was I going to throw myself into his arms, speak at last, tirelessly entreat him, until everything should be said, mingled, merged, his pride and mine, our fears, our angers, our desires? Did we still need to defend ourselves? a tempting inner voice murmured. Was I going to commit this folly? I asked myself in anguish. A moment more and I would throw myself at his feet, confessing, along with my love, all I had done against him: my doubts, my distress, and Stani . . . Did he read this resolution in my eyes, did he guess something?

"And now that we know where we are, my dear Hélène, supposing we have some lunch and celebrate this serious decision?"

The moment had passed when I might have talked to him, and in a cowardly way I felt relieved.

"Yes, let's go," I said, almost joyfully. "Suppose we go to the *Petit Matelot*? That would remind us of happy memories."

Immediately I realized I had made a slip. Happy memories. For Jean, was it not especially the memory of that frightful opening night, of the need he had had for me, things he must not like to remember? Nevertheless, he at once assented, and I dared not suggest something else.

As we left the hotel, the little page boy came up to us.

"A lady was here asking for you, sir. She even offered me two hundred francs to find out if you had really gone out! But you can be sure I didn't tell her you were upstairs! I was sure you didn't want to be disturbed."

His laughing eyes went from Jean to me, with mischievous kindness.

"Was that right, sir?"

"Very good. You're an intelligent young man. You guessed that if you were offered two hundred francs to talk you could certainly count on three hundred to keep quiet, eh?"

His hard voice struck me like a blow. The boy had tears in his eyes. Involuntarily I dropped Jean's arm. He turned towards me.

"What's up? Something wrong?"

188

"Jean, don't you see you've hurt that boy? Look how sad he is."

"Page boys in hotels are a species I don't like," he said, with less assurance. "It's a filthy species. They only think about money and they really despise us."

"Not that one, Jean. You can see he really likes you."

"You think so? Oh well, I'll say something nice to him later on."

I pressed myself against him, content. After all, it was not so difficult to disarm him. All he needed was to believe people liked him. Once more, the threatening presence was there, however, once more the memory of Stani returned, making me feel that confession was necessary. Once more I was afraid. I said nothing until we reached the *Petit Matelot*.

At that hour, the little cabaret was full of dockhands and fishermen silently eating, in a cloud of smoke reeking of frying fat and tobacco. Our little Harlequiness came towards us, no longer costumed as she had been the other night, but fresh and rosy in a big white apron. She recognized us at once.

"Oh," she said, with a laugh, "the cabaret is very different at noon, isn't it? But the upstairs room is empty, would you like to eat there?"

We followed her up to that little room jutting out over the lower room, the gallery where we had danced. A subtle embarrassment clung to us. The Harlequiness turned on the lights, drew up a bench and a table, and we sat down in silence.

"I'll get a tablecloth, then I'll put some flowers on the table, that will be better," she said gaily. From below rose the smoke, the sound of rough voices exchanging a few words, and the tinkling of knives and forks. Our hands met.

"Jean, I . . ."

"You know that . . ."

We had begun to talk at the same time. No, I would not

have the courage to tell him. It was not that I was afraid of his anger; I knew him well enough now to surmise that he would pretend indifference and detachment. But it was precisely that indifference that I feared. And why, too, did he say nothing to me? A tender word, a word of encouragement . . ."

"Let's get things clear," he began. "This is what must be done. You'll go to your father, as soon as you return home, and you will announce that you want to marry me. Surprise, indignation, anger! What, that character? Yes, by now he must have forgotten the protestations of friendship and be convinced that I was responsible for the *Reine Berthe* fiasco. He will talk to you about my age, my infirmity," (he said the word very clearly, without making a wry face) "and he will end up with a categorical 'Never'—since he will have had a little preliminary conversation with Tamara. You will then leave him without arguing—it will be rather hard for you, little donkey, but you must go through with it—and you will hand him a fine letter that I will presently write, in which I will make the official proposal of marriage. You will shed tears for a week, or pretend to, and everything will be settled very nicely. Your father is a reasonable man and will see the advantages of this marriage both to him and to you, and the churchbells of Gers will ring for us."

The soup was brought. The Harlequiness looked at us warmly as she served, confident she was witnessing an episode of romantic love. I began to pull myself together. Jean suited me, I loved him, and I was going to marry him. Did that justify losing my wits and all that tragic feeling I was having in regard to something as contemptible as the Stani affair?

Jean wanted to marry me. He was doing a lot for me, since he was over-riding his mistrust of everyone, his urge for independence, even his pride, for he would be risking laughter at this belated marriage. Why should he, in addition to all that, protest his love for me? Yet we both remained silent, although we felt there were things that should have been said, even if they hurt.

"I believe we're going to get along quite well together," said Jean, as the fish was served. "I can bring you a great deal, I'm sure. To begin with, Parisian life will certainly develop your talent, you'll have more room to spread, you'll acquire a color-sense which you lack—it's something that's learned. And I'm convinced you'll like my home. And then, the young women of Gers are such good housekeepers!"

"I'm not at all sure I'll come up to your ideal of house-keeping," I said, forcing myself to the same light tone.

"Oh, don't imagine I'm going to ask you to cook for me! Your job will simply be to telephone the plumber, buy my shirts, supervise things intelligently! You'll have all the time you want for your drawing, you'll be able to attend classes at the Beaux-Arts, if you like, we'll visit the exhibitions, you'll accompany me to the theatre, it will be a much gayer life than the life here, you'll see!"

"I haven't a doubt," I said, trying to enter his game. "Will I have a pretty bedroom?"

"Why, of course. And with a view of trees—a rare thing in Paris. Are you already afraid of losing your independence? Don't worry, little Amazon, you'll keep it completely. And you won't be jealous, will you? I won't either, I promise you. You know, of course, that I have a mistress in Paris?"

"Yes."

"Of course, I shall immediately take the necessary steps to have her leave the apartment as quickly as possible. I'll set her up somewhere else, and she'll be quite happy. There's not much sentimentality between us. Naturally, I'm not saying we'll stop seeing each other from time to time. You and I are a little far apart. But it will only be for reasons of health."

"Of course," I said, smiling. "I quite understand."

I felt more relaxed now, intoxicated by our easy talk as

much as by a too strong drink. I asked for details of the new life he offered, I forgot to reflect that I, too, would have to contribute something.

The more we talked, the more lighthearted and at ease we became. Jean laughed, interrupted me, acted as if freed from Heaven only knew what threatening danger. And, also reassured, I felt the dangerous and disquieting presence of love recede from us. We would certainly find it again, I thought, whenever we liked, that menacing companion which just a little frightened us. One cannot live every day of one's life in the presence of that encroaching, impossible, and inhuman love. One would need too much patience and abnegation. We had been lifted above ourselves, that night at the *Petit Matelot*, and we were afraid, now, at discovering our love and the demands it made upon us. To satisfy it, we would have to confess all the vanity of our past conduct, disavow ourselves. I would have to recognize not only that I had been wrong to take advantage of his permission to be unfaithful, but also that he had been wrong to give me permission to be unfaithful. Could we all at once return to those values we had overstepped, forget our pride, our quarrels, everything, even to the pleasures to come? Could we admit that just willing it was not enough to create a happy love, but that something else was also needed: a discipline which we had always rejected? No, we could not. At least, not yet. Later on, we told ourselves, as we shut the door upon that intruder who was trying to spoil our pleasures. Later on, when we should have the time, the patience, the courage, love would be there again. Yes, but would it always be humbly waiting there, ready to enter whenever we felt inclined to open the door? This thought troubled me for a moment, then I smiled again at what Jean was saying.

"And we'll not spat ever again, will we, stubborn little mule? What a lucky fellow I am that you're not jealous! If you were, I'm sure you'd not stop halfway."

"And what luck for me, that you're not jealous!" I said, also smiling.

It was the reply to make, wasn't it? Anyway, it was true. I would not be jealous. I thought of Stani for a moment. One of those little affairs without importance, such as Jean himself had in Paris. For reasons of health, he had said. Well, Stani would be my health treatment, or had been. How ridiculous it would have been of me to throw myself at his knees, melodramatically begging forgiveness! Love, bothersome love had almost shoved me into that. I remembered the day in the library, when I had shouted "Never!" and he had made fun of my tragedy-queen attitude. I could just imagine his stupefaction and the slightly shocked irony with which he would have heard my "Forgive me! I was unfaithful!" And I was glad that my pride had stopped me.

"I don't think you'll be unfaithful to me right away," he was saying. "No doubt it will take you some time to bring yourself to it. Just the same, you're rather sentimental, you must admit."

And I denied it, laughing.

"Then, since that's in your line, you'll find some lovely women in Paris, of Tamara's type, what do you say to that?"

I blushed under his teasing, but laughed again.

"Oh, I'm not in such a hurry to be unfaithful, you know . . ."

I was thoroughly enjoying this exchange of futilities, which held out promises of pleasures to come. I recalled Lucette, who kept a bookstore in our street. She had once attracted me, and I imagined other plump, white, beautiful women, the sort Tamara had become, I thought of Stani, and I smiled a little, with a slight feeling of superiority, because Jean believed I would not play around for awhile. I was having fun. How had we been able to hurt each other? We understood each other so well. I had already forgotten that this lighthearted understanding of today had only been made possible because, for a second, the door had opened upon a more dangerous love.

But when, to my impudent "Oh, I'm not in such a hurry to be unfaithful, you know" he replied more gravely, "I do know," I remembered it for a moment, as did he, too, perhaps, and a cloud passed over us.

X I X ·

He had gone. His departure was banal, without tragedy, the train getting under way, Jean giving me a last friendly little wave of the hand, then turning his back to look or pretend to look for something in his suitcase.

I came back home.

"And if Tamara hasn't said anything," I had asked Jean, "will we marry anyway?"

"After all, why not? Marriage it is!" he had replied with a smile.

Julia opened the door. She had nothing really to tell me.

"When you left," she said, "she came down to ask how you'd been able to get out. I said you must have climbed through the other attic window, which was open. So then she didn't say anything more, but it wouldn't surprise me if she's had a talk with Monsieur. She looked furious. What are you going to tell her?"

"Why, nothing but the truth," I said with some satisfaction. "He wants to marry me, so I have the right to see him."

"He wants to marry you?"

"Why, yes!"

"A man as old as that?" she asked, without the admiration I had expected.

"Oh, Julia, he's not old, he's only thirty-two."

"All the same, that's old for you," she said. "Oh, well! You'll find a young man to pay you attentions, like everyone."

"Most certainly not!" I said angrily. Did everything have to remind me of that unfortunate affair with Stani?

I went up to Father's study. Tamara was already there. At seeing her there, sitting familiarly on the arm of Father's chair and talking to him excitedly, I felt a shock.

"Come in, come in, Hélène," she said triumphantly. "We were just talking about you. I wouldn't be sorry to hear you explain to your father your running away this morning. Where did you go?"

"I had an appointment," I said vaguely, adding, " 'a rendezvous'." I could see she had not told Father everything she knew, and so did not want to get in too deep.

"That's just what I suspected," she said, half shocked, half sarcastic. Pretending to know nothing, she was making fun of me. I could see right away what she wanted: it was to make me feel my powerlessness against her, to confront me with an impossible choice—either to tell everything or nothing at all. And then, in calming down Father and minimizing the gravity of my conduct, she would put on a great show of generosity.

"For some time, now," she went on, "I've been aware of a great change in your behavior. That's why, this morning, I asked you to stay at home. Your slipping off like that confirmed my suspicions, and I was obliged to tell your father what had happened. Don't take what I did as a mean trick, my dear, but realize that I wanted to clear myself of any responsibility."

"Yes," Father said in his turn, "I don't even wish to reproach you, Hélène. Considering the frank admission you have just made, I only regret that you did not take us into your confidence sooner, and I ask you now to tell us just as sincerely with whom did you have this . . . appointment?"

This was what Tamara wanted to get out of me by her pretended lack of information. She believed I would have to tell a lie, and would need her to back me up, which would place me completely at her mercy.

"I think, my dear," she said maliciously, "that it would be wise to tell the *whole* truth to your father. He will certainly know better than you how you should conduct yourself. Who was the man you went to meet? The young Mierowicz, perhaps? I seem to have noticed a certain understanding between you two."

How she was facilitating the lie that should save me! How she was arranging things so I would be under an obligation to her!

"No," I cut in rather shortly. "I did not have a date with Stanislas. I had a date with Jean Delfau."

I saw Father's bright blue eyes widen a trifle with surprise. Tamara herself sat up, her eyes flashing with anger, obviously wondering by what miracle I dared attack her, confront her, and what were my weapons. She attempted to frighten me.

"With Jean Delfau! This is much more serious than I had feared. Hélène, do you mean to say you make appointments with that man who is older than you by at least fifteen years, who is no doubt corrupt, and that you do this on the sly, without the knowledge of your family? Why, child, are you aware of the risks you are running?"

She was going to continue, but my father interrupted her with a sharpness that astonished me.

"Tamara, will you be so kind as to allow me to deal with this affair? And even, may I ask you to leave Hélène and me alone together?"

"Why . . ." she said, astounded, "surely it is only right that she should explain herself . . ."

"She will explain herself more easily, I am sure, to her father, than to a kind of tribunal. Isn't it so, Lena? And anyway, this affair concerns only us two."

I thought this was a little hard on Tamara, who went out without a word, obviously annoyed. She must be wondering what excuses I would find for having seen Jean outside the house and must be puzzled at my self-assurance. This amused me sufficiently to be able to support the worried look my father was giving me.

"Now that we are alone, will you tell me exactly what induced you to grant Monsieur Delfau this . . . appointment?"

This language seemed very solemn to me. Clearly, my father counted on maintaining himself in the traditional pose of the outraged father. In another minute, he would be talking about regrettable imprudence, about the cowardly seducer, and even, perhaps, abused innocence . . . I had only to play my part in this scene written in advance.

"I did not grant him this appointment, I asked for it," I said, however, wishing to mix up the cards a little.

"Asked for it! Hélène, I hope I have misunderstood! Come, now! Under what pretext did this man induce you to do such a thing? And how does it come that he's in Gers?"

I saw that Father was absolutely determined to make me play the ridiculous rôle of the lamb led to the slaughter.

"Jean Delfau," I replied patiently, "came to Gers to see me. He came from Paris to see me. And he needed no pretext to tell me he wanted to see me."

"Hélène! What does that signify? What do these rebellious words mean?"

I wanted to check his anger, which I saw was ready to explode.

"He wants to marry me," I said flatly.

"Marry you? What's this? What's this?"

He seemed not to understand, but then suddenly his face cleared.

"I see: he's in love with you?" he said, as if he were translating my words from a foreign language.

"Why, yes."

"Since when?"

"Since we met," I said, deeply embarrassed by the vulgar indecency of his words.

My father inexplicably beamed.

"Oh, so that's it . . ." he muttered to himself.

I began to think that his good-natured behavior with Jean had concealed more jealousy than appeared on the surface. That Jean was asking for my hand in marriage signified to my father that Jean's visits to the house had been for me, not for Tamara, his attentions for me, not for her, and so it had been wrong, no doubt, to become anxious. In his relief, he forgot me completely. He stood up, sat down again, managed with great trouble to resume a serious expression suitable to the head of a family.

"This is more serious—and at the same time less serious—than I had thought, Hélène," he said gravely. "So there's been a proposal of marriage?"

"Yes, papa."

"And . . . do you love him, too?"

Not ever having said it, not ever as yet having been able to say it to Jean, and now to have to proclaim it indecently to my own father!

"Yes, papa."

"I consider," said Father, who had recovered his placid and slightly defiant manner, "I consider that Delfau might have taken the trouble to make this request to me himself. If I had not questioned you today, when would I have been deemed worthy of being informed as to your intentions?"

"Jean is planning to call on you when he returns from London. And anyway, he gave me this letter for you," I said in one breath, so as to end the ordeal. And I handed him the letter, which he took, grumbling.

"Well! After all! They deign to ask my advice!"

Wanting to leave him to his reflections, I started to go.

"Wait!" he called. "Don't go! We must discuss this, mustn't we? After all, you don't expect me to hand over my daughter in five minutes as if I were selling a length of cloth, do you? Well, now. So you want to get married? Yet you've turned down some of the most eligible men in Gers! Oh, as they say, sooner or later young girls see the light. But I would never have believed it, no, never! Well, my dear Hélène, rest assured that the decision I shall come to after mature reflection will be what I judge the most likely to bring you happiness!"

Did he really believe I was ready to abide by his decisions? True, I was dependent upon him—a thing I had almost forgotten during all those years of freedom.

"Now, my child, supposing we reassure Tamara, who is so worried about you?"

He called her. She came in immediately, no doubt having stayed in the hall, trying to overhear our words, and her face bore traces of a certain anxiety.

I went to the window, disassociating myself from the scene that followed, and Father did the talking.

"Tam, my dear, Hélène and I have discussed this affair very calmly and frankly, and I now realize how wrong you were to get so worked up. Hélène could and should have told us earlier of the attentions Monsieur Delfau was paying her, but those attentions in themselves were in no way culpable."

"Oh, really?" she asked ironically.

But her expression was troubled; this was now beyond her.

"No," said Father, and I noticed he was surveying her with a look of sudden suspicion. "No, there was nothing of what you feared in that appointment. Hélène has been imprudent, certainly, but she has not committed a grave fault: Monsieur Delfau, I have just been informed, intends to ask me for her hand in marriage."

I heard a kind of sob burst out, irrepressible, painful; it

was Tamara, laughing. She was laughing, with her head thrown back and an ugly sneer on her face.

"René," she said breathlessly, when at last she stopped laughing, "this is sheer folly! A man as reasonable as you are must realize that all this is only an idiotic lie, that Delfau supposed we would never find out and fooled the poor child in order to seduce her. Marry her? Why, it's preposterous!"

"Why preposterous?" asked Father in a slow and placid voice, even slower and more placid than the voice he used to discuss business. I could clearly see that Tamara's outburst awakened his jealousy. But she went right on protesting, almost stammering out the words in her eagerness to deny the insult she had been given: Jean wanted to marry me.

"Oh, come, René! A man like Jean"—she called him Jean, in her confusion—"a man who is rich, famous, lives in Paris where he can have any woman he wants, a man as well known as he is can't seriously think of marrying a girl like Hélène! At the most, he's amusing himself with her for a moment! Why, it's as old as Adam, promises of marriage like this! And you believe in it? How can you be so naïve?"

From the way Father was frowning, I could see that a storm was threatening, but she was blinded by her paltry wounded pride and saw nothing.

"I really do not understand," said Father, "why you so obstinately refuse to believe in Monsieur Delfau's sincerity. I have a letter here"—he pretended to rummage among his papers— "I have a letter here in which his intentions seem to be as serious as possible."

She took the letter without a word, read it, and handed it back.

"This does not convince me," she said primly. "Understandably, Monsieur Delfau was told by Hélène that I was aware of what was going on. This letter is nothing but a subterfuge, meant to force us . . ."

"Tamara, I think you are going too far," said Father.

I sensed more energy in him than I had ever seen, and a growing wrath.

"I don't believe that a man, even a Delfau, whose reputation is not spotless, proposes marriage to a young girl, with all the details he gives me as to his situation, his income, and does this simply as a joke. I confess I do not understand your persistence . . ."

"It's certainly normal for me to try to protect Hélène against . . ."

"No! It's not normal!" shouted Father. His anger had at last burst out. They stood confronting each other, Father towering over Tamara, who, divided between hatred and fear, was almost cowering, like a fearful animal brought to bay.

"I do not see what you're trying to insinuate," she said weakly.

"You see it all too well, on the contrary! You even understood me with a rapidity . . ."

He strode towards her, his huge hands doubled into fists, looking redoubtable, now that he had lost his good-natured smile. Tamara did not budge, but I saw that her lips were pale. Did she feel as guilty as all that for having let Jean flirt a little freely with her months ago? I must do something. If she confessed that Jean had made love to her before making love to me, my marriage might well not take place, and my father's jealousy might turn into an irresistible aversion for Jean.

I ran towards Father, stopping him two steps from her. What had he intended to do? Beat her? Kill her? He stood stockstill a moment, his eyes wild.

"Papa! Why, what's happening?" I cried in a tearful voice. "I don't understand! Tam didn't know that Jean and I were in love! I didn't want to talk about it before I was sure. It was perhaps wrong of me, but you mustn't quarrel on account of me . . ."

"You—you stay out of this," said Father. But his first impulse had been checked, and he went back to his desk where he sat down. "To end up with, Tamara," he said in a conciliating tone, "you can perhaps understand that I am astonished to see you so upset over something as normal as Hélène's receiving an offer of marriage, at her age . . ."

She straightened up, recovered her self-possession. She must realize as I did that my father's explosion had momentarily exhausted his reserves of energy and that he was now ready to blush at his brutality.

"You can perhaps also understand," she replied, "that I am astonished to see you consider so calmly an offer which concerns the happiness or the unhappiness of your daughter."

"Of course," he said in a still gentler voice, "I can explain your emotion if you really believed Delfau was lying to Hélène; but now that you know . . ."

She did not give him time to finish.

"Now that you condescend to render me justice, I should no doubt feel very happy at being consulted? No, my dear René, I have been insulted enough for one time. I no longer pretend to mix into *your* affairs, as you put it, so I shall leave you to your discussions."

Thereupon she went out with great dignity. Father remained stupefied at this retaliation. He must be calling to mind what Tamara's wrath meant to him—three or four days when she would not talk at mealtime, would not deign to pay any attention to his clothes, his goings and comings, would refuse to listen to his official speeches or to accompany him to a banquet or entertain his big customers . . . Three or four nights when the door of her bedroom would be shut . . ."

"Well, papa," I said timidly, "what about my marriage?"

He brought down his fist on the table with a bang that made some pencils jump and splashed a few drops of ink.

"What in thunderation do I care about your marriage?" he yelled.

The days passed. Jean wrote little, almost not at all. I was agitated in an incomprehensible way. Sometimes I bitterly groaned, "How happy I was before I loved him!" And then I would pull myself together and try to take a more rational view. "All right," I reflected, "I'm in love, so what? I've talked to Father, he's weighing the question. When he has estimated the weight in gold, he'll say yes, because you can't undo a thirty-year-old habit and for thirty years he has assented to any offer that was worthwhile. Jean and I will be married, we'll live together. He loves me, too. We fought hard against it, but that's over, now, everything is simple and easy, there's nothing to do but just drift." Something inside me was not convinced, however. Something kept saying, "No, love isn't so simple, it's more difficult, more demanding. You've already felt that, so why deny it? You must write to Jean, confess that fault, even if he sees no importance in it. You must turn back, reexamine every issue. One can't just choose a part of love and reject the rest . . ." I no longer took solitary morning walks in the narrow streets down by the harbor.

After Father's outburst of jealousy, he and Tamara had of course become reconciled, and Tamara tried by every means to be alone with me. Was it to thank me for having turned aside Father's wrath? Was it in the hope that I would confess something to her? No matter what it was, I cleverly avoided it, pretending to have something urgent to do, or to answer someone who was calling me, and I fled, upset at the idea that she might notice how confused and tormented I was. I also avoided Stani, whose repeated telephone calls finally became a subject of ridicule in the house. I had already refused three times to see him. He was harassing me now with letters and telephone calls, pretending he needed my advice and my presence, and he was even telling this to my father, who laughed a great deal at such pertinacity.

"You can't say you're not in demand, Hélène. Oh, love attracts love, as the saying goes. What a host of suitors . . . But I must say, I still prefer Delfau to Odette's little painter! Happily, you're not old enough for that sort of thing!"

I received a letter from Jean, once more postponing his arrival, saying he would be detained in London on account of changes being made in the film for which he was doing the sets. "Believe me, I regret it," he wrote, "I'm eager to play the rôle of fiancé, particularly the fiancé of a young woman of Gers. This dignified and Victorian film has completely put me into the mood. I am therefore writing to your father, in the appropriately respectful terms, assuring him no *volte-face* is implied. As for you, I suppose there's no question of doubt; I therefore repeat the assurances of fidelity of the sort worthy of a German melodrama."

A little further on, after having given a few details regarding the difficulties of his life there, he incidentally recounted an affair he had had with one of the English actresses, "disconcertingly stupid, only her accent makes her endurable." As compensation, a few words of tenderness followed.

This letter plunged me into frightful doubts, an infinite distress. Was it simply jealousy? No, for I was almost sure that Jean took very little pleasure in winning the hearts of English movie actresses. And if I tried hard, I could even understand the mechanism of his infidelity, and of the need he had to tell me about it. He needed to have my jealousy, just enough to show him that I suffered; he needed to have my tolerance, to show him that I understood; and he also needed to prove both to himself and to me that the minute he arrived in a town he could seduce a girl without making the least effort. I could so well imagine him sitting in a swank restaurant (did he not have the means to dazzle any woman?) eating the conventional bad-tasting things, flirting, in that detached and casual way of his, with that powdered and painted girl, still naïve, with that naïveté that smells of cheap perfume and tries to assume the look of being used to such expensive places . . . And he, too, trying to play a rôle, the rôle of a blasé, well-known man, out on the town, while in fact his entire happiness resided in the admiring look cast at him by the producer sitting at the other end of the room, who whispered to his faded wife, "That Delfau! How does he do it? He makes all the girls . . ."

And then they would go back to the Ritz (or the Mayfair, or the Savoy) into a room without form or odor, clean and invisible as an operating room, and they would make love, since that was why they were there, without much pleasure, but being sweet to each other like sick people, and next day Jean, who was a good sort, would offer Gloria (or Ingrid, or Jenny or Mariette) money to pay two months rent or buy an electric stove or an up-to-date coat she needed, or possibly even some good regular meals. And Mariette, Ingrid, or Gloria, feeling momentarily surrounded with this slightly melancholy and fundamentally disinterested kindness, and also, even the stupidest of them, feeling in that kindness a secret distress, would fall in love with him just a little and, without knowing it, would bestow charity by writing to him, during two or three weeks, some very silly love letters on perfumed paper.

I could understand that. I could also understand that if he still had to have that cheap solace, it was because I did not provide him with enough. I decided to write to him, that very evening, a letter in which I would tell him everything, about my distress, my doubts, my brief affair with Stani, and also how much I loved him. I would tell him that I had made a mistake, that we had both made a mistake, but that everything was still new and open ahead of us.

I came back from the postoffice, where I had picked up his letter addressed "general delivery," too engrossed in thought to be able to avoid Tamara, who was on the lookout for me. She called out, in an almost timid voice.

"Hélène!"

I was already going up the stairs, impossible not to reply, impossible to avoid her.

"Yes?"

"For several days I've wanted to talk to you. Won't you come into my room for five minutes?"

"I don't have much time just now, I . . ."

"I only ask for five minutes."

Resigned, I followed her. What could she want? To shout and threaten and say mean things about Jean? Slowly and carefully she closed the door. She must be thinking up her first sentences, I thought, as I sat down on her bed, ready to fight. Perhaps she would turn my mind a little from the thoughts that were obsessing me? She sat down, too. She seemed embarrassed.

"It's about . . . about your marriage that I want to talk to you."

"Oh, really? Is there something about it you don't like?"

"No, no, that's not what I wanted to say."

"Happily," I said drily. Was she pretending her embarrassment? What was she getting at?

"The other day, you may have thought, you may have believed that I was hostile to your plans, and I must say that, in fact, I was so surprised . . ."

"I certainly noticed that."

"Admit, there was a reason?" she said, not without a faint revival of malice. And with a more assured tone, she went on. "But I wanted to clear up the misunderstanding that may exist between us."

"How will you do that?"

"Why . . . by assuring you formally that you will no longer find me in the least opposed to your plans, either openly or secretly."

I did not understand very well.

"And may I ask what has caused this rather abrupt about-face?"

"You may perhaps have remarked," she said in a lower tone,

"that the scene of the other day rather . . . how shall I say?
. . . rather upset me?"

"I certainly did remark it. And I wasn't the only one."

I expected an angry retort, but she merely said, "I know. I
was afraid."

"You, afraid? Well! That was the only thing that lacked!"

"You don't understand me, Hélène," she said quickly. "Or
else, you make a point of not understanding. I was not afraid
for myself. You might say I had less fear for myself than for
him."

I supremely disliked her serious air. And what signified these
unsolicited confessions?

"Really! Afraid for him! And why, may I ask? That he might
have had a heart attack?"

She sighed.

"You are answering me as you would have answered me a
. . . a year ago. I did not expect this."

"Why not?" I asked fiercely, sensing danger. "What's
changed, since a year? Aren't we just where we were?"

She looked at me with a surprise that seemed sincere.

"Just where we were? Why, Hélène, after all, aren't you in
love with Jean?"

"Let's not talk about Jean, I beg of you. Jean has nothing to
do with this conversation, and the feelings I may have for him
are still more out of place."

"Even so, I had hoped . . . See here, Hélène, you can understand how I felt when I saw that look of suspicion on your
father's face, and when I realized, during the following days,
that the regrettable scene was haunting him, threatening his
tranquility, our understanding, our . . ."

"Your very home, go on, say it, I won't laugh. At this point,
a little more or less melodrama . . ."

"Exactly, our home!" she cried, suddenly rearing up. "What
do you know about my relations with your father? How can

you judge us or understand that, when someone places total confidence in us and we betray it even to the slightest degree, we suffer remorse, regret, to the point of facing the worst—and the worst for me, Hélène, is, I swear it, to endure your stupid obstinacy, your contemptuous airs—in an effort to make amends and regain that confidence?"

"And after all, you do suffer remorse?"

"Yes, I do, and it's nobody's business but my own," she said, with a hard look on her face which for a second resembled the one I had loved. "Anyhow, that's not what I wanted to tell you. I merely wanted to assure you that I will back you up, if you ever need it in regard to your father. And I wanted to tell you that the other day I only gave in to a feeling of spite, perhaps animosity—you see, I'm being frank—but that was all. I'm not in love with Jean, never was, and I'll even go so far as to hope that this marriage will take place. It will bring serenity to your father and, I hope, happiness to you."

"Not counting that it will assure your own tranquility, which was a little threatened the other day by your touchingly frank behavior," I smiled.

I could not but recognize, in the confession she had just made, something superior to the state of mind in which she had lived up to then, a certain courage, and even a kind of grandeur. But I did not want to help her justify herself or clear her own conscience. She was using my love for Jean, was daring to invoke my love for Jean, in order to obtain a cowardly approbation from me, and I would not give her that satisfaction. She too, like the dog, like the beggar, thought she had the right to make demands upon me and what she demanded was for me to forget these years of deceit, bitterness, contempt, these years which had been so hard, so costly, so laboriously constructed, maintained at such a price, and for which suddenly, thanks to love, I was to forgive her and, without more delay, bestow upon her a gift of that serenity which I myself did not enjoy. She could have asked it of me a hundred times, a thousand times, and I would not have pronounced for her that phrase which would end everything and make everything for the best in the best of possible worlds.

Meanwhile, she was nervously pacing the room, her black hair flung back, her wan face distorted in the effort she was making to convince me.

"Hélène, what you say is not true. You yourself know its not true. If I wanted to fool myself, wouldn't it be easier to pretend that I never failed your father's trust, that I never indulged in anything more serious with Jean than a trifling flirtation, not worth thinking about? It's so easy to convince ourselves that a slip of that kind is not a fault, that we're not really being unfaithful when we're not in love, and the only thing to do is just forget."

What she said had stung me to the quick. Was it possible that Tamara knew . . . No, it was only a coincidence. Her agitation and confusion proved that she was thinking only of herself, that no allusion to me had intentionally slipped into her words. Yet what she said stung me, accused me, oppressed me atrociously. Every one of her words was a reproach to me: I did not want to hear any more. Angrily I turned upon her.

"It's not true, what you say! It's not true, all your edifying remorse, your Jeremiads which come a little too late! You're talking like those women who have lost their looks and convince themselves they are chaste for religious reasons. But what you said a while ago was true: you were afraid, and that's all, of losing your comfort, afraid of being alone again, afraid of sinking again into that poverty you don't deserve now. And because you are ashamed of having been afraid, you're trying to be admired by making a spectacular repentance. It would be a triumph for you, wouldn't it, if you could convince me? It would be your master stroke, your final performance as an illusionist! The Illustrious Tamara will now, before your eyes, turn herself into a Magdalene! Silence, roll of drums . . . Well, I don't believe in your repentance. I don't believe in your tears, your cries, your clever little stage-setting. It all happened a little too conveniently, don't you think? You'll have to think up something else, next time. Oh, you'll have no trouble doing so, I know you. And supposing you tried playing the vamp again, just for a change? Languishing eyes, exotic writhings, all the rest of it, the way you did with Jean. Oh, come now! Think up something else. Surely, you're not stalled, are you?"

I stopped, out of breath, waiting for her to scream, protest, show noisy and voluble indignation. But she stood there motionless, her face flaming, her eyes almost wild, and her voice seemed changed when she said, almost inaudibly,

"You don't love Jean, Hélène."

X X ·

That evening, I climbed towards the Plain of Camp. The prairies were all white, it was the indistinct hour when evening resembles morning, because it, too, is about to give birth to something, but the evening is lovelier, for the "something" is the night. A horse stood on the pale prairies, its head raised, Apocalyptic and sad. The lines of willow trees separating the fields stretched their shadows towards each other, without being able to touch and without knowing that in a little while the night would merge them. And the white farm houses were not yet reassuring, because the peasants, wishing to use the last scrap of daylight, had not yet lit the porcelain lamps. From this incertitude was born a kind of peace.

I sat down on a bench in the shadows. I remained a long time there, thinking about Jean's letter and about Tamara's last words. Yes, I did love Jean, I could have gone so far as to forgive him for that infidelity he bragged about; but I did not want that forgiveness to be the first of many. "You don't love Jean, Hélène." And to think it was Tamara who had said that, Tamara who set herself up to judge this love! It was almost comical. That scene with Tamara had been perfectly absurd, the only thing to do was forget it. Well then, where did it come from, this malaise I could not shake off?

A dark, slender figure was climbing towards me, I did not recognize Stani until he was two steps away. I would have gladly avoided him, but he was so obviously looking for me, and there I was on the bench.

"Hélène! You can't imagine what a time I've had finding you. They told me at your house that you'd gone for a walk on the Plain, but I wasn't sure it was true."

"What, you went to my house?"

I felt almost sick at the thought of Stani's and Tamara's encounter. This made me forget my displeasure at seeing him.

"I don't see why I shouldn't go to your house from time to time, you used to come to the Rue d'Ecosse to see me," he said aggressively. "And then, I wanted to talk to you, and it's become almost impossible to reach you by 'phone. I'm sure you've had a lot to do, but after all, you might have told me, at least."

I did not understand what he was talking about in that odd, peevish way.

"Told you what?"

"Why, that you've taken it into your head to marry Delfau. When your stepmother threw out the idea the other day at Odette's that he was in love with you, I thought she was joking, everyone did. You might have told me then what it was all about. Oh, well! What's done is done, and I must say you've managed rather well. Delfau! I have to admit, he's a good catch. The firm of Delfau, Gunther, and Company—that's something."

"So, if I understand correctly, what you came here for was to congratulate me?"

"Well, yes and no. I also wanted to ask you about our future, what arrangements I'm to make, see. You know, I've got to get the maximum out of Odette before I leave her, she's absolutely crazy about me, wants to make over the apartment in the Rue de l'Anneau to me, is going to buy me a car, and so on. But I mustn't seem to hurry her; it'll take about a month."

"Stani, what in the world are you talking about? You seem to be mixing up things frightfully: my marriage, Odette and her gifts. What do you mean by the arrangements you've got to make? And to begin with, why do you want to leave Odette? You'll not find another like her, there aren't many women who'll give you cars and apartments."

I was forcing myself to take an interest in his affairs, so as to forget my own tormenting thoughts. Sitting beside me on the bench, he stared at the ground, an obstinate look on his face.

"You're the one that doesn't understand a thing," he said testily. "Tell me, is he thinking of living in Gers, your Delfau?"

"Certainly not."

"Then what will we do, what about the two of us?"

With stupefaction I grasped his meaning.

"The two of us? Why, Stani, there's no problem about you and me. We are not united for life. Heavens! I found Odette for you, so get all you can out of that. But don't imagine I'm going to drag you after me for the rest of my life."

"Oh, surely now, you're not going to drop me like this," he said coaxingly, and I was amazed to see that he thought I was joking.

"Stani, I'm going to live in Paris with Jean," I said, as if talking to a child. "I'm going to marry him. What in the world could I do with you there? Be reasonable . . ."

He shrugged.

"I can see why you're marrying Delfau. It's to checkmate your stepmother, who was in love with him. And then, of course, you don't exactly spit on his fortune, and he's famous. That's all understood. But all the same, you love me, Lena, and you can't just go off and leave me."

I began to laugh. This was too much, he was overdoing it. He must be dying to go to Paris and begin all over again with me the seductive stuff that had succeeded so well with Odette Périer. Perhaps he was even going to try a little blackmail? But he was too weak, I knew, to go that far, and his mother, his saintly mother who was so devoted to me since I introduced Stani to Odette, would be able to stop him.

"All you have to do is persuade Odette to take you to Paris, if you want to go there that much. But don't count on me to pull you out of here. Don't you think I've done enough for you? You're well housed, you're spoiled, you're covered with good tweed and flannel, you'll soon be driving your own car . . ."

"But, Lena, we can't separate like this, coldly, without . . . without . . ."

That was what I expected. Without a doubt, he was now going to talk about a farewell present, perhaps a rather important one, and if not, then a little talk with Jean would . . . I smiled in advance at what I was going to say in reply. But the demand I expected did not come. Instead, I suddenly heard a curious sound, and raised my eyes. Stani's face was streaming with tears. Stani was crying! A warm, beneficial flood of anger overwhelmed me. If Stani, Stani himself was beginning to play at being sentimental, where on earth would I ever find peace?

"Stop crying at once," I said furiously. "Stop it, or I'll go right off and leave you."

Already, with a too elegant silk handkerchief, he was wiping his eyes. His smile of a weakling reappeared.

"I was sure you were joking," he said, raising his pale lips to me. I pushed him away, but without roughness.

"I'm not joking. I don't want to see you again, I haven't the

213

least desire to see you, I can't imagine any reason for it, that's all. You bore me, I don't like you any more, I don't even want to hear anything about you any more."

His deathly pale face, no longer trying to be attractive, had the rather terrifying beauty of a corpse. It was the first time I had ever seen him absolutely motionless like that. He was no longer using his charm, no longer showing off, no longer convinced that all he had to do was be himself, that to look upon him was to love him. His long hands lay inertly on his knees, his eyes were full of an immense surprise which greatly added to his good looks.

"But Hélène," he went on after a moment in a hushed voice, "after all, you needn't be afraid of having me on your hands. I'm not poor any more. A month from now, the apartment will be in my name. I'll even be able to sell it, mamma could still stay on there. And in addition"—he was speaking feverishly again, his color had come back for a moment, and as he counted up his fortune on his fingers, he looked like the remote little Polish peasant who must have been his ancestor—"in addition, look. There'll be the car. New. It'll be worth around five hundred thousand. The garage man will buy it back right away. And there's the sketch by Degas that's in my room, it's worth a lot, too. And I have some clothes I could hock. I don't need all that. And the watch, the big bracelet is platinum, have you noticed?" He bared his wrist. "It's heavy. With all that, I must have two millions to begin life in Paris, don't you think? Delfau knows people, you'll find me another woman like Odette, and I've saved some money. So I'll be able to hold out a little while and not seem to give a damn. You know, I'll not cost you anything. Hélène, won't it be nice to be together there? We'll save a little money, later on we'll have an income, and we'll never leave each other. Okay?"

At one point I had almost laughed at this bourgeois aspiration—to save money, invest it, live on the income, do nothing. But the touch of his hands on my arm and the new tenderness on his face filled me with horror. Was he, too, demanding tenderness and comprehension? Did he also, he whom I had believed more insensitive and indifferent than a cat or a horse, did he also want to cling to me, be consoled and understood? I had kissed the indifference and cowardice that lay upon his lips; and now he was turning into a desolate little boy whose fretful face badly concealed the tears ready to spring again, whose eyes implored pity, even tried to stir remorse. Oh, of course! It was my fault that he loved me! I shook him furiously. It wouldn't have taken much to make me slap him.

"Even if you had more money than Delfau I wouldn't want you, get that into your head. Even if I were dying of hunger I wouldn't want you any more. Even if you had the power to kill me I wouldn't want you any more."

His bewildered look filled me with joy.

"But I love you, Hélène," he said stupidly. "You're the one that came to me, you're the one that found Odette for me, why did you do that if you didn't love me?"

Again that responsibility they were all trying to saddle me with! In another minute, as Tamara had done, he would be clamoring for pity, in the name of my love for Jean.

"I came to your house for the very reason that I didn't love you," I said very gently, "just because I held you in contempt and because I found it impossible ever to love you. There, that's why I came to your house!"

He sat there, apparently crushed, his arms outstretched, his fine hands clutching the back of the bench, his face lifted, as if my words had stabbed him in the heart, and with his pale lips making him look so like a marvellous corpse that I could not resist, before leaving him, pressing upon those lips a last possessive kiss. It was a rather melodramatic gesture, as theatrical as one could wish, lacking only a murmured "Adieu!" to ring down the curtain in a Dumas cape-and-sword play.

Stani not seeming to respond, I left him, returning towards the town. Just when I was on the point of entering the narrow

215

lighted street that led down towards the railway station, I turned to look. Playing his part in the tragedy, Stani had not budged. In the growing darkness I could see his distant silhouette, motionless on the bench.

"What a reserve of emotions beneath that cold exterior!" I said to myself, lightly parodying the style of a serial-story. "He loved me in silence! Well, all he had to do was suffer likewise. That will teach him to love me! He, too, will learn."

After this summary execution, there was nothing for me to do but go home and to bed. However, I had no wish to find myself alone in my room, reflecting . . . So I continued to walk, going beyond the park. Stani's outburst had been too much. I had been right to jump down his throat. After all, why should one feel obliged to accept protestations of love from a man one doesn't love? From a man . . . I recalled his pathetic, distorted face. "Why, then, did you come?" he had whimpered, naïvely. I was right to repel him brutally, he now knew what to expect. Considering my relations with Jean, it would not have been very nice of me to go on listening to Stani's absurdities.

I continued down the steep streets until I reached the station, where the dingy lights were being turned on. In vain did I try to check the thought that was turning round and round in my mind, as regular as a clock: "My relations with Jean . . ." Was that really true? As far as Jean was concerned, wouldn't a confession have been enough—that confession I hadn't been able to make? "If I were a man," I reflected, "I'd go to a brothel." I yearned for oblivion, for degradation, even. Alcohol? But it took too much time. While I was sitting on a café terrace drinking enough wine or beer to black out, I would have to go on listening to the continual murmur of that thought and it would bore me to tears. I could not face going back to that house where Tamara would still, perhaps, not be asleep—Tamara, also demanding, also pitiable, Tamara, who had said, "You don't love Jean, Hélène!"

I went past the station and up the long boulevard lined with trees. In the beer-houses they were already stacking the chairs for the night, impatiently waiting for the last customers to leave. Stani's bewildered face . . . The face of a child I had intentionally hurt, Stani whom I had wanted to keep in his state of depravity, but who might escape it through grief . . . I could hear his reproachful voice saying, "Why, if you did not love me?" And I could hear another voice saying, "You do not love Jean, Hélène." How could she, of all people, know the trouble I had had not to love him at once, the trouble I was now having as a result of loving him. I reached the Post Office square, so neat and naïve with its standard lamps of wrought iron and its plane-trees. The *Café de l'Imprimerie*, a little old dump, was still open. I went in, and sat down at one of the greenish marble tables under the spiral staircase leading up to the telephone.

"Bring me a glass of rum," I said.

The white-haired old waiter with the twitching mouth looked at me in surprise. I must seem very young to him, too young to give such an order, and especially so late in the evening. He tried to look pleasant and managed to utter some harsh sounds with that twitching mouth.

"Coca-cola with a little rum?" he suggested.

"No. A straight rum," I said shortly.

His nervous tic became exaggerated, he squinted up his eyes, and I thought how terribly like an old duck he looked. He brought me the rum and while I drank it he stood in front of me, leaning against the bar, blinking his eyes, twitching his mouth, visibly upset because a young girl came at nightfall and asked for a glass of rum.

"Another rum, please," I said sweetly.

He almost jumped.

"Well?" I asked, "is it closing time?"

"No, no, Mam'selle. Closing time—one o'clock. Account of Gazette men—they work late."

"Well, then, bring me another rum," I said firmly, disgusted with myself for having entered the one café in town where my timid excesses would reduce the waiter to despair. I drank down the second rum, my eyes on the wall decorations behind the counter. Apparently representing the seasons, four women, very *fin de siècle*, disported themselves in various landscapes— in the snow, in a meadow full of primroses, in the sand dunes (that one was naked, she represented Summer) and in the midst of purplish trellises—with such an identical swaying of the hips that they could have been taken for music-hall girls of a rather special kind. But their four evils—even the naked one wore a hat —showed that, despite their physical seductions, these ladies knew how to stand on their dignity.

I studiously surveyed these old-fashioned ceramics. Winter was a beautiful brunette with a fur collar, Spring was a blonde, a pale and anemic Englishwoman. I called to mind Jean's little English actress. Why couldn't he just have taken private satisfaction in that conquest? Why did he also have to tell me about it? And afterwards, there had been a few words of tenderness, as if to take the venom out of the preceding lines . . . The fat round clock, framed in plaster curlicues representing foliage and birds' nests, made a loud, very regular tick-tock. Two men in shirtsleeves entered and immediately went into the back room, where a billiard-table could be glimpsed. They shut the ground-glass door behind them.

Inplacably, the thought pursued its way, like a persistent animal burrowing its hole and knowing that it is going towards the light. As if to take the venom out of the preceding lines . . . Suddenly the words seesawed and, viewed upside down, they became clear, crushingly clear. Why did he talk about the little English actress, if not to take the venom out of the following lines? It was not the tenderness which should soften the brutal frankness, it was the frankness which should render the tenderness innocuous, harmless, unimportant. I was not the only one to fear the disquieting power of love. He, also, felt, already knew that we had not with impunity stepped into this domain. He, also, was struggling against getting too much involved. What better proof that I was not mistaken, that the danger was there, close, close to us?

"A glass of rum, please."

The waiter gave it without further protest, but in definite despair he poured himself a glass and gulped it down. On the ground glass of the door could be seen the silhouettes of the billiard players. The light sharp sound of the colliding balls could be heard.

So I would have to begin all over again, revise everything? In order to love Jean and be happy with him, I must forgive Tamara, regret the few hours accorded Stani, accept the English actress, admit that Tamara's repentance was sincere, and ascribe Stani's love to my imprudence? As for Jean, he acted in his own way; he would always manage to do that, I was sure. Never would he admit that he needed me, that he suffered on account of his paralyzed arm, that he blushed at his wealth. "The patience of an angel," Manuelita had said. I did not want to be an angel.

My heart pounded. There was nothing I could do to stop the rebellious little thought. I might as well leave, go on wandering in the streets, be afraid of going home, instead of staying there in this too peaceful café. I paid, and, wanting to say something to that unfortunate who, grimacing, brought me the bill, which he had scrawled on a scrap of paper, I remarked, "Isn't it tiresome to stand such long hours on your feet?"

The pathetic lips twitched still more and his eyes blinked several times before he managed to articulate a reply.

"No matter . . . I live alone . . . I'm an orphan."

"Oh!" I said. "What a shame . . ."

"No matter . . . We all have our troubles . . . Don't worry."

Outside in the darkness, I leaned my back against the wall, feeling a little sick. That terrible mouth, that fifty-year-old man saying he was an orphan. And above all, that smile which tried to comfort me, me . . . Again I felt the same pity that had overwhelmed me for the toothless woman, it had sneaked up on me again, and there was nothing I could do about it. I did not want, no, I did not want them to enter into my love, I wanted to enclose Jean, alone, in my heart, leaving outside all the rest of the world. But was this possible? Did not every veritable love open up a breach, letting in more and more love? I was filled with an aching revolt, and yet that burrowing thought in me was still climbing towards the light. Wasn't there anything to do to escape it?

I do not know whether some power came to my aid—if so, it was a power of darkness—but suddenly I perceived a familiar figure, walking on the other side of the square, and a cry of triumph almost broke from my lips: "Yes, there is still something to do!"

Since Jean was trying to take all venom out of our love, why should I not do the same? Of course, it was Stani. Had I forgotten that he had to pass by the post office to reach the Rue de l'Anneau? Or had I dimly calculated on meeting him when, almost home again, I had continued my walk? What did it matter, in the long run? I went towards that shadowy figure.

Stani turned quickly, as if fearing an attack.

"What's this? My God! Hélène! Is it really you?"

"Who else?" I said. "A ghost?"

"I don't know. What are you doing here? I don't understand," he stammered.

He still had that haggard look of awhile ago, his eyes were red.

"You came to look for me, I'm returning the compliment," I said suavely. "Are you in a hurry?"

"No, no, but . . . Lena, would you mind coming home with me?"

"Why, I'd like to."

Momentarily disconcerted, he blushed, then his fatuous smile suddenly beamed forth.

"Yes," I slowly said, "I still love you."

I had never said those dangerous words to Jean, but to Stani I said them. With a spontaneous and graceful movement, he laid his head on my shoulder.

"Kiss me," he said.

I gave him a long kiss. Two men who were coming out of the print shop on their way towards the café bumped into us, laughingly excusing themselves.

"Come home with me," Stani implored.

But I had thought of something better.

"No, no, I don't want to disturb your mother. I know a very good place . . ."

He followed me without a word. Twenty minutes later we were standing at the front door of Clara Vaes' house. I rang the bell furiously. After a few minutes, she came to open the door, her head bristling with curlers, her barrel-like body bundled up in a Japanese kimono, her eyes heavy with sleep, but affable as usual.

"Well, well, Mademoiselle!" she cried, ready to shower me with cordialities, but as soon as she glimpsed Stani she pretended, with infinite tact, not to recognize me.

"Glad to see some customers," she said, "I was just thinking to myself what a very quiet night it was here. So, my lady and gentleman, you would like to have a room. Let me see, there's room number six free . . ."

"Give us the red room, Madame Vaes," I interrupted. It mattered little whether Stani found out that I already knew the house, and for what I wanted to accomplish, the red room was *necessary*.

"Oh, all right," said the stout creature, a little annoyed at finding her discretion was useless. "In that case, you know the way . . ."

We went upstairs.

"It's Delfau's room, eh?" said Stani, smiling. He easily lapsed into vulgarity.

"Yes."

"Isn't it a little dangerous?"

How I liked the fearful look on his face! And he pretended to love me!

"No, it's not dangerous. If Madame Vaes took it into her head to tell all the secrets she knows, not many people in town would be able to get a good night's sleep."

Yes, it was the same red room, a little dormant, a little neglected during the several weeks we had not come there, having by this absence of ours lost some of its maleficence, but quite ready to revive and stretch forth its venomous flower.

"Ritually," I told myself in a kind of daze. It must take place ritually, like an exorcism. For what was it if not that?

"There," I said to Stani, indicating the garnet-red chair. "Put your clothes there."

He obeyed without a word. This succession of events must have bewildered him slightly. His face was not quite the same, it was swollen like the face of a stunned boxer who still remains on his feet but no longer understands what's happening. I felt no pity for him. For the toothless woman, and for the waiter in the café I had felt pity. For Tamara, I could have felt pity if I had allowed myself to. But for him, no, it was his own fault. All he had to do was stay out of a domain which should have remained closed to him. I had chosen him to protect me from love, and he had made himself an accomplice of love; he had only himself to blame for what was going to happen.

The glided caryatids gleamed in the shadows, and as always arched out their polished breasts. I went towards Stani, where he stood by the window, and clasped him in my arms. I kissed his face, smooth as a pebble, kissed his throat and his perfect shoulders. Trembling slightly, he surrendered to my embrace.

"Oh, I love you terribly!" he suddenly declared, with such an infantine enthusiasm that he was rejuvenated by five or six years and it was almost the face of a little boy that I was kissing. "I know why you were angry just now. You're jealous of Odette, perhaps you think I oughtn't to have accepted the apartment, you're afraid I'm in love with her. But you know, I don't love her at all, and if you like, I would even . . . Well, if you *really* like, I won't take the apartment. Now that mamma's there . . ."

Sincerity could be read on his face. I felt like bursting out laughing: Stani, regenerated by love! And just as I had been indulgent towards a scheming, hypocritical, and indifferent Stani, so I was correspondingly filled with anger and cruelty towards this love-sick Stani. Did he imagine love was that simple? A man and a woman were attracted to each other, they went to bed together, said "I love you" and henceforth lived tranquilly until the day when they fell in love with someone else? Then what about my sufferings? And what about our hesitations, Jean's and mine, before that word which we had not said? All that did not exist for Stani. I envied him, I detested him. How could I have the least remorse in using him as an instrument?

We lay down together. He was in Jean's place exactly, his dark hair lay on the same pillow. He was much handsomer than Jean, incontestably. Anyone would have believed, seeing us together, that Jean was the rich protector whom I was deceiving and flouting, while Stani was my true love, my "paramour." After this sacrilege, would love leave me in peace? I pressed Stani's brown body to mine.

"I love you," I said intently, "I love you."

"*I've* reserved some excellent seats where you'll have a fine view of the Carnival," Father said affably. "You've never witnessed a Carnival in our country, I believe?"

"No," Jean replied, "and it's a cause for regret. I've been told that some of the customs observed are exceedingly strange."

"Yes, people come from a distance to see this. Tamara, you have, I hope, attended to reserving those seats for Hélène and her, uh, fiancé?"

He had hesitated a trifle but the word was finally pronounced, to everyone's relief.

"Yes, yes, they are excellent seats," she said, without raising her eyes.

"And you'll have the pleasure," Father went on with slightly forced joviality, "you'll have the pleasure of seeing me go by in the float of the Fools. I have a new and gorgeous costume; old Maalens' outfit was decidedly too tight for me."

"What? You mean to say the Mayor's place in the procession is with the Fools?"

Jean and Father were doing their best to make conversation, while Tamara and I remained silent.

"Why, my dear fellow, not only the burgomaster but all his associates, the aldermen, all the leaders of the city government! Once a year the entire citizenry have the pleasure of treating those in power like fools. It's an old tradition, you know. And you'll not find any city official who would ever dare not to adapt himself to the requirements of the masquerade; there'd be a real scandal if this ever happened!"

"A very healthy custom, it seems to me," said Jean. "They

ought to establish it in France. I can just imagine how our ministers would love it!"

We went into the drawingroom for the coffee. It was all over, and my father had given his consent to my marriage. Now, a little disconcerted by this unexpected son-in-law, he was nevertheless trying to carrying it off. He and Jean exchanged polite civilities, discussed politics. Tamara scarcely looked at me. She still held a grudge against me for not having entered into her game of repentance. And I was stiff, constrained, quite conscious, from the surprised glances my father gave me, that I should have shown greater joy and more expansiveness and shy modesty in this ridiculous role of blushing fiancée; I was not doing what was expected of me.

After coffee, my father jocularly and almost naughtily suggested that Jean and I take a walk together. "You don't have to hide any more, now that you're engaged!" he said. And Jean smiled tolerantly.

We strolled down to the harbor. Everything was tranquil there, the boats had come in, the nets were drying in the sun. Near a Chinese restaurant, two golden children were playing with a kind of yo-yo, quietly and charmingly. We went across the pier to sit down at the end of the jetty.

"It's sad, like Sunday," said Jean, "but perhaps Sundays aren't sad until one's grown up."

"Sundays are always sad," I replied, calling to mind the melancholy afternoons spent in listening to the church bells, waiting for the horrible next day of school, unable to take advantage of a freedom that was too brief.

"Why no, I assure you I remember some very gay Sundays in my childhood. When I was six years old, for instance, I always went for a drive on the boulevards or in the park with my grandmother. Her carriage was drawn by a frightful little yellow horse she was very fond of. I was always wanting the sun. I would say to her, very reasonably, 'Grandmother, I want the sun.' "

"And did she say Yes?"

"Invariably. She was as serious about it as I was. She would pick up her acoustic horn and give orders to the coachman. 'Leopold,' she would say, 'go faster. And towards the sun, if you please.' And I would lean out of the carriage window, holding my sailor cap ready to catch the sun as soon as it came within reach. For the duration of the trip we drove at a gallop. When we returned home my mother was always in the drawing-room waiting for us and my grandmother would exclaim, 'We failed again to catch the sun, my dear! I really don't understand it!' And mother would shrug her shoulders, gently amused."

It was the first time he had talked so freely to me, calling up his childhood, his mother. My heart sank at the idea that he now, at last, believed he could confide in me.

"And what did your mother say?"

"Oh, nothing at all. Anyway, I told her very little about those rides, I sensed her skepticism. I believed she was discouraged, too, at our repeated failures."

"And you never captured the sun," I said, giving him an affectionate smile.

"No. And I even gave up those rides after that day when my grandmother was told to 'stop telling such nonsense to that child!' I remember how she blushed when she explained things to me: like a mother preparing to enlighten a young bride on her conjugal duties. She was quite disconcerted, her bonnet was rakishly tilted, as she told me that our dominical pursuits of the sun were hopeless. 'Why can't we catch it?' I asked, and she could not give a logical reason. All she said was, 'Because we would burn our fingers.' 'I wouldn't mind that,' I said, 'I'd let go of it right away.' She then sadly told me that when I grew up to be as old as she was I would understand how impossible it was to catch the sun in your cap, like a big butterfly."

"And you believed her?"

"Not entirely. I think she wasn't very convinced, herself. If not, why would we have been seen in the carriage all those

Sundays, I with my sailor cap, grandmother enveloped in scarves, and the fat coachman, Leopold, whizzing along, drawn by the little horse, Champagne, in pursuit of the sun?"

I said nothing, and he went on in the same quiet voice.

"It was at about that period that I had my accident. At first I did not suffer much over it. But later on . . . Later on, I made others suffer. I made you suffer, Hélène."

The words had passed his lips with difficulty. He seemed to be waiting for a reply, and I, too, was waiting for the reply that I could not make, that I intended to make . . . No words came. Yet I was touched at his confiding in me and felt that a serious moment was approaching, when he would break down and free himself of all his troubles, confiding them to me as one suddenly hands over to a trusted friend a burden that has become suddenly too heavy. And I could say nothing, could do nothing to help him. The same fear that had seized me at the sight of the toothless woman, the stuttering waiter in the café, Stani in love, and Tamara asking me to believe in her sincerity, the same fear had come back. "But today, this is not just anyone," I told myself, "this is not Tamara or Stani or strangers asking for pity and love. It is Jean, Jean whom you love and want to help." But it was useless to try to rouse myself with such thoughts. The words stirred nothing in me but an incomprehensible feeling of impotence.

And he went on, mistaking my frightened silence for emotion.

"All my life," he said, "I wanted to remain apart from others. I thought it was the only way not to suffer at human contacts. Perhaps I fooled myself. Perhaps I would have suffered less, otherwise? I'm not very sure, now."

He was no longer sure. And I, who should have helped him and who, for a moment, had known how to help him, said nothing, immured in my silence by a thought that had slowly taken form: I no longer was free to choose my attitude. It was not today, sitting there motionless on the bench at the end of the pier, that I was refusing to help him. It was yesterday, when

I flouted Stani's love, a week before, when I laughed at Tamara's regrets—that was when I had refused to help him. And now it was too late, I feared. Could I still do something and save him? I hoped so, despite everything. My feelings would return, love would revive again, and then I would run to meet it, without hesitation. Meanwhile . . . Meanwhile, I would try to fool him, make him believe in my comprehension. And so, I rested my head on his shoulder, I pressed his hand harder, to stimulate his confidence in me. Whether or not he was fooled, I did not know. He said nothing more, but as we turned to go he leaned a little against me.

We were passing in front of the Carlton, where Jean had again taken a room, when the page boy ran up to us.

"Monsieur, a lady has been waiting in the lobby for you since two o'clock this afternoon. Had you forgotten her?"

"I haven't forgotten any lady that I know of," laughed Jean. "What is her name? Is she good looking?"

"She did not mention her name, Monsieur. As for the rest . . . Honestly, Monsieur, she's well on in years."

"That's what I call an inadequate description. All the same, I'll go see who she is. Could it be one of my admirers? Hélène, will you wait?"

"I'll go home to have a look at the 'Floral decorations' as papa says, since I'm supposed to be in charge of them."

"In that case, I'll see you later."

He entered the hotel, and I continued on my way.

By the time I reached the house, Father was superintending the final preparations for the festivities. Traditionally, hay wagons passed through the streets of the town all that day, and especially the following night, picking up drunks and taking them home. No less traditionally, on the eve of Carnival, the drivers of those carts went on strike and demanded of the town notables a gift in money or kind (one or two kegs of wine).

"So," I said, "the strike's settled?"

"Naturally," said Father. "This Carnival is costing me a pretty sum, but rarely will there have been one as successful! And what about you," he added, absent-mindedly, "is it going well, this, er, this engagement of yours?"

"Why yes, papa."

"Good, good."

And he hummed in a falsetto voice, "*L'amour est un oiseau rebelle!*"

Jean arrived a little late to dinner, which was brief and without frills. Father and Tamara seemed entirely absorbed in the preparations for the banquet which was to take place next day at the Hôtel de Ville. I did not dream of asking Jean about his mysterious lady admirer. Against my will, I was also obliged to busy myself with the portion of organizing the festivities that had fallen to me. Jean took leave rather early, pleading fatigue, which surprised me a little. But he promised to come for me in the morning towards ten o'clock, to take a walk in the town which was now invaded by tourists and the peasants of the surrounding countryside.

"Fundamentally, he's a very nice young man," said Father, when Jean had left. "I'm sure we're going to get along well together. Do you know, Hélène, I've even started something that may bring your fiancé into my business?"

"Oh, really?" I said, without much enthusiasm.

"Why, yes. I was looking for an original designer, who would think up something new for our line of cotton prints next summer. Well, haven't I found one in him? Oh, I'm well aware he doesn't need work, but working in the same business will make him feel more like one of the family!"

And upon these edifying words, we went off to bed.

The harbor was swarming with people. In the little cafés they were already dancing; confused sounds of music streamed out of them and mingled with the cries of street hawkers—for which this was a day of triumph—selling wine and beer. Only the children were as yet wearing disguises, but they were enjoying themselves thoroughly, assaulting the passersby, throwing floods of confetti from windows, linking arms in gangs of ten to dance inextricable sarabands which blocked the traffic in whole streets. Here and there, strange machines encumbered the sidewalks, monstrous forms, covered with sacking and looking like somnolent dragons. These were the floats which, in the afternoon, would parade for the much coveted gold cup of the Carnival. We had gone to the courtyard of the Hôtel de Ville to look at the biggest one, the float of the Fools which, drawn by symbolic oxen, would deliver up the notables of the town to the laughter of the general public. We had admired the fishermen's float, in which the prettiest girls of the harbor would parade, disguised as sirens, despite the cold. And now, in front of the Petit Matelot café, a beer seller was offering to the rubbernecks gathered round, all the beer they could drink at one gulp, for fifty francs. A fool's bargain which always drew the sailors, confident in their powers, but who always went off a minute later choking with the overflowing foam. A ring of people gathered round the merchant, laughing at the discomfiture of the sailors. Bets were being laid upon some whose capacity seemed above average.

"Charming custom," said Jean, who was thoughtfully surveying these performances. "While I think of it, do you know a certain Madame Mierowicz?"

"Don't you hear what I'm saying? Yes, a Madame Mierowicz, how many times must I repeat it to you? The mother of a certain Stani."

An enormous sailor in a striped jersey had just approached the beer that was being poured out. He opened his mouth and began to gulp down the amber-colored stream, without apparent embarrassment. Apprehensively, the beer merchant slightly increased the pressure. The sailor's comrades protested noisily.

Had Madame Mierowicz told Jean everything? That one

question dominated my mind, in the midst of such a confusion that it was the same thing as serenity.

"Yes, I know her."

The sailor's face had become purple, but he was still drinking with disquieting persistence. Silence now hovered over the crowd, astonished at such prowess.

I contemplated the scene in a kind of daze.

"Well, what's the story? Say something, for Heaven's sake, Hélène."

"What do you want me to say?" I murmured. "I don't know why she went to see you."

"If you're anxious to know what she told me, I can inform you right away. It's not worth your while to give me the details, she spared me not a single one. As for why she came to talk to me, it's simple. It would seem that her son is dying of love for you, he no longer eats or sleeps, in short, is going into a decline and is the despair of his family. So she came to ask me to intercede for them. I'm to ask you to cease your sudden cruelties! A rather ridiculous rôle, but I'm playing it, as you can imagine, with some amusement."

I made no reply. The sailor had at last stopped drinking and was now regally acknowledging the compliments of his friends. Like a good sport, the beer merchant handed over a plush monkey to him as a prize, pinning it to the sailor's jersey. The crowd dispersed. Jean took my arm.

"Come," he said in a strange, harsh voice that I did not recognize. "It's time to go home. Should I, in this affair, play an active part? Or will you yourself take charge of replying to the lady?"

"I'm sorry they bothered you with all this," I said faintly.

"But they didn't bother me at all! I once said you were full of surprises; it pleases me to note that you haven't changed."

A group of children dressed in rags passed by. As an economical way of costuming themselves, some of them had simply covered face and hands with charcoal and imagined, as they let out inarticulate yells, that they were marvellously evoking savage Zulus. Others had adopted still simpler disguises: wearing a collar of potatoes strung round their necks and with long strings attached to their feet, they represented the tuberous vegetable, entangled in its roots.

And Jean continued his monologue, while guiding me at a quick trot towards the house.

"Why didn't you tell me about this little adventure before? When I think how bored I was in London! A romantic novel in the form of letters would have brightened up our correspondence a bit! Oh well, let's say no more about it. It's a grotesque affair, quite in keeping with this Carnival."

I was amazed to feel no tears on my cheeks. I was beyond grief, absolutely annihilated.

At lunch, Jean was very animated, managing to cheer up Tamara, who looked worried about something, and falling in with Father's rather boisterous gaiety. During our walk, a brass band had come to give him an impromptu serenade, much to his delight. Jean raved about the floats, about the fool's costume Father was going to wear, about everything on the program of that afternoon's celebrations.

"You intend to stay for the three days of Carnival, of course?" asked Father.

"Oh, Heavens, I'm really afraid not. I have a tremendous amount of work to do in Paris just now, and shall be obliged to curtail my trips to Gers quite a lot."

Was he suffering? He had resumed his detached attitude, and was again speaking in the affected and drawling voice of former times. Would I never again see him as confiding as he had been the night before? Would he never again be confiding, not even with someone else? I felt a pang of grief. If I had been alone, I might perhaps have approached him, implored him. But Tamara was there.

"Going so soon?" she exclaimed. "Hélène will certainly miss you, during these days of folly."

"She'll find some masquerader or other to entertain her," he said with an ambiguous smile.

"Could it be you're jealous, my dear Jean?" smiled Father. "In that case, I advise you to drop all work and stay on here, for Gers, though it's the most respectable place in the world during the year, really goes mad during the Carnival season."

"I have no fear that Hélène will go mad," said Jean. "She is much too prudent for that. Aren't you, dear?"

Tamara looked up. Had she caught the rather spiteful accent of irony?

"A young girl cannot ever be too circumspect!" said Father pompously, getting up from table.

Since we had remained a little to the rear, I managed, under the stairway, to say a few words to Jean.

"Jean, listen to me. That Stani affair was . . . after all, I only wanted . . ."

He cut in ironically.

"Now, Hélène, don't make a tragedy of it, child. I know perfectly well what you're going to say. You're not dying of love for that boy, and as far as you were concerned, it was only a passing amusement. That's what you were going to say, isn't it?"

I did not say a word in reply. How could I explain my reactions, how explain what I had felt was threatening me? No danger lay in wait for me, now. Even Jean's words scarcely touched me.

"Come, come, don't be afraid," he said, patting my cheek. "I don't intend to go to your father and break our engagement on account of that trifling episode."

I experienced a faint rush of anger. Well, why didn't he do just that? Why didn't he break off with such a violent outburst that my heart could be reached through the hardening shell in which I was being encased? Why didn't he insult me, decide never to see me again, why didn't he tell everyone about my abominable conduct? Then I would have been relieved of the weight I was carrying inside me, then I would have found the words, the gestures that were needed to convince him, implore him . . . Surely, he would not go on playing this rôle of his for long. That afternoon or that night, once alone together, he would drop that acquired attitude of dispassion and I, too, I would find ways to move him. He must not go away immediately, without listening to me. That was the main thing, wasn't it?

We arrived late, the parade had already begun. Tamara had given us our tickets and had slipped off to her own place in the reviewing stand, which was decorated in the purple of authority. Schoolchildren were marching past, and behind them came a brass band.

From the top of the reviewing stand, with regal gestures, the municipal councillors were pouring out floods of caramels from urns of gilded cardboard upon the children, who had flocked from the surrounding countryside and the neighboring villages. We reached our reserved seats with some trouble, since even the passageways were blocked with people who were shouting greetings and instructions to their children. When at last we were seated, I was horrified to see, only two seats below us, Stani, who was pretending not to see me. Tamara! It was she, I knew, who had distributed the tickets for the best places in the grandstand. It was therefore her hand that had seated Stani there, three yards away from Jean and me. Had she guessed something? Stani's repeated telephone calls and my eagerness to avoid him, perhaps some rumors had been enough to put her on the alert, and Jean's ironical remarks at table must have confirmed her suspicions. She was sitting there in the reviewing stand, watching us, perhaps rejoicing over her idea. I was about to straighten up and turn my eyes away from Stani, when I suddenly noticed that Jean had also seen him. Jean had met Stani once or twice at Madame Périer's and so must know who he was.

I was ready to beg for mercy, to implore Jean to take me home, and I leaned towards him.

"Jean, supposing we leave?"

In his eyes I saw a flash of the old hardness.

"Where do you want us to go? Don't you feel well?"

No, I must not burst into sobs, there on that grandstand, with everyone spying upon me.

"We could go back to the house," I murmured.

"Oh, now, Hélène! Your father would never forgive me. After the *Reine Berthe* scandal, another one? After all, there's no reason to pile it on!"

"But . . ."

"There's no room for objections," he said icily. "I know what's troubling you. But you've always managed quite well to dissimulate, so you can just manage to go on dissimulating."

The big floats were beginning to pass by, hailed by the crowd with enthusiastic yells.

"Admirable!" said Jean. "Really admirable! And the slightly faded colors of those old costumes! I should have brought my sketchbook."

He took my arm and squeezed it almost spitefully.

"And here comes the float of the Fools! Buck up, Hélène, give your father a little smile. He happens to be looking in our direction. Smile, for Heaven's sake. Haven't you any kind of pride?"

Stung by his insulting irony, I burst out into a forced laugh.

"There, that's what's needed. All the same, you surely aren't going to ruin this entire beautiful day for such an insignificant happening. Surely you won't go so far as to hate me because I found out? It was quite involuntary, I assure you. But I'm going to prove that I don't hold a grudge."

Before I realized what he was doing, he leaned down towards the lower rank of seats.

"Supposing you come up here and sit with us, young fellow?" he called out gaily. "I'm sure you'll not mind sitting beside

235

Hélène, and it's about time you and I got acquainted. I saw you once before, I believe, at the Noris' one night?"

Stani pushed his way towards us and dared to sit down beside me, look at me, even smile at me, though with some constraint. I did not make a gesture, concentrating all my thoughts on one sole aim: to stay there, motionless, with stiff back and impassive face. Jean appeared to be very much at ease.

"You're a painter, I understand, so you must appreciate this astonishing Carnival to the full. How suddenly animated this town has become! It's fundamentally a charming place, that's clear. In France, people have lost the festive feeling, they don't know how to let themselves go like this. Perhaps there's too much freedom there, in Paris especially, so that no need is felt for this kind of release?"

"No doubt," said Stani politely.

Jean's serenity reassured him. He must have feared a scene. At present, feeling himself tolerated, without wondering by what miracle, he tried to be pleasant, laughed at Jean's quips, lent his sketchbook. And Jean went on with his persiflage and I did not budge. I did not expect him to forgive me. But if only he would have admitted that I needed forgiveness! If only he had allowed me to be guilty!

A roar of enthusiasm hailed the apparition of the fishermen's float with its Sirens. Daringly undressed, they writhed and swayed in their sequin-covered tights, waved with awkward languor at their families, who were seething with excitement.

As always, each year, at the passage of this float which brought together the prettiest girls of various districts, arguments broke out, then little fist-fights, at first good-natured but soon envenomed by the comments of the spectators. From the top of their float, forgetting their languishing poses, the sirens encouraged or defied the combatants. They passed on, yelling, like a chariot of Valkyries.

Night was already falling, and torches were being lit. Little by little the grandstands emptied. People were going home to put on their costumes for the masked balls. No one was parading now except troups of dusty and slightly intoxicated children.

"Suppose we go have some dinner?" Jean suggested. "Your father has solemnly authorized us, Hélène, to dine together in a restaurant. But it's too bad to go off and leave your friend. Shall we have an apéritif together?"

Stani agreed to it immediately. Apparently nothing in this situation surprised him and he calmly sat down with us at a table in a boulevard café, where we could see the masqueraders pass by. From time to time he looked slyly at me, then quickly turned towards Jean, and they began talking animatedly, like conspirators, cruelly in league against me.

"What's wrong, Hélène, why don't you say something?" said Jean with palpable irony.

And, encouraged by Jean's presence and spiteful, since he felt in a position to attack, Stani had to add his word.

"That's so," he said. "You don't look any too gay, this afternoon. Yet I thought you were fond of the Carnival."

Anger plucked me out of the lethargy in which I was sunk. That instead of keeping Stani away from me, Jean was delivering me up to his sarcasms, was too much. That he pretended to find Stani likeable, that he drew him out, made him talk about himself, his paintings, that he went so far as to make a veiled and impertinent allusion to the "mutual attraction" which must have brought Stani and me together—no, I could not stand this in silence. Perhaps I deserved this cruelty; but Jean knew me well enough to know that I would reply. By acting thus, he condemned me to make a reply. Up to then, I had only felt an aching numbness, an unaccountable impotence before the disaster. But now I was completely overwhelmed with fierce resentment. After all, he, too, was responsible for what I had done. Was he not the one who had formerly preached the virtues of infidelity, had granted, almost recommended it to me? Had he not been unfaithful to me first, thus putting me under the obligation of finding some passing comfort in Stani? Was it not he who was now, once again, obliging me to defend myself, to counterattack—just when I had been searching for words of peace?

"On the contrary, I feel quite well," I said. "Perhaps we had better dine together now? It will soon be eight o'clock, and the night still has some surprises in store for us. For the first time in Gers, thanks to my father's wish to dazzle the citizens, you are going to witness a superb display of fireworks on the lake shore!"

"What next?" murmured Jean, who had seemed disconcerted for a moment. "But you forget, Hélène, that I'm taking the morning train. I don't want to go on too much of a binge to-night! No, we'll just dine calmly, as a respectable engaged couple should, and afterwards I'll take you home. I don't want to face the wrath of Monsieur Noris, who extorted some pretty solemn promises from me!"

As he stood up, I mechanically tried to help him into his overcoat.

"For Heaven's sake, Hélène! Do you want our friend to think I'm an invalid? I may have only one arm, but for all that I'm a man," he joked. And with his right hand, he picked up a paper napkin from the table. "Here, watch this, Stanislas. Could you do as much?"

Quickly, and with inconceivable dexterity, he folded the paper, cleverly transforming it into a smaller square, into a boat, then into a kind of rectangular box. There was something frightful in the rapidity of that hand.

"It took me two years to learn that. But it was worth the trouble, don't you think? And then, there's also the litle ship, the two-seated airplane . . . Such tricks always entertain the girls. But you, of course, don't need that sort of thing to attract them."

"Why, you don't either, Monsieur," said Stani politely.

Jean laughed.

"Oh, you're implying that I can also offer them gifts, take them for drives in an elegant car, surround them with luxury? But it's also necessary to make them laugh a little!"

Why was he lowering himself like this in front of Stani, who was enjoying these confidential remarks and who visibly hoped to see me again soon, thanks to this display of tolerance?

"My dear Stanislas, I believe you will realize why I do not invite you to dine with us. It would create a scandal in Gers. But I certainly hope that some day in Paris . . ."

They parted with a great show of politeness, apparently delighted with each other. As always Stani simply accepted any situation which turned to his advantage. Perhaps he was not far from thinking that Jean recognized his worth and was treating him with consideration as a rival.

"Alone at last," said Jean pleasantly.

"I'm not the one that wanted to invite Stani."

"How wrong you were, my dear. He's a charming young fellow, discreet, modest, and quite handsome, which is nothing against him, and I entirely approve your choice. I understand he is poor and very deserving, to boot. At least, that's what his strange mother implied. How romantic all this is!"

"Yes, isn't it?" I fumed. I knew very well that each of those words was hurting him, that Stani's good looks and poverty were affronts to him. But was he not wounding me, as well? Every moment that passed increased the sum of abnegation and humility it would take for me to allay his bitterness. And why should I try to do that, if he enjoyed being bitter?

"Are we going somewhere to dine, Jean?"

"Why not, since we have the time, why not go for a while to the red room?"

This was his final challenge and I realized it. To go there with him was to admit definitely that nothing had happened, it also meant thrusting aside all possibility of forgiveness. But was I as keen as all that to have his forgiveness, did I still even see the necessity?

"All right, let's go," I said, with a great feeling of fatality.

X X I I ·

He detested me, I felt it at once by the way he pressed my body to his. He hated me for having understood him a moment, for having by chance learned his secrets, for having guessed his weakness. I hated him for having revealed the most difficult love to me, and for not having prevented me from killing that love. As we lay down on the bed, I knew that this was our last evening together.

Later on, Jean, who was pretending to be in a most light-hearted mood, suggested supper. I agreed immediately, caught up a little in his fantastic and ruthless gaiety. The red room had never been richer in shadows and evil spells, cancelling the world around it.

Clara Vaes soon appeared in the doorway, as beribboned as a poodle, jangling her vulgar adornments, bringing with her strong whiffs of cheap perfume. Standing before us, in a hieratic and benevolent pose, her two hands on her stomach, overflowing with good-will and curiosity, this goddess of furnished rooms was ready to gratify all our desires.

"Supper? Why certainly, Monsieur. Anything you like, the house is well stocked. We just happen to have with us"—her voice lowered a tone—"Monsieur Brennendonck, of Barfleur, the deputy, you may know him. Well, he's having supper with a pretty little creature and he just told me he'd never eaten better in his life. Oh, you know, I could open a tip-top restaurant if I liked. But I'm too fond of rendering services, that's my weakness, and when I see a couple in love like you two, well, believe it or not, it warms my heart, and I say to myself, 'They've got to have someone to help them'—you see what I mean."

Her glistening little pig's eyes, half sunk in her pudgy face, surveyed the room as if looking for traces of our revels, and they seemed monstrously to deform everything they looked at. Those ingratiating ways, those fat little hands rubbing together, that flood of unctuous words were usually enough to make my flesh creep. But suddenly, that night, I put up with it easily, as I put up with Jean's gaiety and my own passivity, bathing in a strange, unreal euphoria, such as precedes certain voluptuous deaths.

A beaming and bosomy waitress who, on occasion, served as consolation to certain forlorn clients, came to set up and arrange a little folding table. Madame Vaes gave it a final inspection.

"We have a wonderful *foie gras!*" she said, in a gormandizing way, "and a burgundy that's better than any champagne, believe me. The gentlemen who come here always ask for champagne, and I let them have it. But believe me, the burgundy's better. What's their champagne, after all? Nothing but fizz. An odd thing: because it's expensive, that impresses the girls, at the time. But afterwards? Champagne's for the brains, but burgundy's for the belly!"

I went so far as to laugh at the ignoble pleasantry.

Everything was ready for the meal, but I was still in bed, half naked, waiting until Madame Vaes left to get up.

"Now, Mademoiselle's surely not going to dress!" she exclaimed, perhaps sensing that tonight she could get away with anything. "If you'll permit me, Monsieur, I'll bring her a kimono, I always have one for such occasions, I know how these young ladies can't bring their own lingerie. Wait a minute, wait a minute. I'll be back."

Trotting on her short, deformed little feet, she left the room, returning almost immediately with a black negligée, more than a little transparent. Jean gave me an ironical and attentive look. And I, too, looked at myself, smiling at the dreadful creature with naked bosom who was getting out of bed and putting on that kimono which had a strange smell. Everything was new tonight: the imitation candles with pink shades, the pink lamp, too, the supper on the table, the caryatids with glistening breasts, and the red bed in the red shadows. As I went towards the table, I saw that Jean had opened the big cheval mirror which had always remained folded until that day, and in that mirror I felt I was seeing myself for the first time. My hair was dishevelled, my body showed through its new garment, and I, who usually avoided the sight with embarrassment, I now contemplated that body with satisfaction, and felt a new life inundate every particle of it. I scarcely heard Jean, who invited me to sit down, I kept looking in the mirror at my body and face, trying to understand what had just come mysteriously to life—or was it something that had vanished away?

It mattered little to me. To descend to the depths of degradation like this gave me a particular pleasure. I could have wished to go still further, to ask that servant girl who was discreetly withdrawing to remain, and have myself washed and perfumed by her, like a courtesan . . . Jean was holding me round the waist, and I could read in his eyes a desire more keen perhaps than I had ever seen in them before. This thought intoxicated me, a kind of diabolic vivacity insinuated itself in me, like a good wine. I joked in my turn, and was irresponsibly provoking. The blue and white china plates, the carafe of tepid wine, the roughness of the red plush of the chair which I felt through the thin dressing-gown, everything intoxicated me. Jean poured some wine for me and I, who almost never drank, pressed my lips to the thick edge of the glass with pleasure. Clara Vaes came and went, changing the plates. Her presence in no way embarrassed me, I continued to laugh, resting my head on Jean's shoulder.

"Now, how are we going to get you home?" he asked. "I think I'd do well to order a taxi for you, you don't seem in condition to go home by yourself."

"I have no intention of going home all alone," I laughed. "Why shouldn't I stay here till tomorrow morning? Tam and Papa will come in so late, they'll not think of me, and tomorrow Julia will tell them I've already gone out to see you off at the station. I'll telephone her now. I'm going to telephone her."

Once more I was standing, not far from the mirror. Jean drew near and put his arm around me.

"You don't ask me if I want to spend the night with you?" he murmured, holding me close.

"With whom will you spend it? With Sandra?" I asked, looking him smilingly in the eyes. Only the day before, I would have died rather than allude to what I had heard about Sandra. But what had I left to lose, now?

"It's not just a question of Sandra," Jean said, releasing me and moving away. "I simply might not like to spend a whole night with you, isn't that possible?"

"No," I said in the same tone, "I don't believe so."

I fully realized how ignoble my behavior was. How would I ever again be able to face a man with whom I had descended so low? And yet, I felt ever more strongly drawn towards the dizzy abyss of the irreparable.

As Jean approached me, I gave him another smile of the same brazen kind. It was up to him, now, to decide our fate. All he had to do was resist, get angry, go away. But I was sure he could not do that now. He had already passed the point where he could recognize his own hurt. All he wanted now was forgetfulness: why should I refuse it to him?

243

For a moment we faced each other, halting for the last time, as one pauses before leaving a familiar landscape, a tranquil house.

He was near me, now, his face still as calm, though a bit pale. He seized me by the shoulders, but without brutality.

"You little whore . . ." he said gently. "So that's all you were? Dear little whore . . ."

I gave only a slight gasp as he drew me to him and held me tight, I did not resist his cold and precise caresses. The open mirror betrayed my last innocence, the innocence of the eyes, which had been kept until then. And while the last barriers of pride and decency gave way, a frenzied passion drove us still farther, still lower, in search of forgetfulness, that promised land in the depths of an agreeable inferno.

The morning slowly dawned, colorless, like a pale, fragrant rose. Outside, the hay wagons must be carrying home the last drunkards. The public dance halls, reeking with the acrid odor of spilt beer, were being aired, fresh sawdust was being sprinkled on the floors. In an hour or two, the first blood-puddings would be prepared for the evening of the second day of Carnival, and already the blood of pigs was coagulating in the brown earthenware jars. In every house there would slowly spread, hour by hour, the perfume of the festivities, the joyous fever which that evening would at last erupt, in the sound of the sausages frying in the pans and overflowing simultaneously with the white foam of the beer spilling from the porcelain jugs.

Everything was still asleep, like those flowers inside Japanese shells, which wait for water to make them unfold, but everything would spring to life again, was already alive, enfolded in the hollow of this grey, cool morning, streaked, like a shell, with little clouds, still sombre.

Jean was walking up and down in the room.

"How frightful," he said, "these trains that leave so early!

I hope you'll not have any trouble with your family, Hélène. My dear, we've not been very reasonable."

"Oh, there's nothing to fear. Julia must have turned down my bed this morning and she'll say I went out very early."

He calmly pulled on his shirt.

"Of course, but I'd hate to have a scene with your father, be accused of having dishonored you. Oh, well! We have been imprudent, but we'll not begin again."

I was still in bed, still broken by the fatigues of the night, but I, too, was calm. A kind of airy freedom hovered over our remarks. We had been very imprudent, as he said, but we would not begin again. We were saved, now.

"When does your train leave?"

"Eight o'clock. But I've got to pick up my bag at the Carlton. I'm really frightfully sorry to miss this second day of Carnival. It was charming, yesterday."

"Couldn't you manage somehow to stay?" I asked politely.

"Impossible. They're waiting to discuss the sketches with me, and after I've disposed of that, I'll have to leave immediately for Nancy. It seems all kinds of things are happening there! In other words, I'll need a fortnight to straighten out all that. I'll write you a little note, giving you the details."

"Of course," I said.

We would have to correspond a little. That would facilitate breaking the engagement, which would have to be done slowly, without violence or gravity. I would tell Father that upon reflection I found I was really too young and wanted time to think. He would not put up any resistance, I was sure.

We would not see each other again. Never would he be able to forgive me for having caught him off his guard, never would I be able to forget that I had been afraid of loving him. Never would we forgive ourselves for losing the beauty of what might have been.

"Aren't you getting up, child?"

"I'll get up soon, when you've gone. Anyway, it would be better for us not to be seen together this early in the morning."

We had been imprudent. I pondered those words. His face was unchanged, showed perhaps a little fatigue, but we had hardly slept. He was a little tense, his smile was a trifle forced, but he had always been like that. He had become transformed only for a few days. Could I have kept on transforming him much longer? Carelessly I put aside these thoughts. They were not even dangerous now. We were saved from love, free of its demands. We were saved from dependence, from solemnity, from confession, from forgiveness. We were saved from others and from ourselves.

I could see Jean standing in front of the mirror, on the point of knotting his tie. He drew the comb through his hair, put the comb down, took hold of the tie. His fingers hesitated, his gesture was too slow, no doubt, and the knot slipped. Like an icy arrow, pity, a remnant of love, pierced my breast. I wanted to speak. But the night separated us to such a point that I hesitated—scarcely more than an instant, but too much, just the same. Jean had composed himself, his tie was knotted, and he was now humming a tune as he put on his coat.

I remembered the day when, in the church, I had almost prayed. I had asked for hardness, not indulgence, for force, not weakness, and for unhappiness rather than pleasure. All this had been given me, since I had found love. All this had been given me, and I had not been able to bear the burden, I had set it down as soon as received. And today I was empty-handed, barely conscious of what I had lost, and nevertheless feeling that the gravest loss, the true punishment was not so much having lost Jean's love as having, by dint of blasphemy, deliberately stifled my own. Not a tear rose to my eyes. That night I would be able to dance with no heaviness of heart and doubtless Jean, on the train which would bear him away, would be able to think about his sketches without melancholy, keeping only a dim memory of me, perhaps licentious.

"Now, it's time to go. My dear, we'll meet again soon, I hope. Three weeks from now . . ."

I bore his kiss very well. No more defiance, no more violence, nothing but a peaceful and cold pleasure. We were extricating ourselves from this adventure, unharmed. Never more would I ask myself if I should forgive Tamara, regret Stani. We were saved forever. We were lost.

Jean was ready.

"If you ever have any difficulties with your father, be sure to write me immediately. I'll fix it up, he and I get along marvellously. And in three weeks, I'll come back to see you. Be good!"

He laughed, I laughed too. While talking, he had gone towards the door, as if the silence between us might still hide some trap.

"And don't forget to write. Tell me all the little things that happen in Gers, and all about yourself. I enjoy that terrifically!"

He opened the door.

"Goodbye, darling. I'll be seeing you soon!"

The smell of raw onion penetrated the room. No doubt Madame Vaes was also preparing to celebrate worthily the day of blood-puddings.

"See you soon, Jean," I said gaily.

He shut the door very softly, as if afraid of wakening someone, or something. I was alone in the red room.